A Chain of Pearls

A Chain of Pearls

The Martha's Vineyard Murders

Raemi A. Ray

TULE
PUBLISHING

Dedication

For the island.

Chapter One

KYRA GIBSON TIGHTENED her grip on the rails of the *Island Home* as it pulled into the harbor at Vineyard Haven. The ferry's horn blared, notifying the passengers to return to their vehicles. Kyra hesitated, wanting a glimpse of the island her father had made his home nearly five years ago. The dock looked weather-beaten, the boarded-up, cedar-planked buildings just beyond, desolate under April's gray afternoon sky. A chill snaked down her spine, and Kyra pulled her leather jacket tight around her shoulders. She descended into the belly of the ferry and returned to the warmth of her rented SUV. With a deep, steadying breath, Kyra prepared to disembark.

She guided the SUV off the boat and into a small village consisting mostly of closed shops and cafés. *"Turn left onto Vineyard-Haven Edgartown Road,"* her GPS barked. Deeper into the island, the town gave way to farms and spindly pine woods. The apprehension she'd been ignoring for weeks, resurfaced. *Am I right to have come?*

Make a U-turn!

Kyra cursed. She'd passed the turnoff. "How did he even find this friggin' place?" she muttered. Looping back, she

1

spotted the gravel drive and pulled up to a large house surrounded by a thicket of pine and brush. The house, a traditional New England colonial, was painted white with black trim. Empty flower boxes hung below shuttered windows. The garden beds were well cared for. Someone had spread fresh mulch and pruned back the rhododendrons and hydrangeas.

She parked next to a blue Range Rover. Taking a deep breath, she opened her door and stepped out from the safety of her rental car. The air was heavy with briny moisture. The damp clung to her hair and clothes. Kyra shivered. She gripped the key the lawyer had sent. Its spiny blade dug into her palm. She squared her shoulders and walked up the porch stairs, pausing before the door. Her breathing turned shallow.

She had never expected to be here. But she also thought she'd see him again. She'd thought she had time. Kyra unlocked the front door. It swung open, and she stepped into her dead father's house.

In a stark contrast to the bleak weather, the interior of the house was bright and airy with tall ceilings and lots of glass. She scanned the open living space, her attention drawn to the wall of windows at the back. Kyra's eyes went wide. The view was stunning. From her position just inside the entryway, she could see the sloping lawn and dark, swirling water below.

"Crackatuxet," a voice piped up from behind her, and Kyra whirled around. A woman had appeared on the threshold, almost out of thin air. "Oh, I'm so sorry. I didn't mean to startle you. The pond down there, it's called Crackatuxet

Cove." The woman held out her hand. "I'm Grace. Grace Chambers. I live next door. Mr. Entwistle, your father's lawyer, said you'd be coming over on the ferry. He asked if I could check in on you."

Kyra's brow creased with confusion, as she stared at the woman. Kyra blinked, then accepted the offered hand.

"I'm Kyra. Umm, yes, the key worked. Thank you." Grace's handshake was firm, her smile warm.

Grace dropped her hand and pointed to the windows. "Beyond the cove to the south is the Atlantic. You'll hear the waves and wind at night. It can get pretty rough this time of year. Don't worry, though. Those are all hurricane panels and can withstand pretty much anything."

"I didn't see another house." Kyra tried not to sound suspicious but wondered where Grace Chambers had come from.

"Oh, we're just to the right, behind those scrub pines. There's a little path through the trees." Her voice had softened, and she gave Kyra a sympathetic look. "We were close friends of your dad's and saw him often enough that we wore a shortcut between the houses. I'm so very sorry for your loss."

Kyra nodded. Grace Chambers was probably in her sixties with a perfectly styled blond bob and dressed casually in designer trousers and a cashmere turtleneck under a down puffer vest that did not seem warm enough for the chilly weather.

Grace didn't wait for a response and with another bright smile stepped into the house. "So, let me give you the tour. I can show you the thermostat, the fireplace, the water, and get you all acquainted."

"You know about all of that?" Kyra asked, following Grace as she made her way through the living area and kitchen.

"Oh, sure." Grace gave an emphatic nod. "My wife sold this property to your father, and we've been over hundreds of times over the years. We even helped Ed with the renovation."

Kyra's chest tightened. Grace was describing a familiar and warm relationship with a man she had barely known. Kyra's face was a mask, concealing the tines of jealousy and irritation that pricked her whenever Ed Gibson was mentioned.

Grace opened a door in the kitchen. "Down here is the basement. There's storage, the wine cellar, and the utility room." Kyra followed Grace down the narrow staircase and along a hallway. "The maintenance team should have been here earlier this week to make sure the HVAC system was up and running. It still gets cold at night, so you may need the heat." Grace tried the knob on a door at the end of the hall, but it wouldn't move. She frowned and tried again. Locked. Grace gave Kyra a sheepish look. "That's strange. I'll let Char know, and we can get you the key. I'll show you the rest of the house.

"The house has three bedrooms, all upstairs." Grace pointed to the staircase on the other side of the house. "The primary suite is at the back. It has glass walls, like the living room. If the waves bother you, you may prefer one of the guestrooms. They're quieter." Grace strode through the living room and stopped in front of two doorways. "That door goes to the garage." Grace pointed to a closed door. "And this…" Grace pushed open a set of French doors. "This was Ed's study."

Kyra followed Grace into her father's study and looked around. Like the rest of the house, this room also had floor-to-ceiling glass windows and a view of the cove below, but unlike the other rooms' white walls and sparse, contemporary furnishings, this room was filled with crap. Everywhere. Collected from Ed Gibson's life as a news correspondent. Kyra recognized some of her father's things from when they had shared a life years ago. Turkish rugs, Afghan bowls, a wooden elephant he'd brought back from a highway tourist shop in Tanzania. In the center of the room, facing the windows, sat the large desk her mother had found in an antique shop in a small village outside of Nimes, France. An armchair laden with papers was positioned in front of a stone hearth surrounded by built-in bookcases exploding with books. This was the Ed Gibson Kyra remembered. Chaotic and messy and full of life.

Her eyes fell to the desk, covered in papers and old issues of the *Boston Globe*, *Washington Post*, and *New York Times*. Among the clutter was a brightly colored, handmade, ceramic dish Kyra recognized as one of her art projects from when she was a child, maybe seven. She'd made it at school and gave it to her dad for Father's Day. Her eyes lingered on the dish. It held more junk—key fobs, coins, paperclips, and a gold medallion about three inches in diameter, molded with the bust of Benjamin Franklin. Kyra pulled her eyes from the coin, realizing Grace was watching her. Her phone pinged with a text message, and she pulled it from her back pocket.

"Call me ASAP!"

"I'm sorry, it's a work thing." She gestured toward her phone.

"Oh, of course." Grace pointed to the desk and the nest of wires coming from the wall. "The phone and internet should be on, so you should have no trouble there, though cell service on the island is spotty. Here's our number. If you need anything at all, call us." She grabbed a Post-It from a stack on the desk and jotted down her number. "And please come over to our house this evening for dinner. Char would love to meet you."

Kyra protested, but Grace interrupted her. "No, please, I insist. We were so shocked and heartbroken when we heard about his accident. I can't bear the thought of you in this big house alone on your first visit. Just come through the path, there." She waved in the fireplace's direction as if that clarified where a path would be. "We'll expect you at six-ish."

Kyra's phone pinged again and another three times with more messages. Kyra glanced at her phone's screen, then back at her neighbor.

Grace beamed. "Wonderful. We'll see you at six," she called over her shoulder and flittered out of the study.

When Kyra heard the front door latch closed, she dialed her office.

"Gibs!" a man answered on the first ring. Kyra grimaced at the nickname. "About bloody time. Where are you?"

"I'm in the States, Assaf. I'm here to settle my dad's estate."

Her boss went quiet, and Kyra could picture him frowning, trying to remember the conversation they'd had only last week.

"Right." He cleared his throat, and Kyra heard him shuffling papers. "When's the service? Should I have an arrangement sent?" What he meant was, *when will you be back?*

Kyra ignored his first question. "My flight back is booked the Thursday after next." She walked behind Ed's desk, taking in the disarray.

Assaf made a strangled voice in the back of his throat. "What about the Omega account?"

"It's handled. We don't expect anything to come in until the end of the month, and Loriann can reach me here if she needs me. She has my mobile."

"Oh, it's a working holiday?" Assaf's voice brightened, and Kyra scowled. *It is now.*

"It's not a *holiday*, Assaf, but yes, if you need anything, send it over."

"Excellent. You're tops, Gibs." Assaf hung up.

Kyra slumped into her dad's office chair and dropped her head in her hands.

KYRA STEPPED OUT of the shower and reached for the soft Turkish cotton towel hanging on a warming rack. She couldn't help but smile. *Dad appreciated the finer luxuries.* After years working in the field as a respected correspondent, often living for months at a time among the people he was writing about—sometimes without power or running water, sleeping on a pallet on the floor—she supposed her father had earned the luxe linen bedsheets and soft down comforters piled high on each bed. The towel warmer might have been a bit much, but walking into the cold bedroom, she was grateful for the heated robe.

Kyra had chosen the southern guestroom toward the front of the house. It had been decorated in soft creams and ivories. An inviting peacock-blue velvet chaise was tucked under a large window overlooking the front yard. A thick rug covered the hardwood floors. Like Grace had said, from this room, unless Kyra really listened for it, she couldn't hear the ocean. In what was clearly a theme throughout the house, and in character with her father, this room also held a bookcase chock full of books. Kyra scanned the titles on the bindings and was surprised it contained several she'd owned as a child—*The Black Stallion, Nancy Drew*, and even children's books like *The Velveteen Rabbit* and *Puff the Magic Dragon*. She pulled *The Complete Sherlock Holmes* from the shelf and flipped it open. Her name was scrawled on the title page in the bubbly print of a twelve-year-old girl. She re-shelved it, her finger lingering on the spine. Seeing her childhood things carefully displayed was disorienting. She wasn't sure what it meant or if it meant anything at all. Her father had cleaned out their apartment after her mother died, but she hadn't known he'd kept any of her things.

She zipped open her suitcase and pulled on clean jeans and a thick sweater. She unpacked. From her bag, she pulled the papers she'd printed off before leaving London. She was here to arrange for the sale of Ed Gibson's personal items, then the house itself. There were things she probably should give away to friends and family. *If there's anyone who cares enough to want anything.* Her eyes fell on the bookcase. If Grace was evidence, though, it looked like her father had made a nice, comfortable life here. Kyra gritted her teeth, envisioning dinners filled with laughter, her father captivating Grace and her family with his animated storytelling in front of a warm fire or drinking sparkling wine on a crowded beach. She took a deep breath, making an effort to abate her anger and resentment. *I can't begrudge him for enjoying his retirement.* She attempted diplomacy. He deserved it after his long and hard career. She just wished he'd paid her half as much attention as he had his retirement plan.

Kyra left her room to explore the house and found herself in the kitchen. Her stomach reminded her how hungry she was. She hadn't eaten since she'd left London, rushing from the airport to the car-rental service and driving to the Woods Hole ferry terminal. She checked the fridge. To her surprise, it contained a bowl of fresh fruit and a small jar of cream. There was a Post-It note stuck on the bowl and in elegant cursive it read: *Dinner at 6!* ♥ *Grace.* Kyra smiled despite herself. *She's relentless.* The oven clock read 5:15 p.m. She drummed her fingers on the fridge door. *Do I have enough time to start clearing out one of the rooms?* She was surprised that she was actually considering going. *I am hungry*, she rationalized as she headed to Ed's office.

She stopped in the doorway. It was a jarring experience, leaving the clean crisp lines of the modern living room and entering the dark, cluttered study. The room was chilly, and she turned on the gas fireplace. The flames leaped and danced around the faux logs, throwing off heat and giving a realistic-enough impression of a wood-burning fire. She sat at her father's desk and shuffled through the papers. Besides the months' old issues of national and local newspapers, the pile also contained copies of transcripts from what she thought might be investor calls from a company called Wetun Energy Industries. *Rubbish.*

She pushed the papers to the side and flipped through the stack of mail—bills, coupon mailers, catalogs, invitations to community events … junk mail. *Where's his laptop? His phone?* She opened the drawers, shuffling the contents. Not there. She moved about the room, checking the side tables and various piles of bric-à-brac. Nothing. *He probably had his phone on him when he had the accident,* she thought, surveying the room. *It might have been lost. But his computer?* She racked her brain. Did anyone tell her about items they'd found on him? His wallet? She fetched her own laptop from her bag and booted it up, looking for the email from the lawyer.

Dear Ms. Gibson,

I regret to inform you that your father, Mr. Edward Gibson, has recently died in a tragic accident. My firm represents your father's estate, and we have attempted to reach you via phone and at your office unsuccessfully. Please contact me at your earliest convenience to discuss the particulars.

Sincerely,
Augustin Entwistle, Esq.

She'd received the email three months ago, nearly a week

after her father's body had been found. She hadn't noticed how businesslike and impersonal the tone of it was. Not unlike correspondence she'd written hundreds of times, herself. Detached. Efficient. Cold. When she had finally gotten in touch with Mr. Entwistle, the lawyer had been vague about the details of the accident. Her father, she learned, had drowned after falling from a boat docked in a Martha's Vineyard harbor. Kyra hadn't asked many, or any, questions. She'd convinced herself that boat accidents were the norm on an island, especially during the holidays.

Looking back, she knew she'd been, was still, irrationally angry. Last summer, he'd asked her to visit for the Christmas holidays. He'd texted her weekly for a month. She'd ignored him every time. Then he'd died. She didn't know whether she was angry with her father or herself. Perhaps both.

Her subsequent conversations with the lawyer had been perfunctory. He provided her with Ed's will, and in accordance with his wishes, there was no service, and Kyra was only contacted to finalize the bequest and the sale of the house— if she did not want it for herself. Mr. Entwistle had assured her she need not come to the island at all. That he could have everything arranged and would ship those items that were not to be sold or thrown away to her in London. Originally, she'd accepted the offer. It relieved her of the hassle of taking time off of work and traveling to a remote island off the coast of New England, but the judgmental looks, only thinly veiled by exclamations of concern from her friends and colleagues, eventually guilted her into calling Mr. Entwistle and seeing to the estate's affairs herself.

She planned to help go through her father's possessions,

sign the papers to sell the house, and distribute the estate, then return to London as quickly as possible. Mr. Entwistle had sounded relieved when she'd notified him of her change in plans. He'd sent her an inventory of items her father had instructed to be packed and sent to her and her aunt but assured her she could make any additions or changes as, of course, this was all hers now.

The list of things her father had wanted her to have was eclectic, including various books she could have purchased anywhere, some of her mother's jewelry, art pieces of questionable value, and other odds and ends. Conspicuously missing from the list of items her father thought she would cherish were the professional awards embodied in sculptures, plaques, and medallions he'd received throughout his decorated career. The deep-seated resentment of being virtually abandoned by her father so he could live and report on other people's tragedies while his own daughter was left to grow up alone in England resurfaced. He'd prioritized his job, represented by those awards, above all else, and now, when that was all that was left of him and his legacy, he'd instructed them to be thrown away.

Kyra sucked in her cheeks and punched out an email to Mr. Entwistle, inquiring about her father's laptop and asking for confirmation of various appointments over the next few days. She rubbed her knuckles against her chest. Her gaze wandered around her father's study, and with a frustrated sigh, she snapped shut the computer.

Chapter Two

KYRA FOUND THE path on the north side of the house. It was little more than a trampled patch of dirt through the bramble. Armed with a bottle of wine she'd found in the wine cellar; she made her way to the Chamberses' house. Her father had that unique charisma where he could befriend anyone in minutes. His curious nature invited people to confide in him and share their secrets. His attention was like a spotlight. When you were in his sights, he made you shine, but if he ignored you, if you failed to captivate him, he'd sweep past, leaving you lost in the shadows. *Naturally, his neighbors would have fallen in love with him.* Kyra wondered what it was about these people that had captured his interest. What did they have that she didn't? Everyone loved Ed Gibson. He had not been as generous with his own affection.

The brush pine gave way to a hydrangea hedgerow and a lush lawn that sloped down to the cove and up to a white house. This house was larger and statelier than her father's but architecturally complementary, with the same windows encased with black trim and working black shutters. She climbed the steps to the front door and rang the bell.

A dark-haired woman swung open the door. "Hello. Come in." Her voice was soft and cheerful. She was petite, with dark, wild curls and bright, shining brown eyes. Like Grace, she was dressed in the casual elegance only achievable at great expense.

"Hi, I'm Ky—"

"Char! Love, you're letting in a draft. Oh, Kyra, you're here! Come in. Come in." Grace pushed Char aside, grabbed Kyra's elbow, and half dragged, half guided her into the expansive living room. "Here. Sit there." She pointed to a large couch. Like a child, Kyra did as she was told, dropping into the seat, her palms to her thighs. She stole a look at the woman who had answered the door. Char grinned, then rolled her eyes in an exaggerated arch across the ceiling.

"Oh, my, thank you," Grace exclaimed, examining the bottle Kyra had given her. "Oh, you shouldn't have. You're so kind. Oh, a Sancerre. I love a Sancerre. Look, Char." Grace held up the bottle, and, skipped out of sight without waiting for a response.

"I'm Charlie," the dark-haired woman said with a grin. "Sorry about her." Charlie nodded toward the kitchen and rolled her eyes again. She sat across from Kyra, tucking her legs under her like a cat. "Grace is a bit of a force of nature." She shrugged, but her smile was full of affection. "How was the ferry over?"

Grace reappeared with a tray containing wine and nibbles. She handed them each a glass before sitting down next to her partner. They sat together in that unique way happy couples do, without touching, their shoulders turned slightly toward each other.

"Oh, don't bother her about the ferry, Char. She's come all the way from London. I'm sure she's exhausted. Are you, dear?" she asked, but without waiting for an answer, Grace continued. "It's an island thing. We never stop complaining about the Steamship Authority." She raised her hands, palms up, in an exaggerated shrug. "So, tell us about you." Grace leaned forward, her eyes alight with an eagerness that put Kyra on edge. "Your dad had so many stories. He said you lived in New York, then moved to live with your aunt in London when you were fifteen?"

"Twelve, actually." Kyra winced at the description. Moved made it sound like she went willingly, not dropped on her aunt's doorstep like a FedEx package.

"That must have been exciting. How long were you there?" Grace asked.

Charlie placed her hand on her wife's knee.

"Um, yes. My aunt Ali, my mom's younger sister, isn't much older than me, so it was, well, how about unconventional? I did secondary school in London, then came back to the States for uni, then law school. I moved back to London seven years ago." She thought of her tiny flat two blocks from her office. She'd rarely slept there until recently, having preferred to stay with Ali or friends. Even the couch in her office was more appealing than that drab place. These last four months, though, more and more often, she found herself alone in her sad little flat, feeling like she had nowhere else to go.

Grace's smile wavered, and she shared a look with Charlie.

"So, how long are you staying?" Charlie asked, topping off Grace's glass.

"My flight back is next Thursday." Kyra sipped her wine

and caught Charlie's eye, relieved with the change of subject.

Charlie dipped her head as if acknowledging Kyra's silent thank-you. She hadn't really thought about how her father would describe their relationship to his friends, but she suspected *strained* wasn't the adjective he'd used.

"I have appointments to get the house and its contents prepped for sale, and once that's sorted, I'll return to London. I'm hoping I can get back earlier, if possible," Kyra said, thinking about Assaf's dramatics. She forced an optimistic smile. "There's a lot to go through."

"The house is in excellent shape," Grace said.

Kyra caught another look shared between the Chambers women.

"And this area is very desirable, especially for the summer people. From here you can walk to South Beach, but we're protected from the dreadful storms that come through. The winters can be very rough, you know." She shook her head as if the winters were an annoyance that she'd just have to bear, and Kyra hid a smile.

Grace turned to Charlie. "And, of course, it's a short bike or car ride into Edgartown."

"I sold the house to your dad," Charlie explained. "I do some real estate on the island. If there's anything I can do to help, please just ask." Charlie made the offer with a sincerity that surprised Kyra.

The Chamberses had clearly cared about her father, and seemingly, just by virtue of her being blood, they automatically extended their hospitality to his daughter. She schooled her reaction into a grateful smile, not wanting to appear unappreciative. Grace and Charlie had been nothing but kind. It wasn't their fault that Kyra and her father had rarely spoken since she was forced to move to London, or that before today, she had never heard of the Chamberses. They may have felt like they knew her, but their generosity only made Kyra feel more alone.

"Oh, thank you. I may take you up on that." Kyra looked around the room. "It looks like Ed may have used a similar decorator?" she said, gesturing to the space, which was decorated in the same contemporary style as Ed's house, just on a grander scale.

"Ha, yes," Charlie said. "We renovated our house a few years before Ed moved to the island, and after seeing the glass wall concept, he wanted to do something similar."

"He even told Wes, 'Give me a Grace!'" Grace added waving her hands.

"Wes?"

"A general contractor, dear. He's one of the best on the island. If you need anything fixed, he's the one to talk to. His company did all the renovations on your house and ours, so he can give you any information you need." Grace paused, her perfect eyebrows furrowing. She turned to Charlie. "Oh, that's right, Char. The utility room in Ed's basement was locked. Do you know about that?"

Charlie frowned over her wineglass and jutted out her bottom lip. "Are you sure it wasn't stuck?" Grace shook her head. "I can't think of a reason there would be a lock on that door. That's strange."

Grace hummed her agreement and popped up from the couch. "I'll be right back," she trilled over her shoulder.

"I'll ask Wes about the door. Maybe he'll know." Charlie

munched on a cracker. "His company does good work. I've recommended them to many of my clients."

Grace bustled back into the living room.

"Julia said just a few more minutes." She turned to Kyra. "I've set us up in the sunroom. It's a little cooler in there, but with such a wonderful view of the cove, and Char can light the fire … unless you'd prefer to eat in the dining room?" Grace rubbed her knuckles.

"Oh no, the sunroom sounds lovely. Please, don't go to any trouble."

Grace nodded and sat down, sipping her wine.

"Although, Grace, he has been acting a little odd lately, don't you think?" Charlie mused.

"Who, dear?"

"Wes Silva."

"Oh, I haven't noticed."

Kyra caught a look between the partners, and she could have sworn Grace gave a slight shake of her head, like she was warning Charlie off the topic. Grace glanced toward the kitchen and back to Charlie.

"Maybe it was just an off day." Charlie shrugged and met Grace's eyes.

Kyra sat watching an unspoken conversation unfold between the women.

"Grace, dinner is ready," a slightly accented voice announced, and a woman entered the room carrying her purse and coat. She wore loose-fitting jeans and a thick sweater, rolled up to her elbows. Her mousey, brown hair was lined with gray and pulled away from her face. "Good evening, I'm Julia," she said, pronouncing her name with a silent *J*.

"Hi, Julia. I'm Kyra Gibson." Kyra waved from her seat on the couch.

"Mr. Gibson's daughter?" Julia frowned and glanced down at Grace, but Grace didn't seem to notice. Julia looked back at Kyra. "It's nice to meet you. Grace, I'll be going. If you need anything else, please text me. Tchau."

"Oh, good." Grace clasped her hands together, clearly used to Julia's abrupt departures. "Come, let's eat before the food gets cold."

"Ignore her," Charlie said and bumped Kyra's shoulder.

Kyra looked up in surprise.

"Julia." Charlie nodded toward the door. "She's been here for decades and is suspicious of off islanders."

Off islanders? "What does that mean?" Kyra tried not to sound defensive.

"People who aren't from here. Technically, Julia isn't from here, but she identifies as an islander."

"And you and Grace are islanders?"

"I am. Born and raised. Grace is from New York, originally. We moved here year-round about twelve years ago when she took early retirement." Charlie gestured for her to follow.

They walked through a large formal dining room, through a set of French doors, into a glassed-in atrium with one-hundred-eighty-degree views of the lawn and the cove below. The sunset cast everything in a pink wash, brightening the greens and turning the cove's blue-gray waters a bruised purple.

"Red at night, sailors' delight!" Grace said in a singsong voice.

"It's an old wives' tale." Charlie rolled her eyes. "A superstitious form of weather forecasting. It means tomorrow will be a nice day." She turned to Grace, but before she could say anything else, Grace pointed to the fireplace.

"Light the fire, love?"

Charlie flicked a switch, and with a soft whoosh, the gas fireplace flickered on, casting dancing shadows about the room. Around the square antique table were four large, comfy armchairs. Julia, Kyra presumed, had set the table and laid out platters of food.

"Red at morn, sailors be warned…" Grace continued in the same singsong voice, grinning.

"Shakespeare, it's not." Charlie winked. "Come, sit here, Kyra." She gestured to the chair closest to the fire and took a seat next to Grace.

"Dig in," Grace said and helped herself to a salad, passing the bowl to Charlie.

To Kyra's nonculinary-inclined mind, Julia had gone all out. There was a salad, a spring veggie side, and a golden roast chicken, already carved. Julia had also put out warm baguettes and creamy butter that Charlie confirmed Julia had made herself. *Who churns their own butter?* The meal and warmth of the fire were a comfort to Kyra on this chilly evening. The tension in her shoulders from the long, emotional day melted away, and she relaxed under the Chamberses' affability.

"This was all so delicious," Kyra said, setting down her fork. "Thank you. I wish I could thank Julia myself."

"Our pleasure, dear. Julia is a phenomenal cook." Grace tore off a piece of bread. "And she knows it," she added with a wry smile.

"We can do just about anything but cook," Charlie jumped in, taking Grace's hand. "Without Julia, we'd starve."

"She cooks for us three times a week and keeps our fridge stocked." Grace gave Charlie a mock disappointed look. "And she watches Char like a hawk."

"I'm diabetic." Charlie shrugged. "A badly behaved diabetic." She held up her wine, took a sip, and grinned, a wicked gleam in her eye.

Kyra couldn't help but laugh.

"With a terrible sweet tooth, so we rarely keep sweets in the house." Grace's hands dropped to her lap. "We don't have dessert. Is that okay? I could probably find something…"

"Oh, please, no. I couldn't eat another thing," Kyra exclaimed and attempted a smile that turned into a yawn.

"You must be exhausted." Grace studied Kyra's face with motherly concern. "What time is it in London? Midnight?"

"I think it's after one." Charlie frowned. "Wait, that can't be right." She looked at her watch.

"It is very late for me," Kyra confirmed before they started counting their fingers. "If you don't mind, I think I'd better head back." She faked another yawn for good measure. "Thank you again for your hospitality. It's been a long time since I've had a home-cooked meal. Everything was delicious."

"Oh, anytime, dear. Let me walk you out." Grace stood and led Kyra to the door. She opened it, and as Kyra stepped through, Grace put her hand on Kyra's arm, halting her.

"Oh, wait," she said too loudly, giving Kyra a start. "Wait," she repeated, softer. "I have some things of your dad's. He'd asked us to hold them for him, and with the accident, it was sort of forgotten." Kyra thought her expression looked guilty. "We probably should have notified the police, or at least Mr. Entwistle, but it entirely slipped my mind, and it didn't seem all that important. Then, last week I found them while cleaning out a drawer, and we heard you were coming after all." She was babbling.

"It's okay," Kyra said, gently removing Grace's hand and dismissing the oversight. She guessed her father had lent them some old book on an obscure historical artifact or a type of insect. "I'm sure it's nothing important. I can pick it up tomorrow, if that works for you?"

"Oh yes, that's perfect." Grace's shoulders sagged a little, clearly relieved. "Tomorrow."

Kyra turned to go, then stopped and turned back.

A thought had popped into her head. "Do you have his laptop, by chance?"

"His laptop? No. I haven't seen it. If it's not in the house, maybe the car?"

"Yes, good idea." Kyra nodded. "I'll look there. Thank you again for dinner. It was lovely." Kyra stepped out into the dark and, by the light of the moon, made her way back to her father's house.

Chapter Three

Monday

THE SUN CREPT through the bedroom window, first with soft-pink tendrils, then with bright, golden beams. Kyra rolled over with a groan, and her eyes flew open. *Where am I?* Within seconds, her brain caught up with her body. *I'm in the States. On Martha's Vineyard.* She let out a long, self-pitying sigh. Her phone buzzed, and she checked the screen. There were a few texts inquiring if she'd arrived and another four from Assaf asking after various clients. She confirmed her safe arrival and responded to her boss before he started calling. The most recent text was from her aunt Ali. *"Did you arrive on the island? Are you OK? Call me!"* Kyra texted her back, confirming her status as alive and relatively well, considering she was on a strange island to pack up her absentee father's life and had no idea where to start. She groaned and tossed back the thick down comforter to head downstairs. *Coffee. Start with coffee.*

The main floor was chilly despite the morning sunshine. She padded into the kitchen. "Thank you, Grace," she whispered when she found the pods for the coffee machine. She slid a mug under the spout and pressed the button. While it brewed, she took a survey of the nearly empty fridge. *I'm going to need supplies if I'm to survive a week here.* Kyra added finding a market to her already lengthy mental to-do list and took her coffee into the living room. She flipped on the gas fireplace and held her hands in front of the flame before settling on the white sectional sofa and opening her laptop.

Before she'd left London, Kyra had arranged for her clients to have support from the junior attorneys and other partners on her team, but her highest-maintenance ones would still insist on querying her directly. She scanned through the massive number of emails that had filled her inbox, making sure nothing urgent had come in from Loriann. Despite her best efforts to get some work done, her eyes kept being drawn to the cove below. The water appeared to be breathing. It throbbed with the gentle ebb and flow of the waves that must feed it from somewhere. Birds pecked at the sandy bank and flitted between the tall reeds along the shoreline. Others seemed to float, hovering above the water, searching for fish under the surface. *It is serene*, she conceded, annoyed with herself for agreeing with her father. She could picture him sitting on the couch, book abandoned, taking in the view.

Her phone pinged. A message from Ali. *"You made it! The ferry gets cancelled often in the off-season."* A self-proclaimed expert, even though she hadn't been in decades, Ali had been full of island advice before Kyra had left.

"Yes, it was fine. Everything went smoothly. I've met Ed's neighbors, the Chamberses." Kyra typed out a short description of dinner with Grace and Charlie. *"I also have appointments with the lawyer, estate agent, and a real estate*

agent tomorrow."

"Good!" Ali responded. *"It's nice that you met people. Explore the island. Be nice, Kay, make friends."*

"I'm always nice," she grumbled.

As if she could hear her three thousand miles away, Ali's next message appeared. *"Don't do that polite suspicious thing where you push people away before you get to know them. Don't do the YOU thing. Give the island a chance!"*

Kyra sighed. "Fine." She started typing out a message to her aunt, demanding she butt out, but Ali's next text came in first. *"There are lots of fun things to do! Your mum and I would ride bikes all along Beach Road when we were kids. There are a few pubs on the island that stay open all year. There's one in Vineyard Haven that's a bit of an institution. And don't miss the opportunity to drive up island to Aquinnah."* The three ominous dots kept fading in and out, foreshadowing the forthcoming detailed itinerary. Ali and Kyra's mother, Isabel, had practically grown up on the island, spending every summer and most holidays here when they were children, but Ali hadn't returned since she'd moved back to England. The phone pinged again. This text was short, with no overbearing travel recommendations.

"How's Cronkite?"

"Cronkite?" She typed back.

"Yes, Cronkite. The cat?"

Kyra looked around. *Ed had a cat?* She hadn't seen a cat or any evidence that she shared a house with one or anything else alive, for that matter. Images of finding a cat's corpse flashed before her eyes.

"I haven't seen a cat."

Kyra gritted her teeth, annoyed. Of course, Ed Gibson would have a cat. He always had a cat. He'd often pick up strays during his travels. He even took the family cat, Grimsby, with him when he dumped her on Ali's front porch, after her mother had lost her battle with breast cancer. Ali had only been twenty-two when she took in Kyra, agreeing to watch her niece while her father investigated a story. But one assignment turned into two, then three. Months, then years passed. Money and postcards arrived from all over the world, but her father never did, and eventually Kyra stopped waiting for him to return.

The phone pinged with more texts. *"Your lawyer found someone to take care of the cat until you arrived. You'll need to pick him up if he's not there."* Ali would be in direct conversation with the lawyer. Her aunt was an incessant meddler.

Ali had offered to come with Kyra to the island, and although she wanted the support, and her the company, Kyra declined. Her aunt, and uncle Cam, after years of disappointments, were now the proud parents of a healthy, four-month-old boy, Ignatius. The adoption proceeding had been long and drawn out, exacerbated by frequent hospital visits for Iggy's infant respiratory issues. Kyra would never have forgiven herself if she'd let Ali miss out on even one minute with her son; however, parental responsibilities wouldn't stop Ali from interfering as much as possible.

"Make sure to get him."

"Why do I need the cat?"

If Mr. Entwistle had found a home for him, who was she to take him from his new family? *With a name like Cronkite, it must be a* he, *right?* she thought, chewing her lip.

"Take the goddamned cat, Kay."

Kyra sighed and resigned herself to the fact that she'd just acquired a cat. There was no point in arguing. Ali wouldn't let it go. Kyra learned long ago not to fight her aunt when Ali had her mind set on something. Her aunt had a soft spot for all things abandoned, as Kyra knew personally. She remembered stories her mom would tell of her little sister bringing home a menagerie of hurt and lost critters—birds, squirrels, even a baby goat who terrorized their parents. Kyra responded with a noncommittal, *"K,"* and smiled with satisfaction at her passive aggression, even if she knew she'd lost this battle.

KYRA FOUND THE keys to the Range Rover in the bowl on her father's desk. She headed outside through the garage in search of supplies for the next few days. The garage was neat and orderly. Shelving units along the back and side walls held yard and other tools. Patio furniture was stacked and stored for the winter. An enormous snowblower took up the entire second bay. Kyra hit the button for the bay doors and caught herself smiling at the mental image of her father wrangling the unwieldy machine with snow up to his knees. She had arranged for the rental company to pick up her car later that day, and she dropped the keys on the front seat. Turning to the other car, she unlocked it and climbed in.

She was about to start the engine when she remembered Grace had suggested the laptop might be in the car. Kyra climbed back out and opened the trunk, then the rear doors.

She searched the back and under the seats. Nothing. It wasn't under or on the passenger seat either. She checked the glove compartment and the SUV's little hideaway spots. In the center-console compartment, in a space way too small for a laptop, her fingers hit something. She reached in further, and her hand wrapped around a plasticky brick.

Kyra pulled out an old-fashioned, bar-style cellphone. *Weird.* She turned it over in her hands. She pressed the power button. Dead. She flipped it over and looked for the power port. It was one of those old models with a proprietary connection. Kyra frowned. It wasn't her father's regular phone. From the text messages he had sent, she knew he had a smartphone like hers. She slipped the phone into her purse. *I'll have to find a mobile seller somewhere on the island. Or order it from the manufacturer. That could take days.* She climbed back into the driver's seat and turned the car around. Once she'd set up her smartphone's GPS, she followed the phone's barks toward the closest town, a place called Edgartown.

Edgartown was like something out of a magazine—a Hollywood, glossy version of a quaint New England town. All the houses were painted white with black or dark-green accents, many with white picket fences separating their lush lawns from narrow streets. Some homes had paved drive-ways, and others had the pebbled drives like the one at her father's house. Dribbled among the private homes were guesthouses, small inns, antique shops, and art galleries. She turned onto Main Street and made her way toward the town center. The little downtown had a few restaurants, a bookstore, a movie theater, as well as more shops and galleries.

Kyra parked in a public lot at the bottom of the street next to the harbor. Boats were docked in the slips, and more were moored out in the churning water. Beyond the water was another piece of land, which she guessed must be Chappaquiddick—the small, inhabited island preferred by politicos and celebrities that was only accessible by ferry or helicopter. She turned her back to the sea and walked up a side street, peeking into the windows of the shops until she found an open café with free Wi-Fi.

The little restaurant was bustling compared to the sleepy feel of the rest of the town. More than half of the tables were occupied, many with just one or two people, their attention focused on a newspaper or a laptop.

"May I help you?" asked a little woman with a cheery voice and a nametag that read NINA.

"Yes, just one, please."

"Sure, this way." Nina gestured for her to follow and led her to a table in the corner. As she sat down, Nina handed her a menu.

"Coffee?"

Kyra nodded.

"Take a look. I'll be right back."

Nina returned with her coffee as Kyra was setting up her computer. "You can plug it in there." She pointed to an outlet.

Nina took her order and disappeared again. Kyra sipped her hot coffee and stared at her laptop screen. The change of scenery didn't help with her concentration. Her attention wandered as she tried to read through her work emails.

Gradually, she became aware that the other patrons were whispering and interacting. She abandoned her work and focused on the activity in the coffee shop.

A woman switched tables and engaged in a hushed conversation with a man who set down his newspaper with a frown. At another table, a couple was engrossed in their phones, which ordinarily wouldn't be strange, except that they were pointing to their screens, as if they were discussing something they were both looking at. Nina, behind the counter, was also scrolling through her phone. Kyra turned to her laptop and searched "Martha's Vineyard News:"

"Fire at Senator Hawthorn's Martha's Vineyard Farm"

"Senator's Island Estate Destroyed in Fire"

"Fire on Martha's Vineyard"

"Mander Lane Farm Aflame"

Nina came by with Kyra's food and paused, the plate hovering over the table. Kyra glanced up.

Nina was looking at her laptop screen, reading the search results. "It's really sad," she murmured, placing Kyra's breakfast down with a soft *plunk*. "I heard they lost some of their animals."

"Oh, that's awful." Kyra shook her head.

"The senator and his family have been coming to the island forever." Nina wiped her hands on her apron.

"At least it was just the old barn that burned," interjected the table-hopping woman.

Kyra caught her eyeing the empty chair at her own table, and she pushed her laptop further away to take up more table real estate.

"Can you imagine if the fire had gotten to the house?

Thank the stars the fire wasn't anywhere near L'Huître, the new restaurant or the site of the new barn they're building." The table-hopper looked pointedly at her tablemate, who appeared less than enthusiastic about his intruder. "Harry?" she nudged.

"Yes, tragic." Harry nodded and turned back to his newspaper. He held it up between them, as if it would shield him from further conversation.

"Bah!" The table-hopper waved her hand at Harry, who didn't so much as blink.

Kyra hid a smile behind her coffee mug.

"Have you heard what started it?" Nina asked.

The hopper's eyes narrowed on Nina, a predator eyeing her prey, and stalked her to the counter.

Kyra couldn't hear what the hopper was saying, but Nina had leaned against the counter, arms crossed, nodding.

Kyra turned back to her laptop and typed in "Senator Hawthorn." Her search returned dozens of hits, including a Wikipedia page. She scanned the page for the highlights—

Philip "Phil" Hawthorn, Democrat, a veteran Massachusetts senator, known for his renewable energy platform and sits on the Energy and National Resources Committee. Currently campaigning for reelection.

She scanned further down the page to a section header labeled "Scandal." Last summer, he'd been subject to an investigation by the Department of Justice for claims alleging the senator had been involved in inappropriate and unethical behavior by attempting to award lucrative government contracts to energy companies with whom he had close ties, including BoSOil Petrol and Wetun Energy Industries. The senator denied the allegations, and the investigation resulted in no conclusive evidence of inappropriate behavior. Further down the page, she found the "Personal Life" section.

Senator Hawthorn resides in Sudbury, Massachusetts with his wife, Margot, and adult son, Chase. The family also runs a sustainable farm in Chilmark on Martha's Vineyard.

Chilmark, she learned, was a small town on the other side of the island. And, according to its website, the farm, named Mander Lane, was a working farm committed to experimenting and expanding sustainable horticulture practices and raising award-winning silkie chickens. Kyra, now committed, continued down the rabbit hole and looked up silkie chickens. Silkie chickens, it turned out, were basically real-life, clucking Muppets. Mander Lane also had a farm stand and a wine bar, which must have been the restaurant the table-hopper had mentioned. Nina reappeared, interrupting Kyra's deep dive to refill her coffee.

"Is there a place on the island where I can buy a cell phone charger?" She asked and held up the burner phone she'd found in her father's car.

"There are no big chain stores on the island, but you can try The Quarry. If they don't have it, you'll need to order it from off island." Nina gave her an apologetic shrug. "Just take Edgartown-Vineyard Haven Road. It's up a few miles, on the left."

Kyra packed up her things, thanked Nina, and paid her bill.

Traveling west on the same main road she'd traveled yesterday, Kyra took in the surroundings. The Edgartown shops and restaurants fell away as she left the little village behind. Cyclists sped down the wide bike path running parallel to the road, narrowly avoiding joggers and dog walkers. Peppered along the street were various services that appeared to cater to more than just the summer crowd—gyms and fitness studios, salons, fishmongers, a butcher shop, and a post office.

Next to the store Nina had recommended was a small gourmet market. She eyed the display of fresh bread in the window and stopped in for groceries before stepping inside The Quarry.

She wandered up and down aisles that intersected and turned around with as much planning as London's Square Mile. It was unlike anything she'd ever experienced. The Quarry was a real-life everything store. It had a hardware section, toy section, a home section, a section for anything else a person could ever need, including an alarmingly extensive selection of jigsaw puzzles. Eventually, she found the electronics aisle in the back of the basement, beyond the knitting supplies. She flipped through the plastic boxes, looking for a cable that might fit the phone, and selected two with connectors that might work. *I'll order one from the manufacturer just in case.* She retraced her steps to the front of the store searching for the checkout.

"It's just awful," a familiar voice wailed.

Grace's perfectly styled blond bob came into view as Kyra emerged from an overstocked aisle.

"What is even happening to the island?!" Grace standing next to the cashier, speaking to a man about Kyra's age, dressed in jeans and a green plaid flannel shirt.

Even though he was leaning against the counter, one work boot crossed over the other, Grace's head barely came to his shoulder. His dark hair was combed away from a face that was good-looking in a rugged sort of way. Kyra frowned. Something about his serious features was familiar, but she couldn't place it.

"Do they know if anyone was hurt?" the cashier asked. Then, after a pause, "What about the son?"

"No, Chase Hawthorn is fine. Probably hungover, but fine." The man in plaid scoffed. "Although it wouldn't surprise anyone if it was Chase who started it." His lip was curled in disgust and his voice hard.

"Now, Wes," Grace chided.

"Remember when he and his friends lit that bonfire on the beach? They almost set the dunes on fire. He's an entitled little shit. Causing trouble wherever he goes." He shrugged, unapologetic.

"*Pffft.* You're still cranky he beat your cousin in the regatta last year." The cashier gently pushed him off the counter.

"And when he got drunk and nearly crashed the boat?" Wes swiveled his head between the women, finally stopping on Grace. "You know, the police still don't know how Ed Gibson ended up falling off his boat that night."

Kyra froze at the mention of her father's name.

"My buddy in the force is sure Chase was involved. They just can't pin him."

How would the senator's son be involved? She bit her lip. Feeling like she was intruding on a private conversation, she called out to make her presence known. "Oh, hi, Grace," she said with forced brightness and stepped out from behind the large display of colorful pool noodles.

"Kyra?" Grace looked uncomfortable. "Hi, dear!" She recovered and awkwardly gestured to the woman behind the counter. "This is Mrs. Lisbon. Her family owns this store, and this is Wes Silva." She gestured to the man in plaid. He turned to face Kyra.

"Pleased to meet you." Kyra smiled and placed her items on the counter.

"This is Kyra, Ed Gibson's daughter. She's come all the way from London," Grace explained, stepping to the side.

"It's very nice to meet you, Ms. Gibson," Mrs. Lisbon said, grasping Kyra's hand in hers. "I was very sorry to hear about your father." She shook her head and gave Kyra's hands a gentle squeeze. "If you need any help while on the island, please ask." Mrs. Lisbon gave Wes a pointed look, then scanned Kyra's items.

No one spoke for a few moments, the uncomfortable silence only broken by the register's beeps.

"Yeah," Wes said. "If you need any help at the house, let me know." He fished around in his pocket and handed her a business card.

"Oh, yes. Thank you." Kyra took the card and flipped it over. She slid it into her wallet. "Actually, the door to the utility room in Ed's house? The one to the heating and cooling systems? It's locked. Umm, do you know how I can get in?"

She looked up at him. Wes was scowling, his mouth pressed in a straight line. She stepped back.

"Why?" he asked.

What do you mean, why? It's my bloody house.

She scrambled for an answer. "Umm, when I put it up for sale this week, the inspector will need to get in." She handed Mrs. Lisbon her credit card. "It's okay. Never mind. I'll figure something out."

Mrs. Lisbon bagged the items and handed them to Kyra.

"Thank you. Grace, when will you be back home? I can pick up Ed's things?"

"Oh, yes, of course." Grace bobbed her head and checked her vintage Cartier watch. "I've a meeting at the historical society and have some last-minute meetings for the fundraiser," she said to herself. "How about three? Would that work for you, dear?"

"Perfect."

"I'll come by around that time too and drop off Cronkite," Wes said.

Kyra's eyes snapped to his, confused.

"Entwistle called me this morning to arrange for the cat to be dropped off." He gave Kyra a look that implied she was slow.

Her cheeks flushed with embarrassment and annoyance. She swallowed back the urge to snap at him, unclear if she was more annoyed with him or Ali's meddling.

"Oh, right." She feigned nonchalance and tangled her fingers in the handles of her plastic bag. That this unpleasant man had been taking care of her father's cat made her uncomfortable. "Yes, that's fine. Thanks. I must get going, but it was nice meeting you, Mrs. Lisbon. Grace. Wes." She raised her hand in a halfhearted wave and walked out.

Once seated in the SUV, her bags in the passenger seat, she fired off a series of angry texts to her aunt demanding she butt out. Ali texted back with a heart emoji. Kyra rubbed her temples and started the car.

When she got back to the house, she put away her groceries and tore into the plastic clamshells holding the phone cables. She tested each one on her father's phone. The second one fit the charging port. "Yes!" She glanced around the room. *At least with the cat here I won't be talking to myself.* Kyra plugged the cable into the wall outlet and pressed the power button. Nothing. *Maybe it needs a bit of time?* She set it down on the counter to wait. Ten minutes later, the phone still wouldn't power on. Fifteen minutes. Nothing. Finally, after twenty minutes, Kyra accepted defeat. Cursing under her breath, she ordered the official cable from the manufacturer. She paid extra for the overnight shipping, estimating she'd get it in three or four days.

Kyra tapped the dead phone with her finger, her nail beating out a staccato rhythm against the plastic. Wes Silva's offhand remark at The Quarry needled her. *Did my father fall from the Hawthorns' yacht? And do the police think Chase Hawthorn was somehow involved?* She didn't know Wes, but it seemed like a strange thing to lie about. Kyra frowned, and her stomach turned sour.

Mr. Entwistle had never said whose boat her father had been on that night, and she hadn't asked. She'd assumed it was a friend's, that he'd been at a party or other event. Not mentioning the high profile of the boat's owner seemed odd, and that the senator's son was connected to the accident seemed even stranger.

Kyra pulled her laptop out of her bag. As she typed, she went over what little she knew about the accident. Her father had fallen from the deck of the senator's boat one night in early January. He had drowned, and his death had been ruled an accident. Kyra bit her bottom lip. She found dozens of articles authored by her father and a bland obituary published by one of the papers he had worked for. Further down in the search results, she found a short blurb from an article in the local paper.

> *Early Tuesday morning at approximately 5:45 a.m., authorities pulled a body out of the Edgartown Harbor. The man has yet to be identified.*

Kyra clicked to the newspaper's website and typed in her father's name. The paper's search function returned a few relevant articles:

"Martha's Vineyard Newest Celebrity Resident: Pulitzer Prize-Winning Reporter"

"Green Design: The Beauty in Sustainability"

"The Islands Go Geothermal"

"Pulitzer Prize-Winning Journalist, Drowned"

She selected the last one:

> *The body pulled from Edgartown Harbor the morning of Tuesday, January 4, has been identified as Pulitzer Prize-winning journalist Edward Gibson of Edgartown. Detective Tarek Collins confirmed the Massachusetts State Police and Coast Guard's investigatory conclusion of accidental death. Detective Collins declined to provide a cause of death, citing privacy for the family of the deceased. Mr. Gibson moved to the island five years ago and has been active in the community. His "Green Residence"*

on Crackatuxet Cove, designed and built by local construction company Forrest & Co., Inc., has been featured in many architecture and design publications.

Kyra searched for Tarek Collins. On the state police's website, she found a headshot of an attractive man with a wry smile, dark hair, and intelligent eyes. He was wearing a slightly ridiculous police uniform and a more than slightly ridiculous hat. The page included his email address and a phone number. Without thinking, she grabbed her phone and punched in the numbers.

"Investigations. How can I direct your call?" an operator answered.

"Detective Tarek Collins, please."

"May I ask who's calling?"

"Umm, yes. Kyra Gibson."

"Thank you, please hold."

An electronic version of an old INXS song screeched through the connection. While she waited, she began to doubt whether she should have called. *What am I going to say?* She mouthed the message she'd leave on the detective's voicemail. A polite introduction. A vague inquiry, and request to return her call. Then, the phone was ringing. Once. Twice. A click.

"This is Collins." A deep, melodic voice answered. *Shit.*

"Um, hi, yes, this is Kyra Gibson. My father was Ed Gibson." She paused. Detective Collins didn't say anything, so she continued, stumbling over her words. "I found your name as the person who investigated his death on Martha's Vineyard a few months ago, and I have some questions ... I was hoping you could answer." She closed her eyes and squeezed the phone. *Eloquent, Kyra.*

"Yes." He lengthened the word out, making it two syllables. Was he hesitating? She heard some noise in the background and realized he was in a car. "I think it makes sense to meet in person."

"Oh, okay. Do I come to you?"

"I can transfer you back to the office to schedule an appointment."

She heard him play with his phone, then he came back on the line.

"When will you arrive in the United States?"

So, he knew she lived abroad. She wasn't sure how she felt about that. What else did he know?

"I'm here, actually. I'm on Martha's Vineyard."

"You're there?" He sounded surprised.

"Yes."

He covered the phone and spoke to someone else, their voices muffled.

"I'm arriving on the island in a few hours. I'll call you when I get there. Where are you staying?"

"At my father's house." *Why?*

This conversation was getting stranger. She had figured the police would just dismiss her. She didn't expect a state police detective to agree to speak to the family of an accident victim from months ago with no preparation. *Does he even know where Ed's house is?*

"Good. I'll see you this evening."

The line went dead.

Kyra stared at the phone and blinked. *What in the actual hell just happened?* She replayed the conversation in her head.

The call had unnerved her. Detective Collin's willingness, almost eagerness, to speak with her felt suspicious somehow. She unlocked her phone to call her aunt, get her opinion, and noticed the time. Ten past three. *Shite. Grace.* She grabbed her jacket, but before leaving, she checked the burner phone one last time. It was still very much dead. *Bollocks.*

Chapter Four

THE APRIL SUN had burned off the morning chill, and the temperature was warmer. Kyra pulled her hair off her neck, uncomfortable just from the short walk to the Chamberses' property. A dark-green pickup sat in the driveway. Kyra rang the doorbell, and Julia opened the door and stepped to the side. "Good afternoon, Ms. Gibson. Grace and Charlie are on the terrace with Wesley. You can go on back." The Chamberses' cook pointed the way through the living room.

"Thank you, Julia." Kyra walked through the house, to the backyard, and to a sunken patio.

It was furnished like an outdoor living room, the furniture organized around an inviting bluestone hearth. Grace, Charlie, and Wes were chatting in front of a roaring wood-burning fire.

"Kyra, you made it. Please, join us." Charlie gestured to an empty seat on the large sofa close to the fire. "Iced tea?" she asked and stood to fill a glass from a pitcher on the coffee table.

"Oh, no, thank you. I can't stay." Kyra suppressed a shiver.

It was much too cold for iced anything.

Charlie plopped back down, tucking a thick throw blanket around her legs. "Have you met Wes?"

"Yes, I introduced them earlier today at The Quarry." Grace sipped from her glass.

Wes nodded at Grace and turned to give Kyra a thin smile. He studied her with strange, watery eyes.

"Yes, hi, again, Wes, Grace." Kyra raised her hands to the flames. Once she was still, the chill of spring crept back in, and she was thankful for the fire.

"Oh, Char, I'll go grab those papers of Ed's. I'll be right back." Grace gave Kyra a bright smile and hurried into the house.

"It's not really warm enough to be outside," Charlie said. She gave an exaggerated shiver. "But after being cooped up all winter, anything warmer than fifty feels like summer."

"Typical New Englanders," Wes added, his voice flat. "The islanders will be at the beach once it hits sixty."

"We force the seasons to change out of pure willpower, I think." Charlie laughed.

Wes turned to Kyra, his eyes locking onto her. "I brought Cronkite. He's in the kitchen with Mom."

"Mom?"

"Julia is Wes's mother. She came by today to use our kitchen for a party she's catering."

"She runs a few small service businesses for the summer crowd," Wes clarified, his lips curling around the word summer like it was sour. "But she'll take an odd catering job or two in the off-season." He looked off toward the house, where Kyra assumed Julia must have been working in the kitchen. "We've been trying to convince her to retire, but she's stubborn."

Grace returned with a manilla folder.

"Here you go, dear."

Kyra tried to hide her surprise. She'd expected a book or a gravy boat, not documents. "Thank you," she said, tucking the folder under her arm, stifling the urge to look through it. She shifted forward in her seat. "I'd better get back. I've some things to take care of at the house."

Wes stood up, towering over her, and Kyra suppressed the impulse to step back. He was massive, well over six foot with broad shoulders and the type of thick muscles gained from long hours of physical labor versus time spent in the gym.

"I'll give you a lift. The carrier is heavy." Wes turned, leaving Kyra with no option but to follow. *I guess I just inherited a cat.*

Like everything else in their house, the kitchen was top of the line, with an eight-burner range, pot filler, warming drawers, even double ovens. A lot of thought went into the design of a room the owners admitted to not knowing and having little interest in learning how to use. On the kitchen floor, against a wall, was a giant pet carrier. She crouched down to peek inside. There, hunched into a ball, looking disgusted with his predicament, was an enormous, long-haired, white cat with emerald-green eyes.

She reeled back. "He's huge!"

"We think he's a Maine Coon cat." Wes squatted next to her and poked his fingers into the carrier. Cronkite glared at them and flashed his teeth.

"He's very friendly but doesn't like his carrier much."

Julia glanced down at them and shrugged. "He's been good company for me these last few months," she said with a doting smile. Her knife flew through the herbs she was chopping.

"I see," Kyra mumbled, eyeing the murderous snowball. "You know, if he's happy with you, Julia, maybe it makes sense for him to stay with you? So we don't stress him?" She looked up, but Julia was already shaking her head.

"I'd love to keep him, but my daughter is allergic, and she comes back from Brazil for the summers." Her mouth turned down in a sad smile. "But I'll visit him often, yes?"

"Of course. Anytime." Kyra didn't tell her that the cat would be on a plane to London in a few days. She eyed the restless ball of fur. *I've inherited a yeti.* Her eyes slid closed. She mentally counted down from ten.

With a sigh, she stood up and wiped her hands on her jeans. "Okay. Does he need food or anything?" she asked, glancing about for any other supplies that came with the cat.

"There should be plenty at the house," Wes said. "I'll show you where it is. I'll take you now." Before Kyra could protest, Wes picked up the carrier as if it weighed nothing. "Tchau, Mama." He gave his mother a quick kiss on the cheek.

Kyra grabbed her father's file from the floor where she'd dropped it and followed Wes out. Wes put the carrier in the back seat of the pickup truck's king cab and hopped in. Kyra climbed in and leaned against the passenger door, putting space between her and Wes. He made her nervous, but she couldn't pinpoint why. He didn't say anything, just started the car and pulled out of the drive. She probably could have just carried the cat, she thought, then scolded herself. *He's a nice man, doing a nice thing. He and his mom took care of this cat for three months. Don't be a bitch. Don't do the* you thing *Ali talks about.* The truck rumbled down an unfamiliar street.

"Hey," she said, attempting an un-you thing. "Umm, thank you for taking care of the cat."

"No problem."

Kyra waited for him to say more.

Finally, after a seemingly endless silence, Wes made an irritated sound in the back of his throat, as if conversation was personally insulting to him. "The crew found him on a job site about two years ago. He was hiding in a pile of trash, half-starved." Wes slid his eyes to Kyra. "I'm talking about the cat. The guys were going to leave him at the shelter, but Charlie thought Ed would want him, so they dropped him off at his house instead."

"That sounds like him." Kyra watched the passing land-scape.

Wait. She wasn't naturally good at directions, but some-thing seemed off. They were traveling away from the cove and her father's house. "Where are we going?" Her voice came out sharper than intended. She clutched the folder against her chest. Her heart skipped. Ludicrous thoughts of escape flashed through her brain, but they were moving at close to thirty miles per hour. She wasn't going to jump out of the truck. *And if I did? I'd die. Why am I thinking of jumping out of a moving car?*

"Grace and Charlie are the last house on Heron's Cove Road. It doesn't intersect with your street. I have to go around." Wes didn't take his eyes off the road. "It's faster to walk, but the cat and carrier are heavy." Wes jerked his thumb toward the back seat.

Kyra kept her eyes glued on the road, looking for anything familiar. They stopped at a four-way intersection that she thought she might recognize. Wes turned right. Kyra clutched her phone in her pocket. If he didn't turn onto a familiar street soon, she'd call the police, she told herself, while the more practical voice in her head chided her for being silly and melodramatic. The road curved through the thicket. About a half mile down the street, he made another right onto yet another scrub-pine-lined road, but this one was familiar. Kyra let herself relax against the passenger seat as Wes pulled into her driveway.

He parked behind the Range Rover, effectively blocking it in, and turned off the engine. Wes turned to her but didn't meet her eyes, staring somewhere over her shoulder. He opened his mouth as if to say something, closed it, and cleared his throat, shifting his gaze to the rearview mirror.

"You ready, cat?" He jumped out of the truck, pulling on a thick jacket, and hoisted Cronkite's carrier. "Can you get the door?"

Kyra scrambled to shut the cab door for him and pulled the house keys from her pocket. "Umm, right. This way." She unlocked the front door, pushing it open.

She turned around, intending to take the carrier, but to her discomfort, Wes walked past her and into the house. He set the carrier on the floor and opened the gate.

"You're back home, buddy," Wes murmured. Cronkite took a few wary steps out of his prison and raised his nose to sniff the room. With a flick of his tail, he sauntered off, out of sight, leaving Kyra to manage her unwelcome houseguest alone.

"I guess he's glad to be back," Kyra said and attempted a grin. *Please go.* She shifted her weight from foot to foot.

"Looks that way." Wes shrugged. "I'll show you where his food and supplies are." Wes strode toward the kitchen.

"You know, it's fine. I can figure it out," Kyra called after him. "I'm sure you're busy."

She could have sworn that Wes paused for a split second, then continued through the kitchen and down into the basement as if he hadn't heard her. Kyra stood at the top of the stairs, her unease growing. *There's no chance in hell I'm following him down there. I've seen enough horror movies.* Kyra held onto her phone and debated calling emergency services, but what would she even say? Technically, he wasn't an intruder. She might not have invited him in, but she hadn't asked him to leave. *Christ, Kyra, he's just being neighborly.* Kyra pushed her hair out of her face. The minutes ticked by, and her discomfort morphed into anxiety. *What's he doing down there?* A few minutes later, she heard a heavy tread on the stairs. Wes emerged from the basement. He'd slung his jacket over his shoulder and was carrying a bag of cat food and a shopping bag. He set the bags down on the kitchen floor.

"There's more stuff down there, in the storage room—a litter box, bowls." He gestured toward the basement. "Did you need me to get that stuff for you, too?"

"No. No, thank you. I can get it," Kyra replied, frowning. "I've had cats before," she added, as if that qualified her to fetch stuff from a basement.

"All right. While down there, I got your door opened. It wasn't locked, just stuck."

No, it was locked. I'm positive it was locked. But she hadn't tried the door herself. *But why would Grace lie?*

"I also checked the HVAC system. It hasn't been serviced. So, I'll need to come back."

"The HVAC system?" she repeated and glanced at the basement door. *Come back?* She did not want this man coming back.

"Yeah, the geothermal heat and cooling system for the house." He spoke to her like she might be dim. Kyra cringed. "It needs regular maintenance to function properly. Charlie would have gotten around to it eventually, but I've added it to my schedule." He adjusted the heavy-looking jacket on his shoulder.

"Charlie's the property manager for the house?"

"Yeah." He turned back to face her. "She didn't tell you?"

"No." Kyra shook her head.

Wes made a grunt and shrugged. Kyra watched with dismay as he wandered into the kitchen and opened a drawer, pulling out a pen and pad of paper. That he knew his way around the house, like someone who had spent time here, was unsettling. *No, I definitely do not want him coming back.* Wes jotted down his phone number and held out the paper. "In case you have any issues."

"I have your card … you know, from earlier."

Wes gave her a blank look, shrugged, and dropped the paper on the counter. "Yeah, that's right." He headed toward the foyer.

Kyra shadowed him to the door, shutting it behind him and turning the lock. Only when she could no longer hear the tires crunching on the gravel did she step away.

Chapter Five

WHEN KYRA RETURNED to the kitchen, she found the large cat lounging on the island atop her father's folder. Pages were splayed out from her careless toss. "Well, I guess it's just you and me now," she said to the cat, and was rewarded with a yawn and a tail flick. "Fine, you're right. Let's see what was so important." Armed with a glass of wine and a snack, she sat on one of the barstools and reached for the file. Cronkite moved off the folder but remained on the kitchen island, watching. Kyra reached out to give him a pat, but he avoided her touch.

The folder contained articles from various newspapers, as well as handwritten notes and other printouts. Many were on the subject of wind energy and a company called Wetun Energy Industries headquartered in Boston. *Wetun?* She drummed her fingernails on the granite countertop, recalling the mess on her father's desk. *I think they were involved in the senator's scandal.* She pulled the pages closer.

Her father had printed out Wetun's financial statements. The company had performed well for years under the leadership of its previous CEO. Under his guidance, Wetun Energy Industries had successfully secured contracts for large wind projects all over the country, including in Texas,

Oregon, and Indiana; however, after a change in leadership, Wetun's luck has taken a turn for the worse. Dr. Maria Alonda took over five years ago, and since taking the mantle, she had seen year-over-year declines in revenue and significant cost increases.

According to her father's notes, last summer Wetun had submitted a proposal to the Energy and National Resources Committee seeking approval to build a wind farm off the coast of Massachusetts. If awarded the contract, Wetun Energy would receive funding to build and maintain the wind farm, as well as secure an exclusive contract to provide electricity to the entirety of southeastern Massachusetts. The contract was worth billions and would make the company profitable for the first time in years.

Kyra set the papers about Wetun aside and flipped through the next stack. Her father had printed out transcripts from sessions of the Energy and Natural Resources Committee, as well as information on Senator Phil Hawthorn. Another article from an architecture magazine was a feature on the "Green Residence" at Mander Lane Farm, built by Forrest & Co., Inc. She skimmed through the article, an interview with Wes Silva and Margot Hawthorn, the senator's wife. *Hmm. Wes Silva's company built the senator's house, too.*

She turned to the last pages. They were stamped by the US Department of Justice and dated last September fifteenth. So much of the report was redacted, Kyra couldn't be entirely sure, but it might be the results of the DOJ's investigation into Senator Hawthorn. The conclusion was *insufficient evidence to support a charge.* "So much for innocent until proven guilty," she muttered, as she read another page, this one of notes from an interview between Ed and an unnamed person from late December on the activities of "A."

Kyra's phone rang. "Hello?" she answered, distracted.

"Miss Gibson? This is Detective Collins."

"Oh, yes."

"I'm on my way to your house. I'll be there in twenty minutes."

Kyra was about to protest, but he hung up. She stared at the phone for a second before turning her attention back to the cat.

"What is wrong with these bloody people? Is it normal to just invite yourself here?"

Cronkite's tail tapped a piece of notepad paper that had slid out from the folder. She picked it up. It was a list of handwritten phone numbers, numbered one through twelve. She recognized a few of them, including one as the direct line to her office in London, and the 212 number was her father's colleague at the *Times*. The last one, just a partial only six digits—was circled at the bottom of the page. *An extension?*

"That's weird." *Why did he give this to Grace? What was he looking into?*

Her father had a habit of hiding his research and notes to protect them against loss or theft, but he'd been retired for years. And environmentalism really hadn't been his thing. He preferred grittier stories, often involving warlords or coups. He loved the danger. Loved bearing witness to the fallout. She'd read everything he'd written.

Kyra fanned the pages out on the island. "What were you doing?" she whispered.

A knock at the front door disrupted Kyra's thoughts, and she slid the papers back into the folder. She opened the door and came face-to-face with the handsome man from the state police website. He was dressed quite unridiculously in the television detective uniform of dark jeans, a light blue oxford shirt, and a loose tie.

"Miss Gibson?" He opened his wallet and showed her his badge. "Good evening. I'm Detective Collins with the Massachusetts State Police Investigative Department."

"Yes, hello." She stepped aside and waved him into the house. "Come in," she said.

He entered the foyer and dutifully wiped his feet on the mat. He stood to the side to let her shut and lock the door. She led him into the kitchen and gestured to the barstools at the island.

"Can I get you anything?" She pointed to her wineglass.

"A water, please," he said and slid onto a seat.

She poured him a glass of water, placed it in front of him, and returned to her own seat at the furthest end of the island. She sipped her wine, waiting for the detective to say something, but after a few moments of silence, when it became clear he wasn't going to, she spoke first.

"Thank you for taking the time to come out here. I really just have some questions about how my father died. I was hoping you could tell me what happened?"

The detective nodded and cleared his throat. "Yes, as you know, I was the detective assigned to the case involving the death of Edward Gibson." He spoke like he was delivering an official briefing, slow and formal. The detective sipped his water. "He died from drowning. Our theory is he hit his head, either during the fall or while in the water, possibly on the hull of a boat docked in the Edgartown harbor. The official ruling was accidental."

"The official ruling?" She'd caught the slight change in his tone. *Frustration? Irritation?* "And what about the unofficial ruling?"

"Pardon?"

"Please, just tell me what happened, exactly," she said, forcing her voice to soften and giving him what she hoped was the encouraging smile of a bereft daughter.

"We believe he was on a yacht owned by Senator Hawthorn, *The Island Pearl*, when he fell overboard, struck his head, and unable to climb out of the water, he drowned."

"Was he visiting the senator?"

"No. To our knowledge, he was the only person on the boat. His jacket was found on the vessel."

Kyra studied the detective's face. "He was on the boat alone? Why?"

"We don't know." The detective spun his water glass on the countertop, avoiding eye contact. "The Hawthorn family claim they had no knowledge that Mr. Gibson was on the vessel." There was something about the way Detective Collins wouldn't look at her.

The tense set to his shoulders made Kyra review all he'd just said.

She took a sip of wine. "You don't believe it was an accident." The words came out breathy, realizing the truth of her statement as she spoke it.

"Ma'am?" His gaze finally found hers, his eyes widened, and in the light, she noticed they were green. He shifted his weight in his seat.

"You could have told me all this over the phone in only a few minutes. You didn't need to come all the way out here. There must be some reason. I'm guessing you wanted something from the house? You think there's something here? Or just wanted to get a feel for me."

Detective Collins stayed silent, but she noticed his lips twitch, almost like he was trying not to smile.

"Did you recover his laptop or his phone?"

The hint of smile disappeared, and he shook his head.

"No, neither item was recovered. It's likely that the phone had been on his person, and it was lost to the bottom of the harbor." He drank down a bit of his water. "His wallet was zipped in his jacket pocket and, as I said, that was found on the vessel." Collins stared at his glass and frowned, the space between his eyes crinkling. He pressed his lips together, as if silently arguing with himself, and sighed. "Look, Miss Gibson."

"Kyra."

"Kyra." He gave her a nod. "The case is officially closed. I don't want to give you hope, or worse, dredge up painful memories. It was a tragic accident."

"I assure you, Detective, I'm not an aggrieved child trying to process her father's death. I just want to understand what happened."

He quirked an eyebrow at her tone.

"The facts don't make sense." She played with her wineglass stem, debating whether to tell him about her concerns, her unanswered questions, the suspicions that had been forming since she arrived. With a deep breath, she let it tumble out. "He didn't drive himself to town that night. Both sets of car keys are here. I haven't seen the jacket or wallet you found, so it's unlikely the keys would have been returned but not his other possessions, correct?" She didn't wait for his response. "And why would he be alone on someone else's boat? Why would he be on any boat in January? We weren't close, Detective Collins, but Ed Gibson wasn't a sailor."

"There was a nor'easter that night with heavy rains and strong wind," Collins offered. "We believe he may have sought shelter on the boat."

"He was in a town but sought shelter from a storm on someone else's boat? Then he took off his jacket but remained on the deck and fell off?" Kyra's eyes met his, challenging him. "Seriously, you don't believe that."

"No." He sighed, shaking his head. "No, I don't. I agree with your instincts that the narrative doesn't make sense."

"What if I told you he was working on a story?"

Collins looked up; his eyes darkened with interest. She pushed the file toward him.

"He gave this to some friends to hold on to before he died. It contains his research for a story he was looking into involving the senator and a contract for an offshore wind farm."

Collins opened the folder and scanned the contents. "Where was this?" he asked, flipping through the documents.

"Grace Chambers, the neighbor, had it. According to her, she forgot about it with the accident, then it just didn't seem important until I arrived. I don't think she looked through it."

"Do you have a draft of the story? Anything more?"

"Not that I've found, but I'll keep looking."

Detective Collins's eyes moved back and forth, taking in the information.

"It seems like an odd coincidence that he was investigating an energy contract associated with Senator Hawthorn, and then he died on his boat, don't you think?"

The detective collected the papers, returning them to the folder, his lips set in a thin line. "I don't believe in coincidences," he mumbled.

"Neither do I, Detective." Kyra glared at him, annoyed at the half-assed job of the police. Their story was absurd. "I appreciate you giving me the information you have. I'll look into this further on my own." Kyra shifted forward to stand up, dismissing the detective, but he ignored her, his frown deepening as if he was weighing his options and didn't like any of them.

His eyes met hers, and he motioned for her to stay seated. "As you're aware, a body was discovered in the aftermath of the fire at Mander Lane Farm this afternoon."

At her blank expression, he raised his eyebrow.

"It's all over the news. I gave a statement a few hours ago."

Kyra shook her head.

"The fire department determined that an accelerant was used to start and spread the fire quickly. It's unlikely it was set accidentally. A body was found in the debris." He paused, watching her, and she motioned for him to continue. "It's purely speculation at this point, since I don't have confirmation on cause of death from the medical examiner, but it's possible the victim was caught in the fire, or it could have been set after the victim died. Needless to say, the Hawthorns are involved in another suspicious death on the island."

"Why are you telling me this?"

"It will be purely unofficial. I'm not authorized to open closed investigations without fresh evidence."

Kyra frowned, still not following where the detective was going.

"But,"—he paused his green eyes glinting—"since I'm already here to investigate the incident at the farm, I can take another look at Ed Gibson's case file and make some inquiries on your behalf. I can't promise I'll find anything more than what you already know."

Kyra nodded. This could be wasted energy, but if she could get a little more information before she left, maybe it'd ease some of her guilt for not asking more questions when he died. For pretending she didn't care. Maybe she'd learn it was just an accident. Kyra finished her wine its tangy notes sour with self-reproach.

"Okay, I'd appreciate that, Detective. Thank you."

"If you find anything else that may be important, please give me a call." He stood and fished a business card out of his wallet. It slid across the granite, stopping in front of her. "I can see myself out. Goodnight, Miss Gibson."

Chapter Six

Tuesday

KYRA GASPED AND her eyes popped open. Her legs were bound. A heavy weight rested on her abdomen, pinning her to the mattress. Panic gripped her, and she sucked in a breath to scream. Then she heard it. A soft rumbling, and her eyes met the bottle green ones of her assailant. Cronkite stretched his large, fluffy paws and put his head back down, his purr intensifying. Kyra huffed a soft, content laugh. *Someone's comfortable.* She snuggled back down, surrendering to the pull of sleep, but a jarring buzz yanked her back to consciousness. She groaned and reached for her phone on the bedside table. Yowling, Cronk jumped down and trotted from the room. "Sorry," she mouthed after him.

"Hello?"

"Are you still asleep? How's the cat? How's the house?" A pause. "How are you?"

"Ali?" Kyra said, still groggy. "The cat's fine." She sat up and rubbed her eyes. Milky light seeped in at the corners of her window. "What time is it? What's wrong?" Kyra checked her phone. It was just past six.

"I'm checking in on you, obviously," Ali tsked. "How are things? Today you're meeting with the estate agent and the sales manager, right?"

"Yes, and the lawyer. Later this morning." *To sell the house, settle the estate, rush back to London. To my job, and my dreary little flat.* Kyra swallowed back an uneasy feeling and rubbed her face.

"You know, Kay, you don't have to sell it right away." Ali's voice was gentle. "If you want to wait and think about it, that's okay. You have time." She always seemed to know what Kyra was feeling, even before Kyra knew it herself. "You can take some time to learn more about our family, the island, your mom and dad… Enjoy a fabulous summer vacation house for a while."

"No, I'm just tired. Jet lag." Kyra rubbed the sleep from her eyes. "There's so much to do, and Assaf is off his trolley. You know how he can be." Her aunt sucked in a breath. "I'm fine, Ali, really. I'll sort everything here and be home before you know it. When I'm back, we can plan our own trip to stay at—what did you call it? *A fabulous summer vacation house?* Maybe France? Spain?" Kyra teased, forcing lightness into her tone.

"Yeah, that's it. I want to go to France." Ali heaved a resigned sigh. She could always see right through her niece's avoidance tactics. Apparently, according to Ali, she'd inherited her repressionist tendencies from her mother. "Even so, Kay. You're already there. You might as well let yourself enjoy it. If you keep suppressing your feelings, you'll age prematurely. Do you want wrinkles?"

"Is that why you have such a youthful glow? You're an oversharer?" Ali was barely ten years older, at forty-four.

She and Kyra were often mistaken for sisters, even if they

didn't look much alike. Long ago, Ali had committed to her signature icy blonde that brought out the creamy undertones in her perfect skin. Kyra's hair was dark, her own skin leaning more olive. They shared the same dark-blue eyes.

"That and a ten-step skincare routine. I mean it, Kay. Don't stick your head in the sand, just your toes. And if you need anything, any help, let me know."

"I will. Thank you." Kyra picked at the seam of her comforter. She knew Ali wanted to support her. Six months ago, she wouldn't have doubted that Ali'd jump on the first flight out if Kyra asked, but things were different now. "How's my Iggy?"

"He's decided that he'll only sleep in eight-minute increments and only if he's held while we walk him around the fucking house. By the time he's old enough to walk on his own, I'll be in amazing shape," Ali grumbled, but Kyra heard the love through her aunt's exhaustion.

"Give him a kiss for me and say hi to Cam. I'll call you later with all the news and I'll send you photos of Cronkite."

"You better. You know how much I want a cat. Stupid Cam and his allergies. Love you."

"Love you, too." Kyra plugged her phone into the charger and forced her still-tired limbs into the bathroom.

Freshly showered and dressed in jeans and a warm pullover, she found herself in front of the coffee machine while an insistent cat yowled at her and wove between her legs. She narrowly avoided falling on her face while feeding him. Coffee and toasted grocery-store croissant in hand, Kyra settled on the couch with her laptop. Between work calls, she perused the global, regional, and local news.

She paused on the homepage of the local paper. The headline was an article about the fire at Mander Lane Farm, including a statement by Detective Collins. The incident also made other papers but wasn't featured as prominently. She was scanning the headlines when one on the *Boston Globe*'s homepage caught her attention. "Senator's Son Expelled from Beacon Hill Hot Spot."

She clicked on the article, scanned its contents, then read it through more carefully. The paper reported that early Monday morning, an inebriated Chase Hawthorn was asked to leave a bar in Boston's Beacon Hill neighborhood for unruly behavior. He wasn't arrested, but police were called and escorted him back to his hotel. The paper reported that his family was spending the summer on Martha's Vineyard at their farm in Chilmark. Kyra tapped her nail on her keyboard. *Wes Silva and Grace had been talking about Chase Hawthorn*, she thought, trying to remember what she had overheard.

She typed in Chase Hawthorn's name. A slew of articles returned, including many from the society pages of DC and New York City papers. The photos alone were sufficient evidence that Chase Hawthorn partied hard and didn't have the good sense to decline a photo op from a paparazzo. He made frequent appearances on the gossip sites. She scanned photos of him at bars and clubs, drinking and dancing with celebrities and models and videos of him driving a red Porsche, entering restaurants, getting coffee. *The media hounds him.* She felt a pang of sympathy for the young man. One of the more predatory sites had resurfaced a years' old cellphone video of him drunkenly mouthing off to police in

New York. Unlike most of the photos, where Chase posed with the same smarmy smirk, in this video he appeared angry. He was shouting, flailing his arms, pointing to something off camera. His clothes were torn and askew. The video ended with him being thrown to the ground and handcuffed. Kyra frowned. *What happened?* She couldn't find any context about that night, but she found another article in the *Vineyard Times*. It reported on another incident, this one a fire on the island. Kyra's breath quickened.

At one of the private beaches up island, Chase and a few other kids had lit an illegal bonfire in windy conditions, and the fire spread. No one was hurt, and no property was damaged. Charges were never filed. That was over eight years ago. He'd have been about sixteen. Kyra frowned. It wasn't exactly damning evidence, just teenagers being teenagers.

Kyra kept searching. Chase had attended a prestigious liberal arts school in Connecticut but didn't complete his degree. A New York tabloid skirted libel claims by insinuating that he'd flunked out.

She was about to close the laptop when she spotted a link referencing an incident from the prior year. She clicked the link and was taken to a back-issue article of a Westchester paper. *Four Rescued from Sinking Pleasure Boat.* The article was archived, requiring an account to read it. Annoyed, she set one up and downloaded the PDF.

> *The Coast Guard rescued four revelers when their party boat sank. At approximately eleven p.m. Tuesday night, in response to a 911 call, the Falmouth police and Coast Guard rescued four individuals from a sinking pleasure boat. The four partygoers, identified as James Hallowell,*

22 of Purchase, NY, Mazie Elmer, 21, granddaughter of media magnate Hedge Elmer of Manhattan, NY, Grant Warren, 23 of Providence, RI, and Chase Hawthorn, 23, son of MA Senator Phil Hawthorn of Sudbury, MA, were partying on the Elmer family yacht, newly delivered to the marina at West Falmouth. The Coast Guard believes the passengers attempted to take the yacht out of the marina and struck a submerged rock or a mooring. No one was injured. Chase Hawthorn was the only experienced sailor on the vessel, having sailed in numerous regattas. He had recently failed the captain's licensing exam. Police have charged him with endangerment, which levies fines up to $1,500. The yacht was unrecoverable.

Kyra shut the laptop. "He gets himself into some unfortunate situations, doesn't he?" she said to the cat. Cronkite opened one eye and flicked his tail. "He probably sailed the boat my father fell from, don't you think? Wonder if the police talked to him? Maybe he has some idea how Ed fell?" She mulled over the idea. Cronk flicked his tail again. It landed on the sofa with a soft *thwap.* "You're right, I'd better get going." She reached out to scratch his ears. He didn't avoid her touch this time. *Progress.*

She climbed into the car and punched in the address of Mr. Entwistle's Vineyard Haven office. The GPS took her through back roads along South Beach. The water sparkled and danced between a bright sapphire and deep navy with white, foamy crests. She followed the curve of the road inland, away from the beach, but remembering Ali's advice this morning, she made a note to walk down to see it before she left.

She entered the village of Vineyard Haven. In the sunshine, the town center was much more vibrant than her first glimpses two days ago. And it was busy. Shop doors were open. Pedestrians milled about, congregating on the sidewalk. People queued outside of a coffee shop. She heard the blast of a ship's horn announcing a ferry's arrival or departure.

Halfway down the street, she found Mr. Entwistle's office. It was on the second story above a home-furnishings store. She entered a dim but tidy sitting room. Thick rugs overlapped each other, muffling footsteps and voices. A few armchairs were arranged around a square coffee table, facing a cold, empty fireplace.

"May I help you?" a creaky voice asked, and a severe-looking woman appeared in a doorway Kyra hadn't noticed.

"Oh, hi. I'm Kyra Gibson. I have an appointment with Mr. Entwistle."

"Of course. Please have a seat." The woman gestured to the chairs. "I'll let Mr. Entwistle know you're here. Can I bring you a coffee? Water?" Before waiting for an answer, the woman turned to go, then stopped, glancing back. "Or a tea?" she asked, probably registering Kyra's accent.

"No, thank you. I'm fine." Kyra took a seat in front of the empty fireplace. The hearth had been painted black, and the dark firebricks seemed to suck the warmth from the room. She rubbed away the chill on her arms and reached for a magazine on top of the stack. She flipped through it without seeing the pages, needing something to do. Her breakfast turned to a hard, uncomfortable lump in her stomach. She glanced at the doorway. *What's the bloody holdup?*

The woman reappeared.

"Mr. Entwistle will see you now. I'll take you to the conference room." Kyra followed her through the doorway and down a hall to a large room that took up the entire backend of the building. Within, the room held a conference table surrounded by swiveling chairs and a buffet table stocked with refreshments.

A woman with dark, unruly curls was already sitting at the table, rifling through a stack of papers. Charlie's head popped up and her cheeks widened into a grin. Someone coughed behind Kyra's shoulder, and she turned around. A dainty-looking man dressed in an old-fashioned, three-piece suit with a bowtie and wireframed glasses approached and held out his hand.

"Augustin Entwistle. Pleased to meet you, Ms. Gibson. Please, sit." He gestured to the empty chairs and took a seat at the head of the table. "Let me introduce you to my colleagues. You've already met Laura, my paralegal and assistant."

Kyra raised her hand to the woman who'd led her here.

"Pleased to meet you." Laura nodded and took the seat next to Mr. Entwistle.

"And this is Charlene Chambers." He held out a hand to Charlie. "I've engaged her company to assist us in cataloging and selling the contents of the property and to sell the house on your behalf."

"Yes, Auggie, Kyra and I've met. She's my neighbor." Charlie waved her hand at the lawyer, dismissing him.

Mr. Entwistle peered down his nose at her, then turned his attention to the folder in front of him.

Charlie glanced at Kyra and rolled her eyes. "He's very proper," she stage whispered, her grin mischievous.

Entwistle ignored them. He leaned back in his seat and steepled his fingers. "Charlene can explain the services she'll be providing. Laura and I will provide legal support and ensure the estate filings are complete." He nodded at Charlie.

"Kyra." Charlie cleared her throat, transitioning to businesswoman. "Here's the proposal." She passed Kyra a folder. "Once you're ready, we'll do a walkthrough to catalog the contents of the house. We'll sell off whatever is salable. Often, my company will buy furniture in good condition that can be used by our managed rental properties. Any items that cannot be sold will be donated or recycled off island. We'll proceed placing the house on the market. It's also possible that a buyer may want to purchase the property furnished. It's common on the island, and Ed finished decorating less than two years ago, so everything is still in great shape. We're at the end of the prime selling season now. Buyers often want guarantees they can use their new house for the summer months. Depending on your schedule, we can try to do a furnished sale now and off-load the property as quickly as possible. Or, if you prefer, we can keep it off the market this season. If you decide to put off selling it until next fall, and you don't want to lose an income opportunity, you can offer it as a high-end vacation rental. You also always have the option of listing it now, leaving the property unoccupied for the summer, and wait for the right offer to come through. Honestly, I don't think you'd wait that long. The house should sell easily."

Kyra felt the weight of Charlie's stare as she studied the

papers. She bit her lip.

"I'm just giving you all the options. You don't have to decide anything now."

Kyra nodded. She tried to swallow the burning in the back of her throat and forced herself to review the folder's contents. It contained schedules and the fees associated with each service. Charlie's fees would be deducted from the proceeds of the rental or the sale. Also included were agreements and the engagement contract. All very straightforward. Charlie knew what she was doing, not that Kyra expected anything less.

"No, I'm ready," Kyra said, but even she heard the waver in her voice.

She looked up. Charlie's smile faded, and her full lips pulled down at the corners. Kyra turned back to the proposal, pretending to read. Entwistle and Laura chatted in hushed tones about another case.

"Auggie, Laura, can we have a minute, please?"

"Of course." Entwistle nodded and left the room. Laura's sensible heels *thudded* after him. Charlie pushed her chair back and stood. She walked to the buffet and returned with two cups of hot coffee, placing one in front of Kyra.

"Oh, thank you," Kyra said still pretending to study the proposal.

Charlie sat in the chair next to her.

"Kyra." Charlie placed her hand on top of Kyra's. "Kyra, look at me."

Kyra reluctantly turned.

"Grace and I got quite close to your dad over the last few years. First working together and then being neighborly.

Eventually, we became friends."

Kyra picked at a scratch in the varnish on the tabletop.

"I may be out of line, but he talked about you all the time. His greatest regret was not being there for you after your mother died."

Kyra opened her mouth as if to speak, but Charlie held up her hand.

"No, let me get this out, and then you can make some decisions." She shrugged. "Or not. He came to the island because it was a place your mother loved. Ed wanted you to come. To see it and perhaps take part in her memory. He was terrified that your relationship was damaged beyond repair, and in respect of what he perceived was your preference, he tried to stay out of your life as much as possible."

Kyra gritted her teeth against the prickle behind her eyes and glanced down. She hadn't cried over her father in years. She'd be damned if she started now.

"I've my own history with estranged family. My own regrets." Charlie turned toward the window. "You don't get to my age without a few." She turned back with a sad smile. "Grace is much more forgiving. She always sees the best in people. She encouraged your dad to reach out. Make amends. She can be persuasive." Her lips stretched into a soft smile.

Kyra remembered the texts she'd ignored and felt her cheeks heat in shame.

If Charlie noticed, she didn't say anything. "Honestly, I think he always wanted to reach out but needed a push. When his efforts weren't successful, he called your aunt Alicia."

Kyra felt that familiar knot of resentment tighten in her chest.

"The first call didn't go so well. From what I heard, your aunt had some choice words for him, but then it got better, and the calls became less hostile. Eventually, he hoped to talk, really talk, with you."

"Ali didn't say anything," Kyra whispered. She couldn't help feeling betrayed by her aunt for going behind her back, but also thankful Ali had protected her.

"Were you ready to listen?" Charlie asked.

Kyra shook her head, half in answer and half in disbelief that so much had happened without her knowledge.

"And then he died in this horrible, tragic accident." Charlie spread her hands wide and reached for the file. "You don't have to listen to what I'm saying, and of course, I'll help you any way you want. And if after this, you prefer to work with someone else, I'll set that up for you. But I think—not that you've asked—you should take some time. If you want to learn about your family, you can, or just enjoy a few days on the island, but just let everything absorb, sink in, then decide. If you still want to sell and return to your life in London, I'll help you." Charlie sat back and sipped her coffee. Her cheeks were flushed, and she squeezed the bridge of her nose.

"You knew him really well, didn't you?" Kyra asked.

"I'd like to think so."

"You really think he wanted to get to know me?" Kyra ran her finger up and down the side of her now-tepid coffee mug, ashamed at how much she sounded like a hopeful little girl.

"I know it."

"And you'll still help me go through all his things?" Kyra's eyes met Charlie's, and Charlie's lips stretched into an encouraging smile. Kyra attempted her own. "He has a shit ton of stuff, you know."

"I'd be honored," Charlie said, and she reached out to embrace her.

Kyra, surprising herself, hugged Charlie back. When Charlie pulled away, releasing Kyra, her eyes sparkled.

"Fantastic!" Charlie clapped her hands. "I love annoying Auggie. Also, he *hates* being called Auggie, but Gran babysat him." Charlie shrugged.

"Wow, your family is really from the island, isn't it?"

"Six generations." Charlie nodded, but something dark flickered behind her eyes.

"What do you mean, pissing off Au, er, Mr. Entwistle?" *I can't call him Auggie.*

"I talk people out of selling all the time." She flipped her hand. "*After* he's done all the paperwork. It drives him nuts." Her grin widened. "So sad."

Kyra couldn't help it. She blew out a breathy laugh. "Tragic."

Charlie wrapped her arm around Kyra's shoulders, giving her a little squeeze. "I'll go get Auggie."

Kyra sipped her cold coffee. *I'm a homeowner in a country I don't live in. How am I going to afford this?* Her breathing became a touch shallower, and she forced herself to stay calm. *I can change my mind whenever I want. Charlie thinks it makes more sense to push the sale until next spring anyway.* She was rationalizing. *Dammit. I don't want to give it up, yet.*

Kyra cursed Ali for knowing her better than she knew herself. Again.

"Miss Gibson?" Entwistle entered the room and made a noise in his throat. "Charlene has informed me you'd like to wait to sell the property." He remained standing, his hands clasped behind his back.

Kyra nodded.

"Yes, of course, understandable," he said, his tone implying that it was anything but. He pushed his sleeve back to check his watch and made a smacking noise. "I've some papers for you to sign to finalize the estate and transfer Mr. Gibson's assets to you."

Laura set a pile of papers all tagged with sign-here stickies in front of Kyra.

"Thank you. I'll look these over and bring you the signed copies back later?"

Mr. Entwistle nodded, and Laura produced a folder.

"Very well. If there's nothing else," Entwistle said, "then please return the documents at your earliest convenience, and Laura will file them with the court, concluding our business." He nodded and turned to leave when Charlie reentered, blocking him. "Charlene, I'll see you at tomorrow's reception."

"Yes, Auggie, Grace received your RSVP." She stepped aside to let him out, rolling her eyes behind his back.

Kyra gathered her things, slipping the folders into her bag.

"You should come, you know." Charlie held the door open for Kyra and let her pass through.

"I'm sorry?"

"Grace is hosting a cocktail-party fundraiser at the yacht club for Senator Hawthorn's campaign and support for green initiatives, like Wes Silva's company, green energy, you know."

Kyra frowned, still confused.

"Grace is very active in the local community and island politics. With the senator on the island…" Her voice trailed off. She dug in her purse and pulled out an invitation on pale-green cardstock. "Here." She handed it to Kyra. "It'll be good for you to meet some people on the island. Ed certainly would have been at this event."

Kyra studied the card. The event was tomorrow night.

"Also, you'll get to see the Edgartown Yacht Club, which is normally only open to members, and it's stunning, right on the harbor, at sunset."

"It says *cocktail attire*." She followed her friend down the stairs.

"Cocktail attire, lite." Charlie grinned. "We're still a summer island." She checked her phone. "I've a showing. Consider it. I'll put you and a plus-one on the guest list." She pushed the door open and nodded to the card still in Kyra's hand. "Free food, open bar, amazing view. Did I say open bar? You'll love it. I'll see you later." Charlie gave Kyra a quick kiss on the cheek and hurried down the street.

Kyra slid the card into her bag and walked down to the harbor. She found an empty picnic table overlooking the water and sat down. Once she turned it on, her phone pinged with missed messages, almost all from Assaf asking after Loriann and a few other clients. She answered his frantic texts and scrolled through her emails. Kyra rubbed her temple. Her phone pinged again, and Kyra mumbled a curse.

"Are you free? I have some updates." It was the detective.

Her heart beat a little faster. *"Yes, I'm free."*

"I'm at the station in O.B. Will be finished soon. Meet at Claire's on the waterfront?"

"O.B.?" she mouthed. *What's that?* Kyra typed it into her phone. It was the neighboring town, Oak Bluffs, just a few miles away.

"I'm in Vineyard Haven." she texted. *"I'll head there now."*

Chapter Seven

CLAIRE'S WAS A little restaurant right on the harbor in Oak Bluffs. Kyra found Detective Collins sitting at a sunny table on the roof deck, his long legs stretched out as he read through some sort of report. She sat across from him just as a waitress placed a beer on the table. At her questioning look, he shrugged then grinned when she ordered a glass of wine.

"Afternoon, Detective." She caught her reflection in his mirrored sunglasses and winced at her too-bright smile.

"Hello, Miss Gibson." His grin morphed into a smirk.

Fucking hell. Kyra rummaged in her bag for her sunglasses, mortified. *Act professional.*

"So, please, tell me. What's the update?" She slipped her glasses on.

His expression blanked and he sat up. "Here." He selected two sheets of paper from a folder and slid them across the table. "This is the medical examiner's report for Mr. Gibson's death."

Kyra picked up the papers and scanned their contents. She gave him a questioning look, but he just nodded toward the documents. The detective drank his beer and turned toward the harbor, giving her privacy to read.

The ME had concluded that by evidence of water in the victim's lungs, the cause of death was attributed to cerebral hypoxia resulting from drowning. Lacerations to the back of his skull suggested blunt-force trauma. The examiner had found wood splinters in the wound. It was tested, but the sample was too small for any conclusive findings. The ME hypothesized the splinters came from the harbor decking or one of the oak pilings and became lodged when the victim struck his head. The injury to the back of Gibson's skull was sufficient to have rendered him unconscious or at least incapacitated enough that he wasn't able to pull himself from the water. With water temperatures close to forty degrees Fahrenheit, he would have suffered from hypothermia, further debilitating his ability to climb from the water.

The report included a blood analysis resulting in trace amounts of her father's blood-pressure medication, as well as detailed descriptions of contusions and abrasions, all post-mortem and likely from the current tossing the body. He also sustained injuries to his lower left leg that had been entangled in a buoy line.

She squinted rereading the paragraph. She looked at the detective. "He was tied down?"

Detective Collins turned back to her, but she couldn't see his eyes behind his sunglasses.

"Strange, isn't it? There had been a bad storm that night, and the current through the harbor would have been strong. It wouldn't have been surprising if his body had been swept out into the harbor or even further into the ocean, but he was tangled in a line anchored next to *The Island Pearl*."

"You didn't know about this until today?" She glared at

him from behind her glasses. *What kind of investigation did they run here?*

The detective made a face and placed his hand on the closed folder. "When I arrived on the island to oversee the investigation, per standard procedure, the body had been pulled from the water and taken to the morgue already. What evidence there was had been bagged and submitted, including the buoy line. I thought it was strange that the line he became entangled in was so close to the vessel from which we believe he fell, but the Coast Guard confirmed it wasn't that unusual. In struggling to get out of the water, he may have gotten tangled up." He frowned, as if he wasn't convinced.

"What's in that?" She nodded to the folder.

"The photographs from the scene and the autopsy." He slid his sunglasses off, set them aside, and his eyes met hers. "Miss Gibson, Kyra, these are ... grisly. Drowning victims ... it's horrible." His voice was soft. "I've reviewed them again, and there's nothing in here that contradicts the ME's report."

Kyra reached for the file, and Detective Collins pushed it toward her, but something in his expression, resignation, maybe, gave her pause.

"It's okay." She pushed it back. "I believe you. You'd tell me if you thought something was wrong."

He nodded and pulled the folder back. Kyra thought she saw relief flicker across his face.

"I'm sorry I didn't find anything more."

Maybe I'm trying to find something that isn't there. Kyra looked beyond him to the harbor and sipped her wine. *Ed had been alone. No one had been there to help him.* She swallowed back her guilt. Her mouth stretched into a humorless smile. She felt like *she*'d let *Ed* down. *The irony.*

Kyra took a deep breath and turned back to the detective. "How's the rest of the investigation? You know, the *real* one?" she asked, needing to talk about anything else.

"Well, not great, actually." He slipped his glasses back on and, after a pause, continued. "The accelerant has been identified as fertilizer." He ran his hands through his hair. "That's a dead end. It's a farm. The medical examiner here on the island isn't equipped to handle the identification processing or provide a cause of death on the body, so it's being sent to Boston. I won't have more information for a few days."

"They can't confirm whether the victim died from the fire or before the fire was set?"

"Not with the equipment they have here, no. It's a small island. We don't have a ton of resources. Boston should be able to, though."

"So, what do you do now?" she asked, watching the condensation drip down the side of her glass, looking anywhere but at her own reflection in his sunglasses.

"Well, if there's nothing to do but wait for more information from Boston, I'll head back tomorrow." He twirled his beer glass on the coaster. "If I can find a lead that furthers the investigation and requires me to stay, then this is a top priority for the department, given the connection to the senator."

"So, you have no leads?"

"I have nothing substantive or credible enough that

would get me a warrant to search the Mander Lane premises, and I can't really go around asking people questions. The investigation has to be handled delicately," he scoffed, saying the words like he was repeating a mandate handed down to him.

"Well, I found out some interesting things about Chase Hawthorn," Kyra offered. She filled him in on his encounter with the police in Boston on the night of the fire and his history of setting fires and crashing boats.

"Yeah, I would have liked to speak with him, but the family is refusing to cooperate without their lawyer present. I have a hard time believing that a habitual party boy with no history of violence would have killed someone, but that they're shielding him doesn't sit right," he mumbled, like he was speaking more to himself than Kyra.

"Accidentally locking someone in a building and setting it on fire, though, you'd believe?"

"It seems less unlikely, but he was in the city Sunday, as you've learned."

"How about on January third? When my father had his accident? Was Chase Hawthorn on the island?" Kyra leaned forward.

The detective flipped open the case file and scanned through it.

"Yes, he was on the island the night Mr. Gibson drowned. The Hawthorns were all questioned, but nothing ties him to the scene of the accident, and even then, what's the motive?"

"Maybe he killed my father by accident and got a taste for it," Kyra whispered, her eyes wide behind her sunglasses.

"You watch way too much true-crime television." Detective Collins chuckled. "It's rare for people to enjoy murder." His smile disappeared. "More often, it's a desperate last attempt, a nasty means to an end. What kind of lawyer are you, anyway?"

Kyra stiffened in her seat, surprised that he knew about her job.

"I pulled a background check on you the day you called. Brown undergrad, Columbia Law, associate at Downe Mastiss, then you transferred to the London office. You haven't been back to the States in years."

"Intellectual property," she said, feeling foolish, revealing how little she knew about what she'd involved herself in. "Most of my clients are press and news media, an odd author or musician here and there. Not exactly crime fighting." She spread out her hands, palms up. She waited for him to poke fun at her, call her naïve, but he didn't say anything.

"Oh, wait," she cried out, suddenly remembering. She pulled the pale-green card from her purse and handed it to him. "I may not be able to help you search the farm, but I can get you access to all the island's posh green politicos. Load the elite up with free drinks, hors d'oeuvres, and lots of flattery, and they'll tell you anything you want to know." Kyra grinned.

The detective slipped off his glasses to read the invitation.

"I'm impressed," he teased. "But how will this help? Do you think I'll wait in a van outside and whisper in your ear over a wire while you schmooze with the senator?"

"No, Detective Collins. You'll be there as my guest."

The detective eyed her and sighed, but he was smiling. "I suppose you should probably call me Tarek then."

Kyra grinned and gave him an exaggerated appraisal. "Well then, Tarek, you're going to need a suit."

Chapter Eight

Wednesday

KYRA STEPPED BACK from the full-length mirror, smoothed her dress, and gave herself a critical assessment. With a sound of frustration, she snapped another photo with her phone and texted Ali. *Black or cream?* She waited for her aunt to respond, desperate for help, but unsure why she was putting in such an effort. For the investigation, she had told herself. At Ali's prompting this morning, after Kyra had filled her in on yesterday's meeting with the lawyer, the conversation about her father, and this evening's *it's not a date* with the detective, Kyra had gone on a mad shopping spree in search of a cocktail dress that made her look fantastic but also said she didn't try too hard. The pickings were thin. Most of the shops hadn't opened for the season yet, and those that were open had limited inventory. She was stuck shopping for last season's pieces. Shopping bags and wrapping tissue were strewn on her bed, adding to the chaos. She hadn't even had the forethought to bring any sort of dress shoes.

Her phone pinged. *"What shoes?"*

Kyra snapped photos of a pair of strappy, black, high-heeled sandals she'd found. They were more appropriate for a girls' night or a nightclub than a swanky charity cocktail party. She also snapped a photo of a pair of nude block-heeled mules that she'd thought were cute when she bought them, but now felt matronly. Then, just for fun, she snapped a photo of the designer, cognac, suede, knee-high boots with the laser-cut cone heel. She'd snatched them from a deep-discount rack. She was awarded with Ali's immediate response. *"Those are fabulous. You've needed those your entire life!"* Followed by too many heart emojis.

Kyra smiled, appreciating her aunt's retail support.

"Can you wear the boots with an oxford and dark jeans? They'll think you're very British, very Princess Di."

Kyra snorted. No one in their right mind would ever compare her to Princess Diana. *"Seriously! Help! And, yes, I'm totes wearing that."*

"Wear the black dress with the black sandals, just wear your moto jacket and your hair down to make it a bit more casual. Send a photo!"

Kyra changed back into the black dress she'd found, also in the clearance section, at a boutique in Edgartown. It was a strapless, formfitting, sheath-style dress with a slit up the thigh. Again, a bit too sexy for a political event, but it fit her perfectly, and the slit wasn't scandalous. She strapped on the sandals and unpinned her hair so it fell down her back. She stepped back to reassess. *Not terrible. That's the best I'm going to do today.* She added the only jewelry she thought to bring: a simple pair of diamond studs and a gold chain that sat at the base of her neck. She slung her leather moto jacket over her shoulders like the girls at fashion week. Kyra snapped a photo and sent it to Ali. Ali responded with heart and fire emojis.

"It IS a DATE! I KNEW IT!!!!!"

"Still NOT a date, Ali."

The little dots faded in and out, and Kyra tapped her foot impatiently. This morning, Ali had badgered her until she'd sent Detective Collins's headshot from the state police website. That had been a mistake. Her aunt had squealed like a tween. She was so loud she woke up Iggy, and then in more dulcet tones insisted her niece go shopping. Kyra was likely going to need another suitcase to get all her purchases back to London.

"Whatever. I showed Cam the picture of the fit detective. He said definitely a date."

Kyra gritted her teeth and made a note to throat punch Cam for encouraging his wife. She typed furiously, needing to stop this immediately or die of embarrassment. *"I'm attending a cocktail party hosted by Grace and Charlie. Obviously not a date!"*

"You don't put in that much effort for your law galas…" Wink emoji.

Ali wasn't wrong. She only went to those events because Assaf insisted, but Kyra was reluctant to consider what that meant. Instead, she tidied the mess she'd made with her purchases and triple-checked her hair and makeup. As she was dumping the recyclables in the bin, she heard a knock on the door. She checked the time. Tarek was early.

When she opened the door, though, she was pleasantly surprised to see the Chamberses smiling back at her. Grace was wearing a mossy-green dress with a wide neckline. The skirt flared out at her waist. She'd accessorized with large, princess-cut, emerald earrings. Charlie was dressed in a tailored dark-gray suit that fit her so perfectly, it was clearly made for her. They both looked fabulous.

"Hi, dear. You look beautiful," Grace gushed, bouncing on her Manolos. "I'm so excited that you're coming. When Charlie told me she'd invited you, I was over the moon. It's going to be so much fun, and you'll meet so many lovely people." Kyra glanced at Charlie. Charlie raised one shoulder and sucked in her cheeks, expressing how *lovely* Kyra should expect these particular people to be. Kyra rolled her lips.

"You can hang out with me. At the open bar." Charlie winked.

"You both look amazing. Come in."

"Oh, no, we try." Grace waved off the compliment but broke into a pleased smile.

"Can I offer you a drink?" Kyra asked, ushering them toward the kitchen.

"Oh, umm…"

"We'd love one," Charlie said and took her wife's hand. "How many of these things have you hosted, love? And how many have gone off without a hitch and would have been perfect even if you hadn't shown up hours early?"

"Fine, yes." Grace frowned, then gave a shy smile. "What can I say? I'm an excellent planner." She eyed Charlie with reproach. "We can have one. One drink before we go."

Kyra opened the bottle of champagne she'd been chilling and found some flutes. She poured three glasses and raised hers.

"Cheers!" Grace sang, turning the word into two sylla-bles. The crystal made a soft, tinkling sound as the glasses touched.

"Did you need to ride over with us?" Charlie asked, setting down her glass.

"Umm, no, thank you. I'm going with Tarek."

"Tarek?" Grace asked, eyes wide in feigned innocence as she pressed her hand to her heart. "Tell us more."

"Yes, Tarek Collins." To her embarrassment, she felt her cheeks redden. Too casually, she raised her fingers to her cheeks. "He's a detective with the state police. He investigated my father's accident."

Grace watched her with a knowing sparkle in her eye that only further embarrassed Kyra. Her face was hot enough she was sure she resembled a roasted tomato. "I'd reached out to learn more about what happened, and..." She now realized her mistake. It hadn't occurred to her she'd have to explain why they were at the event together.

"Grace is just mad because she's already planning your wedding to Wes."

"Char!" Grace sputtered.

"But it's true." Charlie laughed and leaned in closer to Kyra. She whispered behind her hand, "You're getting a string quartet, by the way."

"Wes Silva?" Kyra was at a loss for words. *Wes Silva?!* "But I've only met him once." *And that man gives me the creeps.*

"Once is all it takes, dear," Grace said, patting her hand.

"It's not like that with Detective Collins, anyway. He's offered to help me understand what happened last winter. You know, to my dad." She looked away, embarrassed for a different, more complicated reason.

Grace, somber now, came around the island and put her arms around Kyra, pulling her close. "Oh, my dear, no. Of course. We understand. Char?"

Charlie nodded.

There was a knock on the door, interrupting the moment before it got more emotional, and Kyra ruined her eye makeup.

Grace gave her a gentle squeeze before letting her go. "Go get your detective."

Kyra made a face at her and, ignoring their muffled laughter, walked to the door. She opened it to see Tarek. He was elegantly dressed in a slim-fit, dark-gray suit with a black dress shirt and matching tie. Kyra felt the barest flutter in her chest. Detective Collins cleaned up quite nicely.

"Miss Gibson." His mouth hitched in a peculiar half smile, like he was challenging her to amuse him.

"Hi, come in. We're just having pre-drinks." She dragged her gaze away from him and waved him inside.

"We?" He quirked an eyebrow and followed her into the kitchen.

"Yes, these are my neighbors, Charlie and Grace Chambers."

Tarek shook their hands. "Nice to see you both again."

"Oh, right. I remember you from … before." Grace's voice wavered, and her eyes slid to Charlie with an uncomfortable frown.

"Nice to see you again, under better circumstances, Detective Collins." Charlie poured him a glass of champagne. At Kyra's questioning look, Charlie explained, "The police asked us some questions when Ed died." Charlie's gaze fell to the granite countertop, and when she looked back up, her features were drawn. "Grace and I identified him," she said.

Oh. Right. I wasn't here. Kyra swallowed back the burning sensation in her throat. Guilt for ignoring the request to come visit for the holiday and for exposing these women to something so horrific that she had avoided it again today. Kyra stared into her glass. *I'm a coward.*

"Please, call me Tarek," he said, taking the glass.

Kyra looked up into his dark-green eyes. He was watching her, probably thinking the same thing. He shifted his attention to Grace.

"Grace, I'm afraid I'm unfamiliar with the cause this event is supporting."

"Oh, yes, it's twofold, really." Grace bubbled, shifting into hostess mode. "We're kicking off an information campaign for more sustainable energy on the island." She waved her hand in a circle. "For example, this house is heated and cooled using geothermal energy, and its electricity consumption is offset by the solar panels installed on the roof. Senator Hawthorn is also using this as a fundraising opportunity for his campaign for reelection. He's running on a green platform." She sipped her champagne.

"Oh," he said. "I didn't realize this was a political event."

Kyra caught his fib and gave him a questioning look, but he was focused on Grace.

"So, who will be there?"

"Well, besides the senator and his people, we also have several business owners from the island committed to sustainability, including Wes." She slid an obvious sideways glance at Kyra.

Kyra crossed her arms over her chest. *Absolutely not.*

Charlie made a strangled sound over her champagne flute and pressed a napkin to her nose.

"And there are some campaign donors who have come in from the mainland." Grace ignored Charlie and reached for her purse. "I have the program, including the sponsorship and guest list." She pulled out a pale-green pamphlet from her bag and handed it to Tarek. "You can keep that one. There are more at the club."

"Thank you." He pushed back his sleeve to check his watch.

"Oh, yes." Grace clasped her hands. "We must be getting there. Char?"

"Yes, let's go." Charlie sighed and finished her champagne. "Don't worry, officer, we'll take a cab back."

"I'd expect nothing less." Tarek huffed a laugh.

Grace gave Kyra a quick kiss on her cheek and confirmed she had the address. Charlie followed her wife to the foyer, stopping to look back at Kyra. She pressed her hands together, eyes raised to the sky, a mockery of saintliness before slipping out the door.

"They're characters." Tarek finished his champagne.

"Yes, they really are," Kyra said, realizing in just a few days, she'd become quite attached to her new friends.

"Oh, here. This was out front." He pulled a small packing envelope from his pocket.

"That must be the cable. It came early." She ripped into the package. "Wait here." She ran off as fast as she could to get the burner phone from the office, cursing her stilettos. She brought it back and plugged the cable into the wall outlet.

Kyra stared, almost trembling with anticipation. "Yes!"

The battery signal began fading in and out. It was charging.

She showed Tarek the phone, her eyes shining. "I found this in Ed's car a few days ago. This isn't his normal phone. It could be someone else's? Or a burner?" She waited for him to make a joke.

Instead, he was frowning. "You didn't say anything about finding a phone."

"Oh, I must have forgotten. I'm sorry." Her gaze remained glued to the screen. She tried to power it on, but it needed more charge. "I'd ordered the cable before we met, and I guess I wanted to see if this would work before telling you about it." She didn't know why she hadn't mentioned the phone to Detective Collins. It just hadn't come up.

"Is it working?" He peered over her shoulder at the phone.

"Yes. It's charging. I guess we wait?" She slid onto the barstool the phone still cradled in her hands. She looked up, confused when she heard his soft laugh. "What?"

"Haven't you heard that saying about a watched pot?"

She made a face at him.

"Here, look at the guest list." Tarek slid Grace's pamphlet in front of her. "The Hawthorns and the Wetun Energy CEO Maria Alonda are attending. That's convenient."

"Yes, it is." She sighed, annoyed. "Fine, we can go." She dragged her eyes away from the phone's screen. "Maybe it'll be fully charged when we get back. Wait, did you say

Alonda?" she asked, pressing her lips together. She scanned the guest list. "Do you think that's *A* from my father's notes?"

"Could be. It seems to fit. Only one way to find out." He held out his hand.

KYRA SHOWED TAREK where she'd found the phone while searching through her father's car.

"Are there lots of compartments in here?" Tarek asked looking around the Range Rover.

"I think I found most of them."

"I'm going to ask the forensics team to take a quick look, if that's okay with you?" He glanced at her, then back at the road.

"Sure," she agreed. "Wait, will it ruin the car?"

"No, they'd just be doing me a favor. Normally, unless they find something that requires a more thorough search, they return the car in the condition they received it." He peeked over at her. "If they found DNA in large quantities, for example, then they take the interior apart."

Kyra frowned. "Are you joking?" she asked, recollecting all the crime shows she and Ali had binged where blood was found in the trunk. "You *are* joking."

"A little." He grinned. "But it's pretty close to the truth." He shrugged and slid the car into gear. "I doubt they'll find anything requiring disassembling the car, but maybe they'll find something else in a compartment you missed? Like another phone, a memory stick, papers?"

The sun was setting, casting a golden light on all the buildings along Edgartown's Main Street. Tarek parked, and they walked down to the yacht club on the harbor. The air was thick with the fragrance of lilacs and winter jasmine.

The sleepy little town seemed to have awoken. Restaurants and shops were bustling, their doors open to the sidewalk. The planter boxes hanging below the windows had been filled with colorful flowers.

Tarek pointed to a store. "Main Street opened early to cater to the party attendees."

"That would happen?" Edgartown had been a ghost town just hours earlier.

"For a political-campaign fundraiser bringing in lots of money? Sure." Tarek nodded and slipped his hands into his pockets. "The businesses will go back to a reduced schedule for a few more weeks. The official start of the season isn't until the last weekend in May."

That's a whole month away. I'll miss it, Kyra thought with the pang of disappointment.

"This is it." Tarek stopped in front of a dark wood door with brass accents.

The building was one of the tallest on the road at three stories high. Porches extended out toward the harbor. Here, too, all the windows were adorned with overflowing flower boxes. Tarek held the door open for her, and she stepped into the entryway.

The interior was decorated in a sophisticated boating theme with lots of glossy, dark-stained wood, plush navy rugs and textiles, and polished brass accents.

"Good evening, name, please?" a woman holding a clipboard asked as they entered. Kyra gave the woman their names. "Right through there. Enjoy."

They walked through a hall and up a short staircase into a large room with high-top tables placed around the space. A long bar took up the back wall. To their left, the glass doors had been opened, and people were milling about between the interior and the porch. Guests chatted along the porch railing, standing under heat lamps, sipping cocktails.

Kyra was relieved to see she wasn't under- or overdressed, the other guests having chosen cocktail dresses and suits of varying colors, including an uncomfortable amount of unironic seersucker. Waitstaff bustled among the guests, some carrying trays laden with hors d'oeuvres, others picking up abandoned glasses, napkins, and plates almost as quickly as the guests set them down. At the far end of the room, she spotted Grace chatting with an older man whom Kyra recognized from the news as Senator Phil Hawthorn. At his side was a woman with sleek, black hair. She had that pinched, gaunt face, symptomatic of stress or a lifetime of dieting.

Grace noticed Kyra and waved her over. "Senator Hawthorn, Margot, please let me introduce you to our new neighbor, Kyra Gibson."

"Nice to meet you, Miss Gibson. Welcome to the island." The senator gave her a warm smile and shook her hand.

Margot turned hawklike eyes on her. "I was unaware there was a recent sale on Crackatuxet," she said, her voice haughty and clearly implying little occurred on the island that she didn't know about.

"It's my father's house. I'm just staying there for a while." She turned to Tarek. "This is Detective Tarek Collins."

The senator's eyes widened a fraction.

He recovered quickly. "Ah, yes, of course. You're helping with the, uh, incident at Mander Lane. Nice to see you again, Detective." He clasped Tarek's hand.

Margot pursed her lips in distaste and glared at Tarek. "My love, leave such unpleasantness for another time," she cooed and wrapped a jeweled hand around her husband's elbow.

"It's such a horrible tragedy," the senator said, paying no attention to his wife. "We haven't learned any more information on what happened or who the poor victim is."

Tarek bowed his head. "Yes, it's frustrating waiting on the medical reports, but I've worked with the chief medical examiner in Boston for years. Dr. Khaleng is the best there is. And, given the high profile of the case, I know she's handling it personally."

"I appreciate that." The senator's tone was grim. "What gives me pause is my staff has reached all but one of my aides. Brendan. Brendan ... err. Margot, do you remember Brendan's last name?"

Margot shook her head, her expression still unpleasant. Kyra suspected Margot had never bothered to learn Brendan's first name.

"Perhaps we should ask Bill. He'd mentioned earlier today that he couldn't reach him." The senator adjusted his tie.

He's concerned. Kyra didn't know why that surprised her.

"Sweetheart, I'm sure his phone is just off," Margot said.

"You know how young people are, always off partying." She ran a disapproving look over Kyra and her thin lips twisted into a sneer. Kyra didn't know whether to be insulted or complimented that she was included among Margot's young people.

"Do you think?" he asked his wife.

"When was the last time you spoke to him? Would he have been on the island?" Tarek asked, smoothly switching from party guest to concerned constituent-slash-investigator.

"I'm not sure I've ever spoken with the young man, frankly." The senator had the grace to look sheepish. "I wouldn't know how he spends his leisure time, but I certainly did not invite him to Mander Lane. Bill may know more about him. He liaises with the aides."

"Bill?" Tarek repeated.

"Yes, Bill Grover. He's my chief of staff."

"He's here?" Tarek asked, scanning the crowd.

"Yes, he's over there, the gentleman with the bright-green tie." The senator pointed out another man across the room.

"I'll follow up with him. Thank you, Senator Hawthorn."

"Come, Philip. There are others you need to say hello to." Margot tugged on his elbow.

The senator grasped Tarek's hand in a warm handshake. "Your attention to the matter is appreciated, Detective," he said in a low voice before letting Margot guide him away.

"Sorry. Margot can be a bit … much," Grace grumbled. "Ignore her."

Charlie appeared, carrying two champagne flutes. She

handed one to Grace.

"Hi. What did I miss?"

"Oh, Margot being Margot," Grace said, her voice tinged with irritation. She accepted the glass from Charlie. Grace's eyes followed Margot as she and the senator walked away. "If she continues to insist on attending these events, she really needs to learn graciousness. Tarek and Kyra could have been potential donors." Grace sighed.

Kyra frowned. *I wouldn't give that horrible woman a cent.*

"I'm sure she's just saving it for people with names like Kennedy and Rockefeller." Charlie grimaced at Kyra. "Consider yourselves lucky. The only thing worse than being ignored by Margot Hawthorn is having her attention."

"I hope you're right, Char." Grace sighed, clearly not listening to Charlie.

Kyra followed Grace's gaze to the senator who was standing alone at the railing talking with his wife.

"Ugh, the point of this is for Phil to interact with the guests. Make them feel important so they donate to the campaign. Margot cannot monopolize all his time tonight." With another huff, Grace stalked off.

Charlie said, "Never a dull moment herding the island elite." She gave Kyra a quick hug. "I'd better follow her before she starts lining up guests to talk to Phil." Charlie excused herself.

"Maybe we should get a drink?" Kyra looked at Tarek who nodded, and she followed him toward the bar. "What do you think of the senator?"

"I'd like to speak to his chief of staff," Tarek said, not answering her question. He ordered two seltzer waters. "Let's see if we can learn more about this Brendan." There was an edge to his voice. He handed her a glass, and she followed him as he made his way to the man with the bright-green tie.

"Bill Grover?" Tarek held out his hand. "I'm Tarek Collins, and this is my"—he glanced at Kyra—"friend, Miss Gibson."

Bill Grover shook Tarek's hand, then Kyra's. "Nice to meet you," he said, his eyes on Kyra with an expression she couldn't read.

"I don't want to disturb you, but I'd like to ask a few questions. I'm a detective with the Massachusetts State Police Investigative Unit. It won't take more than a minute, I assure you."

Grover nodded; his eyes narrowed in suspicion.

"Miss Gibson and I were speaking with the senator just now, and he mentioned you had been unable to reach an aide?"

Grover's shoulders relaxed, but his expression was one of concern. "Yes, Brendan. He hasn't been in the office this week, and no one can reach him."

"Do you have Brendan's last name?"

"Delaney. His family is from Framingham. He's a good kid, responsible. That he hasn't called in is out of character." Grover stared into his cocktail glass, the lines on his forehead deepening.

"Have you notified the DC PD?"

"No. Do we need to?" His brow creased in alarm.

"When was your last communication with him?"

"I couldn't say." Grover shook his head. "I've been here on the island with Phil for the last few weeks, but I can check with the staff in DC." He placed his drink on the empty tray offered by one of the wait staff.

"I'll submit a request to follow up on our end." Tarek opened his mouth to say more, but Grover spoke first, his gaze locked on Kyra.

"Miss Gibson? As in Kyra? Ed and Isabel's daughter?"

"Yes, that's me," Kyra said, surprised. She studied Bill Grover but didn't recognize him. "Do I know you?"

"From London?"

Kyra nodded again, taken aback when Grover thrust out both his hands, clasping hers. "Ed was a good friend. I'm so very sorry for your loss." His voice went low, and he squeezed her hand in his own oversized paws before letting her go.

"Oh, thank you," she said. "You knew him?"

"Yes, very well." Grover's smile was sad. "We met years ago in Kuala Lumpur. He was there on an assignment, and I was working with the State Department at the time. We'd stayed in touch over the years and saw each other more frequently since he moved to the Island some years ago. He was a tenacious truth-seeker and a talented writer. He was terrible at golf." He huffed out a pained laugh and glanced at the floor.

"I didn't know he played golf."

"He only took it up in the past few years. I think to keep me company. We'd play whenever we could get a tee time." Grover slid his hands into his pockets. He rolled his shoulders and straightened up, as if pulling himself out of his memories. "Are you here long?"

"No, I'm just settling Ed's affairs before I return to London."

Grover nodded. "Of course. Of course." One of the servers approached them and spoke in his ear. "Thank you, I'll be right there." He looked back at Kyra. "I'd very much like to talk with you before you return home. Why don't you come by the farm tomorrow? The Hawthorns love showing it off." Grover glanced behind Kyra. "Sara," he called, waving someone over.

A trim woman dressed in pressed slacks and a half-tucked blouse walked over. "Bill," she said, her expression blank.

"Kyra, let me introduce you to Sara. Sara is the Hawthorns' farm manager. Sara, this is Kyra Gibson, Ed's daughter, and her guest, Mr. Collins, was it?"

Tarek nodded.

"Nice to meet you." Sara gave a polite nod.

"I've invited Ms. Gibson to come visit the farm tomorrow, see all the work you've done. Maybe get a tour?"

"Ah, yes," Sara said, not looking at her. "Tomorrow afternoon." She stared at something beyond Mr. Grover's shoulder. "Excuse me." Sara walked away.

Tarek raised an eyebrow at Kyra.

"She's an odd duck," Grover said, watching her walk off. "I think it's because she spends so little time with humans." He smoothed his tie. "But she's an expert in sustainable agriculture, and the farm's success is entirely because of her." Grover was about to say something further when the senator's voice called him from across the room. "Duty calls." He handed Kyra his card. "My and Beth, the house manager's numbers. I hope to see you tomorrow. Enjoy your evening." He excused himself to join Senator Hawthorn, who was surrounded by enthusiastic donors jostling for attention. Margot stood a bit to the side, her lips pressed together so tightly they disappeared.

"He seemed nice," Kyra said to Tarek, watching Grover walk away. She looked around the room and took in the little clusters of people all waiting for their turn with the senator. "Are all political events so weird?" Kyra asked.

Tarek drank his water. "Yes, and tiresome," he said with an irritated tone. His hand was in his hair, his eyes scanning the space. "Any idea which one of these people is Ms. Alonda from Wetun Energy?"

"We can ask Grace to point her out or the woman in the front."

"I'll go ask. Why don't you grab something to eat? I'll come get you at the bar when I'm done."

Kyra balked, disappointed she was being dismissed, but agreed with a nod. *Go, I'll just go hang out at the bar by myself.* He stalked off to find Grace or the attendant. She found an empty seat at the far end of the bar, near the wall. She took it, only realizing when she sat down that her feet had been hurting. Her toes started throbbing the second she relieved the pressure of standing. *Stupid sexy shoes.*

"What can I get you?"

"Umm, a white wine, please."

The bartender returned with a glass and a small bowl of salty snack mix.

"Here you go. Anything else?"

She shook her head, thanked him, and placed a few dollars on the bar. Kyra sipped her wine and munched on her snacks, picking through for the tasty bits, the pretzels, and the rye chips. She tossed the offensive wasabi peas onto a spare napkin. Her thoughts wandered as she watched the party's attendees. The temperature in the room had risen, and it was too warm away from the open sliding doors. The crowd had drifted closer to the porch and the refreshing, crisp sea air. Engrossed in people watching, she was slow to realize that she was within hearing range of a hushed but heated conversation coming from the hallway to her right. Her attention shifted from the mass of people to the voices she didn't recognize.

"Don't think I don't know about your activities, Brian," a woman whisper-shrieked.

"This isn't the time or place," a man responded with a steely, calm voice. "You need to go home. You're an embarrassment to yourself, your family, and to me."

"I'm fine," she snapped.

"You're hanging on that Coast Guard kid like a desperate whore. At least have the decorum to remain discrete, Adele. This is your mother's night, and you're making a scene." *Mother's night? Grace?* Grace hadn't mentioned a daughter. Kyra scanned the room and noticed a few people dressed in Coast Guard uniforms.

"Fuck her. She didn't even have the decency to invite us. Her assistant had to make the arrangements. Her *assistant*. And then only when I asked." Adele's voice rose. "That old bitch couldn't even be bothered."

"Not here. I'm warning you."

"What are you going to do about it?" Adele sneered, her voice dripping with contempt. Kyra shifted her gaze to her phone, pretending she hadn't been eavesdropping, as Adele came barreling out of the alcove. A few seconds later, a man emerged. He straightened his shirt cuffs under his suit jacket and walked to the bar to Kyra's left, his hand raised.

"Macallan. Neat," he called down to the bartender, who brought him a pale-green napkin and a lowball glass.

He drank it down in one gulp and brought the glass down with a *thump*. "Another," he demanded.

The bartender poured him another drink and set a bowl of bar snacks down in front of him before stepping away.

Brian pulled out the barstool next to Kyra and sat down with a sigh. "Cheers." He raised his glass.

She raised her own glass, almost a reflex, and shifted away from him.

"Brian Lee." He held out his hand. "And how are you connected to all this?" he asked and gestured to the room.

"Kyra Gibson." His hand was hot and clammy. She picked up her napkin, gripping it in her fist, and hoped he didn't notice. "My friend, Grace Chambers, invited me." She waited for his reaction. Nothing.

"I don't know her." He shrugged, his interest lost.

She studied him from under her eyelashes, pretending to look at her phone. He probably was in his early forties but could pass for much younger. His black hair was cut stylishly, longer in front, falling over his forehead, achieving a rakish appearance he must have been going for. Like nearly all the guests, he wore a business suit, but unlike most of the others, he'd worn no tie, and he'd left the top few buttons undone. He twisted his head around, clearly looking for someone more important to talk to.

Out of curiosity, or perhaps boredom, Kyra said, "Oh,

she's a personal friend of the senator." She turned back to her drink.

Brian's head swiveled back. He appraised her with renewed interest.

"You know Phil?"

"A bit." She shrugged. *Not technically a lie.* "How are you connected to all this?" she mimicked him, hoping her flirting wasn't as awkward as it felt.

He gave her a look that said she'd offended him. Apparently, she was supposed to know who he was, and based on his expression, be impressed.

She thickened her accent. "Pardon me. I'm not well acquainted with American politics."

He sat back and nodded. Her foreignness made her ignorance less unforgivable.

"Margot and Phil are my wife's parents."

I didn't read anything about the senator having a daughter.

"Your wife?"

"Yes. She's around here somewhere, *networking*. Helping to raise money for the cause, campaigning. You know how it is in politics." He knocked back the rest of his drink and motioned for a third. She didn't know how it was in politics, and she was certain the woman she'd seen storm away was in no way fit to be raising money.

"Hey." A soft, melodic voice came from behind, and Kyra felt the fabric of Tarek's jacket graze her bare shoulders. A flush of heat rippled through her.

Tarek angled his body toward Brian. "Tarek Collins." He held out his hand.

Brian's gaze shifted from Kyra's face to Tarek's, and he

pushed his hair off his forehead.

"Dr. Brian Lee." He emphasized the *doctor* part and eyed Kyra. Brian had to shift on his barstool to shake Tarek's hand. He studied the detective for a moment, then stood up. "Nice to meet you, Kate," he said, someone more important already in his sights. Dr. Lee grabbed his drink and, pushing past Tarek, strode away.

Detective Collins sat in his abandoned seat. "Nice guy."

"A proper gentleman." She made a face.

"Who was that?" Tarek laughed and ordered another seltzer.

"*Doctor* Brian Lee, son-in-law of the senator," Kyra replied. "But I don't remember reading about the senator having a daughter."

"He doesn't. The wife does, though, from a previous relationship."

"Oh." Kyra glanced at Margot who was still attached to her husband. "Did you find the Wetun CEO?"

"Grace introduced me to her. Dr. Maria Alonda." He handed Kyra a business card and picked at the discarded wasabi peas. "Lots of doctors here, apparently."

"And?"

"She seems like a nice lady. She's personally donating to the senator's campaign fund but has never visited the island before, or so she says. She didn't seem interested in speaking with me here but invited us to make an appointment at her office." He shrugged.

"So ... what does that mean?" She hadn't expected Tarek would learn much at the party, but she was still disappointed.

"It means I'll meet with her when I'm back in Boston." Tarek slid the napkin along the bar top. "But I'd like to have more information before I harass the CEO."

"And..." Kyra motioned for him to continue.

"We know there's a connection between Wetun Energy and the senator, but we really don't know anything else. I'd like to learn a bit more about that connection. Even if it has no bearing on the case, it may give me some context."

Kyra nodded, frowning at the entirely practical plan.

Tarek wiped his hands on a napkin. "C'mon." He stood and held out his hand.

"Where are we going?" Kyra asked, putting her hand in his and letting him help her up.

"Let's check out the Hawthorns' boat, then get some real food." He eyed a plate of intricately arranged hors d'oeuvres as a server passed by and his mouth turned down.

"Excellent." She grinned. "I'm famished."

Chapter Nine

KYRA SLIPPED ON her leather jacket and zipped it up to her neck. She followed Tarek down the dock toward the boat slips, taking care not to catch her stilettos in the decking slats. Tarek stopped short, and Kyra barely avoided running into him. She peered around him, and there, in the third slip, was a large luxury pleasure boat with a navy hull. Toward the front end, on the bow, painted in silver calligraphy, was the boat's name. *The Island Pearl.*

"This is it?" she asked, her voice barely a whisper.

"Yes," Tarek said, his voice just as soft.

Kyra blinked, taking it in. She crept closer for a better view, but Tarek held out his arm and nudged her back, angling his body in front of her.

"Hello?" he called, raising his voice to carry over the lapping waves. "Police."

"Oh, uh. Hello?" a voice responded, and a young man emerged from the shadows. He was holding what Kyra thought might be a beer bottle. The dark blue of his Coast Guard uniform made him nearly invisible until he stood right beneath the boat's lights. "Can I help you?"

"Good evening. I'm Detective Collins with the Massachusetts State Police. Is this the Hawthorns' boat, *The Island*

Pearl?"

"Umm, yeah." The man raised his beer and gestured to himself. "I'm Brody. With the Coast Guard." He pointed to his uniform and sloshed his beer. "Goddammit." He swiped at his chest. "You need something?" he asked, frowning down at his stained shirt.

"Brody?" Tarek asked. "As in Brody McAllister?"

"Yeah, what of it?" Brody's eyes snapped up to Tarek.

"You found Ed Gibson."

"Who?"

"You found the man who drowned in the harbor last January." Tarek's tone was patient and conversational, like he was asking for directions, not talking about finding a dead body.

"The dead drunk guy?" Brody barked a laugh.

Kyra stiffened.

"Yeah." He shrugged. "So what?"

Her indignation at Brody's callous response to finding her father turned to surprise when Tarek found her hand and gave it a reassuring squeeze, silently telling her to remain quiet.

"When do you return to the station on the mainland?" Tarek asked.

"I'm here for a while. Why?"

"I just had a few follow-up questions. I've got my card." Tarek dropped her hand and pulled a business card from his pocket. He held it up. "Can we meet up?"

Brody made a doubtful face.

"I'll buy you a drink."

"Yeah, sure." Brody descended to the stern to meet Tarek

and held out his hand to take the card. Tarek stepped up to *The Island Pearl* and gave a low, appreciative whistle when he was close enough to get a better look.

Kyra choked. *You've got to be kidding.* Tarek glanced at her. A warning flashed in his eyes.

"Beautiful," Tarek said as he turned back to the boat.

"Yeah, one of the nicest in the marina, which is saying something." Brody rolled his shoulders back. He took the card and glanced at it before slipping it into his back pocket. "I'll catch you soon, Collins. Ma'am." He raised his beer to Kyra, turned, and disappeared into the shadows.

"Ma'am? Really?" Kyra hissed. "I'm offended. I'm not that much older than that guy."

"Come on, granny. Now *I'm* famished."

They walked up the street along the harbor, their backs to the yacht club.

"There was someone else on that boat he didn't want me seeing," Tarek said.

"Really?" She turned back, squinting in the darkness. The light from the moon and the club seemed to converge on the silvery script on the yacht's bow. "You know, Dr. Brian was reaming out his wife for flirting with a Coast Guard officer at the party."

When Tarek raised his eyebrow. Kyra filled him in on the argument she'd overheard. "She stormed off. Maybe it was her?"

"Maybe." He tilted his head, considering it. "This is it." Tarek guided her toward a door set in a fieldstone foundation covered in English ivy. It opened into a warm, low-lit pub. Kyra paused in the entryway while her eyes adjusted to the dim interior lighting, cast from mismatched brass and pewter sconces. The room came into focus. A fire roared in a deep stone hearth on the far side of the pub. The paneled wainscotting absorbed the din, muffling the voices of the patrons sitting at simple wooden tables shoved into every nook and cranny. The air was tinged with a dampness that came from decades of spilled beer and stone walls.

"It's just like the ones in England." Her voice came out breathy.

"I thought you'd like it." Tarek's warm breath tickled her ear, and her heart stuttered.

She hadn't realized he was standing so close behind her.

"Tarek!" a voice boomed. An enormous man wearing a flannel shirt, the sleeves rolled up past his elbows displaying his tattoos, appeared. He'd tucked dishcloths in various pockets, and they fluttered around him like streamers. He strode up and clasped Tarek's hand, then gathered him into a bear hug. "Good to see you, man." The giant stepped back. He was at least a head taller than the detective, making Kyra feel tiny. He slapped his big hand down on the detective's shoulder. "This way." He stepped toward the dining area, then turned around and looked Kyra up and down. His eyes narrowed. "Bar or table?"

"Bar," Kyra said, raising her chin. "Please."

"I like her already." He grinned at Tarek, who let out a long-suffering sigh, earning a chuckle from the giant. He held out an enormous mitt of a hand to Kyra. "Gully."

"Kyra. Nice to meet you, Gully."

"Come on back." He led them toward a bar in the rear of the pub. Tarek pulled out the barstool closest to the fire for

Kyra to sit. Gully walked around the bar and, wiping his hands on one of his towels, asked, "What can I get you?"

"You're tending bar?" Tarek asked.

Gully shrugged. "You know how it is in the off-season. I've got eight bartenders scheduled to start Memorial Day weekend, but until then, it's me, or no drinks." He grinned and turned to Kyra. "Don't order anything too fancy."

She wasn't sure if he was teasing her.

"This place is open all year round," Tarek explained. "It's a few hundred years old, built by an English sea captain."

"So goes the legend." Gully nodded. "But take that with a grain of salt. The island has an unreliable but colorful history of drunk sailors and teetotalers. This part of the building has always been a tavern, though." He pointed to the ceiling. "Above us is storage space for the fancy hotel next door." He gestured toward the ocean. "The legends say the tavern was even open during prohibition to those islanders who knew about it, and they used the hotel as part of the bootlegging trade."

"Really?" Kyra asked, looking at the pub in a new light.

Gully winked at her. "The tourists love a good story."

"How long have you been coming here?" Kyra asked after Gully had taken their order. "The island, I mean."

"Since high school. Gully and I would get summer jobs. Gully worked in the restaurants and eventually bought this one a few years back. I worked at a bike shop, in construction, and for a few hours I drove a tour bus."

"A tour bus?" she repeated, unable to picture it.

"I crashed it…" He shrugged. "And then for the last few summers, I was a lifeguard on the beach by your house."

That fit. Of course, he's a swimmer.

"Wait, you crashed a tour bus?"

"First, it was empty. Second, it wasn't my fault, not really. No one explained emergency brakes to me. How was I supposed to know? I parked it, and it just rolled down the hill and slammed into the seawall." He mimed a car rolling down a hill and exploding. "Completely totaled. I was fired on the spot. That's when I started lifeguarding. Worse pay, better view."

"You swam, then?" she asked, laughing at the image Tarek had described.

"Yup, high school and college. Scholarship."

"And you know Gully from home? Where's that?" To her surprise, she wasn't just trying to make polite small talk. She was genuinely interested in the detective's story.

"We grew up together in Worcester, a city west of Boston." He focused on her, and she felt a not uncomfortable warmth radiate from her collarbones. "And how about you? Where did you grow up?"

"Our house was technically in New York, but we were rarely there," Kyra said, guessing he probably knew everything about her since he ran checks. "After my mom died, I went to live with my aunt in London." She gave him a thin smile. "It's not a great story." She met Tarek's intense gaze, then dropped her eyes to her wineglass, feeling self-conscious.

"And your dad? Where was he?" Tarek asked.

"He was a war correspondent, so he traveled a lot. I think after my mom died, he went to Beirut or Aleppo? He was rarely in one place for long." She didn't look up, afraid he'd look at her the way everyone did, with pity, when they realized she'd been essentially orphaned as a child.

"That must have been hard." Kyra's heart sank at his sympathetic tone.

Gully brought their food, setting the plates down on the bar. Kyra gave him a grateful smile.

"This looks delicious," she exclaimed as Gully slid a cheeseburger in front of her and a lobster roll in front of Tarek. Between them, he placed an enormous plate of fries.

Gully took Tarek's empty beer glass and grinned. "Another round?"

Tarek looked at Kyra. She nodded and grabbed a handful of French fries.

Kyra snuck another fry from the depleted plate. "I couldn't eat another thing."

Tarek leaned back and patted his flat stomach. "Me either," he said with a smile.

"Amateurs." Gully cleared away their plates and wiped down the bar. "Can I get you guys anything else?"

"No. Thank you. My burger was delicious." She sighed. "The English just don't know how to make a proper burger."

"It's the fat content. See, most countries and departments of health recommend a higher meat-to-fat ratio, but not here in the good ol' US of A. We like a solid fifty-fifty."

Kyra gaped at him. *No.*

"He's kidding," Tarek said. "It's closer to seventy-thirty."

"Next you're going to be telling her we don't use bacon fat in the fryer." Gully shook his head in mock disappointment.

Kyra's eyes went back and forth between them. She

didn't know if they were teasing her.

"How long you in town?" Gully asked Tarek.

"Just a few more days, probably."

Kyra caught him watching her before turning his eyes back to Gully. Gully's beard twitched.

"You're on the case of the fire at Mander Lane?"

"Yeah." Tarek spun his beer glass on the bar. "I need to follow up with some people in Boston, but I think I'll have to come back at some point."

"You be careful." Gully wiped his hands on his dishcloth, then his eyes traveled back to Kyra. His head tilted to the side while he studied her through narrowed eyes. "You, too."

Kyra straightened in her seat. Goosebumps rose on her arms.

"I'm always careful," Tarek scoffed. "You ready?" he asked, turning to her.

Kyra nodded and pulled on her jacket.

"Don't be a stranger." Gully shook his friend's hand. "And bring her back. I like her."

Tarek ignored him and ushered her out. She was aware of his hand on the small of her back, guiding her out of the restaurant. Before stepping outside, she looked back over her shoulder. Gully was still standing behind the bar, watching them. He raised his hand in a halfhearted wave and stepped out of sight.

The crisp evening air was a welcome change from the warm stuffiness of the pub. Kyra inhaled the refreshing scents of flowers and the sea. They turned away from Gully's place and walked up the street. She zipped up her jacket and stuffed her hands in her pockets, wishing she was wearing something warmer … and her sneakers. Her feet were murder.

"The car is that way, I think." Kyra pointed in the opposite direction.

"I texted the station, and they sent us a ride. Also, it gives forensics the opportunity to search your car. They'll pick it up, give it a once-over, and drop it off in the morning."

It was then she noticed the patrol car parked at the corner. The officer gave them a wave through the window. Tarek opened the rear door for her. She slid in, and Tarek climbed in behind her. The bench seat was made of a hard, slippery plastic, as was the floor, making it difficult for her to find a stable, comfortable position.

"It's a short ride." Tarek gestured to the bare-bones interior. "All set," he called to the driver and tapped on the ceiling.

The officer's head swiveled around, and he gave them a thumbs-up. The patrol car lurched forward, throwing Kyra into Tarek's chest, and his arm went around her shoulders, steadying her.

"Sorry." The officer glanced back at them in the rearview mirror, the creases at his eyes deepening. "The roads are terrible this year."

The car snaked out of town, weaving to avoid potholes.

"It's so dark." Kyra peered out the window. The only light came from the moon and stars.

"Yes, ma'am. Not a lot of lights out here."

Kyra made a face at the second ma'am of the evening. She felt, more than heard, Tarek's chuckle at her back.

Kyra took in the island at night. The darkness made it

difficult to make out recognizable landmarks, and they pulled into her driveway much earlier than she'd expected. The officer brought the car to a halt close to the walkway. Tarek grabbed her arm to keep her from sliding off the seat from the change in momentum.

"Sorry," she mumbled, untangling herself.

"Boy, Wes Silva sure did a good job on this old house," the officer said, dipping down in his seat to get a better view through the windshield.

"You know Wes Silva?" Kyra asked, leaning forward.

Tarek's hand slipped away.

"Yes, ma'am." Kyra bit her tongue. *Seriously!?* "He was a few years above me, but he was in the same grade as my cousin," the officer said, as if that explained everything.

He came around and opened the car door to let her out. She debated whether to invite Tarek in for a drink. Her heels caught in the gravel, and she stumbled.

"Whoa, careful there." The officer gripped her elbow, keeping her upright. "Good thing the detective got you a ride, huh?"

"Yes, um, thank you." She turned back to Tarek, who was still in the car, watching her. He looked like he was trying not to laugh. *Right, then. No drink.*

"Goodnight, and thanks for coming to the party. Um … and for dinner." She turned to the officer. "And the ride."

"No problem." The officer grinned and climbed back into the driver's seat.

"Night, Kyra," she heard Tarek call after her. "Talk to you tomorrow."

She pushed open the door and felt along the wall for the

light switch. Her fingers found the panels, and the room flooded with light. She shut the door behind her and locked it. Sighing, she slipped off her cursed heels and tossed them in a corner. She headed toward the kitchen, turning on lights as she went. The police cruiser's wheels crunched on the gravel as it left the driveway. A loud yowl welcomed her home. Cronkite announced his presence with another meow and rubbed his face against her calf.

"Hungry?" She reached down to scratch the cat's ears. He pushed into her hand and purred. Kyra pulled down a bowl and poured out his kibble when her eyes fell on the phone, still plugged into the wall. "The phone!" She dropped Cronk's bowl on the counter and reached for it, ignoring the cat's withering stare. She pressed the power button, and the phone booted up. "Yes!" She fist pumped into the air. Before she could open the menus, Cronk jumped on the counter. He let out a cry, demanding her immediate and unwavering attention to his dinner needs. "All right," she grumbled. "I'll feed you."

Kyra fed the cat and reached for her own phone. She snapped a photo of the burner's lit-up screen and shot a text off to Detective Collins.

The phone powered on.

He responded a few seconds later. *I'll bring your car back in the morning. Don't do anything until I'm there.*

Kyra frowned, annoyed. "Whatever. I won't *do anything.*" She stalked upstairs to bed, leaving the phone plugged into the wall.

Chapter Ten

Thursday

KYRA RUBBED HER eyes and stumbled down to the kitchen, Cronkite on her heels. She'd slept in, and for the first time since arriving on the island, she felt fully rested. The sun streamed in through the wall of windows, flooding the living room. On autopilot, she fed the cat and made coffee. While she waited for the machine, her gaze fell on the burner phone, still plugged into the wall. It took all her willpower to wait for Detective Collins. She mumbled a few choice English insults, smiling at her crass creativity. The coffeemaker stopped buzzing, and she reached for her mug. She savored the first taste of the hot liquid as she went through her mental to-do list. Today she was going to start cleaning out her father's things. She felt her phone buzz and pulled it from her pocket. A message from Tarek. He'd be by around one.

"We have a few hours to kill, Cronks." The cat blinked his absinthe eyes at her. "Yeah, probably should start with the office?"

Kyra carried her coffee to the study. The cat trotted along beside her. "Do you think we'll find anything interesting?" He jumped up onto the desk and stared at her, swishing his feather-duster tail. Kyra surveyed the papers scattered on top of her father's desk. "We're going to need trash bags."

Bags in hand, she began sorting. Bills, junk mail, old magazines, newspapers. It all went into a bag. She set aside things that could be important for a more thorough review later, but most of the paper was destined for the recycle bin. In hardly any time, she had cleared the top of the desk. Next, she moved to the drawers, again filled with mostly junk. "Did he know about the secret compartment?" she asked the cat. Cronkite flopped onto his side and pawed a paperclip.

Kyra ran her hand along the desk. She had been there when her mom had bought it from an antique shop in France. The shopkeeper had told them it was well over a hundred years old. It wasn't made by any known craftsperson or particularly valuable, but it was unique. The second drawer down on the left was built out with cubbies, a large, rectangular compartment in the front and twelve smaller ones behind it of varying depths. Isabel thought it may have been made to hold a scale and weights.

They had made up stories about the lives of the women who'd sat behind the desk over the centuries. Sometimes she was an apothecary distributing herbs and tinctures or an alchemist mixing potions and turning lead into gold, but Kyra's favorite version was the lady jeweler for King Louis's Versailles. Their master jewelry maker made tiaras out of daisies and bracelets out of the long grasses that grew in their garden. Kyra played for hours, putting her treasures in the cubbies for safekeeping until her father returned from his assignment when she could tell him all about their adventures. She never told either of her parents about the hidden cubby, though.

She pulled out the drawer until it reached its stoppers, then she carefully grasped the sidewalls of the interior compartment box and pressed them in toward each other until she heard a soft click, and the entire compartment lifted out, revealing the false bottom. The drawer was actually a few inches deeper than it appeared from the exterior. Kyra let loose an involuntary squeak. *There's stuff in here.*

She pulled the papers into her lap. At the top was a yellowed packet folded in half and bound with yarn, like a booklet. She recognized it immediately. It brought her back to a Christmas in Lima. They'd stayed in an apartment with blue tile floors. She'd made her father's present that year. The *Gibson Globe*, a newspaper reporting on their family activities while he'd been on location. Kyra remembered working on it for weeks, writing each story and drawing each picture, then carefully copying out the final version. She was eight.

"I can't believe he kept this," she whispered, her voice hoarse.

She placed the *Gibson Globe* in the junk pile and turned to the rest of the papers. The pile included a few articles about her and some high-profile deals she'd worked on in London, Ali's wedding invitation, photos of him and Isabel, and one of the three of them on a beach somewhere smiling. Clearly, he'd learned of the false bottom at some point. She couldn't help but feel like he'd put these items there for her to find. *But why?* Kyra felt too many emotions at once. Resentment, accompanied by sadness, guilt, and annoyance.

She settled on anger. *Keepsakes and family photos don't make up for dumping me.* Kyra let loose a breath and lifted the papers to toss in the trash. A sealed envelope slipped out and landed in her lap.

She flipped it over, and there, across the seal, written in her father's spiky script, was his nickname for her. *Kuddlebug.* Kyra tore it open. She reached inside and pulled out a folded piece of paper ripped from a notebook. *The hell?* She unfolded it. Her father had written the name of a cloud-storage service and an account number.

She turned it over. "Where's the password?"

Cronk blinked at her.

Gripping the paper, Kyra hurried to the living room and booted up her laptop. Cronk trotted behind her. She found the website for SkyCloud Data Storage and entered the account number, which, of course, prompted her for a password or pin number. She tried her mom's name, her name, Cronk's name. Nope. Nope. Nope. She tried important number combinations, like Isabel's birthday, their wedding anniversary. She tried her own birthday—not that he'd ever remembered it. Nothing. Kyra pushed the laptop away with a huff.

"When were you born, Cronk?"

The cat cocked his head and began licking his paw.

"Do you think Tarek can get SkyCloud to give us the password?"

She scratched the cat's chin and was rewarded with a deep rumbling.

"There's no harm in asking, though, is there?" She swore Cronk blinked his agreement.

"WHAT DOES IT matter? It's a *farm*." Ali grinned from the laptop screen on the bed. She squinted at the different tops Kyra held against her body. She'd called her aunt needing last-minute fashion advice, but Ali's smug smile had her rethinking the wisdom of that decision.

"I didn't bring enough clothes." Kyra threw them to the side, frustrated. A dull ache radiated from her arms and back, sore from all the trash bags she'd filled and lugged to the bins in the garage. Cleaning out the office had taken forever, and then she was stuck on a two-hour call talking down Assaf and Loriann. Tarek was going to arrive any minute, and she wasn't dressed.

"Wait. Is this another *date?*" Ali shrieked, then winced. "Shit, if I woke the fucking baby." She tipped her ear up. "No, thank god."

"No, of course not." Kyra rustled through the clothes on the bed. "I'm not even sure he's going to come with me, actually."

"Oh, but you want him to. You fancy him!" Ali's grin widened.

"Seriously, Ali, don't be ridiculous. I'm leaving in a few days."

"So? You were in Majorca for less than three days and had a magical time with Marco."

"It was Marius," Kyra snapped, then frowned. "It's not the same. I'm not on holiday."

"You *do* like him." Ali's tone was gleeful. "Tell me every-thing. What happened last night, Kay?"

"Nothing." She sighed and glared at her aunt. "It was a professional outing. We went to the party, Detective Collins asked a bunch of questions while I waited around, then after we got some food at a pub. He dropped me off before ten. That was it."

"Well, that's … disappointing." Ali made a face. Cam's grease-stained coveralls popped into the frame. He tapped his wife on the shoulder. "Honestly, you can't deal with it?" She gestured toward Kyra.

"Tinkering today?"

"Hi there, Kay. Doesn't look like I'll get to it," Cam said and raised his two fingers in a tired wave. He turned his pleading eyes back to Ali. "He won't go down. I don't know what else to do."

"Wait, he's still not asleep?" Ali grimaced and sighed. "I'd better go. Wear the new boots. Love you."

"Love you, too," Kyra said as the video call disconnected. Kyra considered her options splayed on the bed, disappointed with her packing choices.

She crossed the hall to her father's room. It took up the entire back wall of the house, and like Grace had said, had floor-to-ceiling windows overlooking the cove. She opened the door to the walk-in closet. It was well organized. *He was never this tidy.* She scanned the contents until she found her father's sweaters folded on a shelf. There, on the top shelf, she found what she was looking for, a creamy merino-wool, Aran-style pullover. She'd purchased it while on a girls' trip to Ireland as a birthday or Christmas gift for her father a few years prior. She wasn't surprised he never wore it. Kyra yanked it from the pile, tore off the tags, and pulled it over her head.

Back in her own room, she zipped her new suede boots over her favorite jeans and gave herself a once-over in the mirror.

"Meow!" Cronk yowled from his position on the bed among the mayhem of knitwear and denim.

"I know. I'm being stupid." She cleared away the clothes despite the cat's protests. "Of course, it doesn't matter how I look or what I'm wearing. Or that I've spiraled into insanity, talking to a cat." She gave Cronk a kiss on his furry head. "I'm off, Cronker," she murmured and headed downstairs.

She was eager to go through the phone with Detective Collins. *What could be on there? Likely nothing.* But the likely reality didn't diminish her excitement. She was still itching with anticipation.

Kyra froze on the landing. Wes Silva stood in her foyer, a backpack slung over his shoulder.

"Um. Excuse me?" she said.

Wes stared up at her.

"I'm sorry. I didn't hear the doorbell."

Why am I apologizing?

"There isn't one. Ed didn't like them. And the door was unlocked." Wes jerked his thumb over his shoulder.

Kyra hesitated. *No, that's not right. I locked it last night, didn't I?* She tried to remember.

"What can I do for you, Mr. Silva?" She reached for her phone in her back pocket, clenching her teeth when she realized she'd left it upstairs.

"I came to check on the geothermal system. Like I told you."

"Oh, right. I'd assumed you'd make an appointment. Now's not a great time, actually." Silva stared at her through narrowed eyes and with a scornful expression that said what he thought of her assumption.

"It needs to be serviced, and I'm here now." He patted the backpack strap.

Kyra blinked unsure about what she should say. Her mouth opened and closed.

"Is there a better time, then? I can let myself in." He held up a large keyring and jangled it at her.

"But you just said the door was unlocked."

Wes shrugged. "I can't remember."

Kyra stepped back, her heel hitting the riser of the step behind her. Her heart banged against her ribs.

What the hell is happening right now?

Wes shifted the backpack, hunching his shoulders under the weight. Realization dawned on her. He hadn't known she was home since her car was still with the police.

Kyra swallowed and forced herself to descend the staircase, slowly, casually, keeping her hand on the rail. "Thank you for your attention, but your services may not be immediately necessary."

"What?" Wes glared at her.

Kyra shrugged.

"Have you turned on the heat?" he asked.

Kyra frowned, confused by the question. She hadn't. She'd been using the gas fireplaces for warmth.

Detective Collins appeared in the doorway. He looked between Wes and Kyra, and something in his expression darkened as he stepped inside.

"Ah, Detective. Right on time." She flashed him a courteous smile. "Thank you for coming to see me."

Tarek's forehead creased in bewilderment, and she willed him to understand her silent message. *Please. Play along.*

"As you can see, Mr. Silva, now is not a convenient time. I'm busy. I'll let you know about rescheduling." She jerked her chin toward the door. "Good day."

Wes didn't move. His eyes shifted between Kyra and the detective a few times, finally resting on Tarek.

His mouth twisted into a sneer. "Fine." He turned on his heel and stormed out, almost barreling over the detective, who stepped out of the way just in time. His truck door slammed shut, and the wheels spun over the gravel drive.

"What the fuck was that?" Tarek glared at her. A muscle in his cheek twitched.

She sagged against the console table and pushed her hair away from her face. "I don't know," she said, her voice shaking. "He just walked into the house."

Tarek closed the door and turned the lock.

"He said the door was unlocked, but I'm sure I locked it last night." She racked her brain. "He has a key. He can just let himself in. I don't think he knew I was home."

"You didn't invite him?"

"No, of course not." She ran her hands over her arms.

Now that Wes had left, she felt cold, chilled down to her bones.

Tarek pulled out his phone, tapped the screen a few times, and pressed it to his ear. "It's Collins. I need a favor." He walked into the kitchen, still on his phone, and Kyra ran upstairs to grab her own. When she came back down to the kitchen, Detective Collins was leaning against the counter. "I called a locksmith. They'll have someone out here in a few hours to replace all the locks. He'll text you the details."

"Thank you." Kyra poured herself a glass of water. "You didn't need to do that."

Tarek didn't respond, but there was a stiffness to his posture.

"Did they find anything in Ed's car?"

"No." Tarek studied her for a moment. "Did you want to show me the phone?" he asked and sat down at the island. Cronkite jumped up, demanding scratches.

"Oh. Yes. It's right here." With the unexpected appearance of Wes Silva, she'd almost forgotten why Tarek was here. Kyra unplugged the phone and handed it to him. "Would you like a coffee?"

"Please."

Kyra popped a pod into the machine. They waited for it to brew, the only sound the whirring and sputtering of the coffeemaker. "How do you take it?"

"Black, one sugar."

Kyra added sugar to the first coffee and passed it to him. He waited for her to repeat the process for her own cup. Tarek seemed to understand she was trying to calm down, that she was more rattled than she was willing to admit. Finally, cup in hand, she sat next to him.

Tarek turned the phone on. He navigated to the call log and scrolled through the numbers on the phone. "Look." He pointed with his thumb. "He had inbound and outbound calls to the same number on the day he died. The last one connected for a four-minute call at seven p.m. That's interesting."

"How's that?" She peered over his shoulder. He shifted closer to give her a better view.

"Well, at the very least, he was still alive at seven. He had the phone and was in or near his car." Tarek rubbed his jaw.

"The area code is 781."

"That's the Boston suburbs." Tarek's brow furrowed. He pulled a small notebook from his pocket and jotted down the phone number. "I'll have the number run, but I suspect it's another burner phone, probably bought from a convenience store outside of the city." He continued to navigate the phone's rudimentary interface. "He didn't seem to have any stored numbers, and there are no voicemails."

"What about text messages? He texted." Something in Kyra's chest gave a painful tug as she remembered all the unanswered texts her father had sent in the months before his death.

"Hmm... Yeah, there are a few outbound ones. What is that? A series of numbers?"

Kyra read the texts. Each one contained groupings of seemingly random numbers, not unlike SPAM messages: *1311-730-05, 3411-20-04, 3212-20-04, !!2601-13-08!!* She chewed her bottom lip, thinking. She sipped her coffee. Something clicked in her memory.

"Meeting times and places," she said, annoyed.

"What? How do you know that?"

"He loved that old cloak-and-dagger, spy-vs-spy shit." At Tarek's still confused face, she tried to explain. "When I was a kid, he'd always make everything a search for clues, like for birthday presents or whatnot. Believe me, it sounds fun, but it got tiresome quickly. Sometimes, I just wanted to eat my birthday cake, you know? He used this system all the time. It was part of a silly code he'd made up, and he used it with his confidential sources. The first set of numbers is the day, the second the time, and the third relates to a set of predetermined meetup places. See here." She pointed to the first one. "He was telling the recipient to make contact on the first Tuesday of November at 7:30 a.m. at the fifth designated place, and the next one, the third Wednesday in November at eight p.m. at the fourth place. They connected again there on the third Monday in December at eight p.m."

"Okay." Tarek didn't sound convinced, but the more she thought about it, the more she knew she was right. That there were only a handful of people who knew about her father's system and could decipher his code gave her pause. "Are those the only messages?"

"It looks that way." He glanced up at her. "What?"

"It's just weird he saved them. He didn't save the responses, just the outbound messages. All to the same number, right?" Tarek gave her a look that hovered between confusion and curiosity. *Who are these messages for?* She came up blank. "Never mind. I don't know what I'm saying."

"How do we figure out the places represented by the third set of numbers?" he asked, turning back to the phone.

"There should be a key somewhere. Or at least there was for me." She glanced around the kitchen and raised her hands in a helpless gesture. "The third set of numbers would refer to something different, depending on the context. Sometimes coordinates, sometimes names of places, or people."

"So, the last one was a one p.m. meeting on the second Friday in January?"

Kyra nodded. *That would have been a few days after he died.*

"What about the exclamation points?" Tarek asked.

"Maybe the last meeting?" She furrowed her brow, thinking. At Tarek's doubtful expression, she shrugged. "The end or something important was always noted. Sometimes to mark a celebration, like my birthday. That would be where my present was. I think he'd also use the markers to communicate with his sources, exchange some other bit of information, like he was leaving or bringing a witness? The code was his way of communicating with us and his paper. If something happened to him, someone could figure out where he was. He started it as a joke, I think, marking a celebratory thing after he escaped from a tough spot once. Then it became a part of his life. Record everything. He was held hostage more than a few times, and maybe he thought the codes could help the newspaper find him?" That hard, little spot in her chest moved to the base of her throat and lingered there, burning. She felt a tightness across her shoulders, and she rolled them, trying to ease the tension.

Kyra stood up and walked to the sink. She turned on the water and washed out her mug. When she turned around Tarek was watching her.

"You okay?"

"It's nothing. He was an idiot." Her words were clipped.

He stood up. "Kyra..." He stepped forward like he was going to reach for her.

"No," she said, and he stopped. "It's just so fucking stupid. He traipsed all over the world. Ran toward actual war zones, and he gets himself killed in retirement by getting pissed and falling off a goddamned pleasure boat." She brushed at her cheek. *I'm not fucking crying.*

"He wasn't drunk."

"What?" she snapped.

He was close enough now she had to tip her head back to see his face.

"The tox screens came back normal. It was in the report I showed you. There was no sign of alcohol or any other questionable substances in his system."

"Whatever." She looked back down. "I don't see how that matters." She grabbed a dishtowel and wrung it through her hands. "Another coffee?"

"No, thank you." He stepped back, and Kyra moved around him to pick up his cup. She felt Tarek watching her, but thankfully he didn't say anything more.

He went back to his seat and picked up the phone. He ran through its contents again while Kyra dried each mug and restacked them in the cabinet. "If you're okay with it, I can try and get some cell phone-tower pings? See if we can locate where this phone has been? I can also run the number, see if it's registered to someone."

"Yeah? That would be great," she said, her voice flat. She sat back down, deciding the best way to handle her emotional outburst was to ignore it. Pretend it didn't happen. She picked up the phone and scrolled through the menus. "How about getting a password?"

"What do you mean?"

Kyra explained about finding the envelope and account

number with the cloud-storage company. "He'd hidden it with a bunch of junk, so it may not amount to anything. It could be just a backup server he used years ago." She felt silly playing at being a detective, sleuthing for clues.

"You don't have the password?"

"No." She shook her head. "I've tried everything I could think of. Can your computer people figure it out, or can we make the company give us access?"

"Without a warrant, it depends on the company's policies. Some are more willing to work with law enforcement than others. You may have more luck persuading them as his daughter. Or go through his papers again? People normally write their passwords down somewhere."

Kyra didn't want to think about opening all the trash bags she'd filled or going through it all again. "Are you busy now?" She ran her hands down her thighs. "I was going to go to Mander Lane Farm and meet with Ed's friend from last night, Mr. Grover." She paused then rushed on. "If you're not doing anything, did you want to come with?"

Tarek's eyes widened, and his lips twitched into a half smile.

He hesitated, then nodded. "Okay. I just need to make a call."

Chapter Eleven

THEY TRAVELED WESTBOUND up island to Chilmark. Tarek had made a quick detour into Oak Bluffs to drop off Ed's cellphone, but now they were on their way to Mander Lane Farm. Kyra fidgeted in her seat, still unsettled from her earlier encounter with Wes and nervous to talk to Grover about her dad. She couldn't fathom what Ed would have told his friends about her.

"If you continue on this road, up that way," Tarek said, pointing beyond the intersection. "You'll hit Aquinnah and the clay cliffs. If you have time during your stay, you should go. If you go that way," he pointed to another road, "you'll go to Menemsha."

"What's there?"

"It's a fishing village. It has a deep harbor, so there are a lot of large boats and the best lobster roll on the island."

Kyra turned to him, surprised.

He feigned an innocent smile. "Don't tell Gully."

She grinned. She could imagine how well that conversation would go.

Up island, the landscape changed from beach grass and sand dunes to pine trees and scrub forest. She could smell the smoky, heady scent of wood-burning fires. Stone walls partitioned off fields peppered with sheep and cows, even a few horses.

"It's so pretty."

"It is. This side of the island is totally different from the Edgartown and O.B. sides. It's quieter out here. More remote. A lot of farms." Tarek turned off the main road and onto a wide gravel drive bordered by thick bushes. "This is it."

They drove under an arbor covered in climbing morning glory. A carved sign painted dark green with gold lettering, reading MANDER LANE FARM EST. 1974, hung from the arch. They pulled into a parking area next to a farm stand and restaurant. On the other side, the drive followed a low stone wall, circling up behind a house sitting atop a hill. The house itself cut an impressive image against the blue sky. Once a standard-issue Victorian, it had been extensively remodeled with glass and metal accents. A hodgepodge of classic and contemporary styles keeping watch over the property like some sort of steampunk sentry.

"Subtle," Kyra deadpanned, staring up at the monstrosity.

"Yeah…" Tarek peered through the windshield, taking it in with a frown. "I'm not sure I like it. I think we can park up at the house." He followed the drive past the PRIVATE NO ENTRY signs and parked next to a red Porsche.

They climbed the stairs to the front door and rang the bell. They waited a minute, and when it opened, a slight woman appeared in the doorway, smoothing her hair, tucking the loose pieces behind her ears.

Her chest heaved like she was out of breath. "Yes? How

can I help you?"

"We're here to see Mr. Grover. He's expecting us. I'm Kyra Gibson."

The woman checked a tablet. "Ah yes. Please, follow me."

They stepped into a round foyer. A massive floral arrangement sat on a round table in the center of the room. Nearly life-size portraits hung on the walls. Three in total. One each of the senator and his wife and another of them together with a pair of sleek hunting dogs. There were no paintings of the senator's children. They followed the woman down a hall until she stopped at the door of a solarium and ushered them in.

The room was encased in glass on three sides as well as the vaulted ceiling. It was decorated in complementary shades of greens and blues, mimicking the colors of the land and skies. "Please, take a seat. I'll let Bill know you're here."

Kyra stepped up to the nearest window. From her vantage point, she could see the farm stand and the restaurant down below. Just beyond was a construction site, where a foundation was being poured.

"That's the site for the new barn."

Kyra turned around.

Bill Grover entered the room and came to stand next to her. "I'm glad you were able to make it, Kyra." He shook her hand and turned to Tarek. "Nice to see you again, Detective."

"It's just Tarek," he said. "I'm just a visitor today."

"No more information about the fire, or the victim's identity, I take it?"

"No, sir. Nothing yet."

"Mmmhmm." Grover pressed his lips together in a thin line and nodded. He sucked in a breath and pointed to the worksite. "The Hawthorns started construction on the new barn last fall. Over there," Grover said, moving to the other side of the room. They followed him to the other window. "That's where the old barn stood. Margot planned to keep it as an events venue, but now it's scheduled for demolition."

At the bottom of the hill was a blackened skeleton of what had once been a large structure. Yellow police tape cautioned people from entering.

"I'm terribly sorry," Kyra murmured. Her words felt forced and inadequate, but she was unsure what else she could say.

"It's such a tragedy." Grover shook his head. "We're all very upset." He stared out at the black stain on the otherwise pristine landscape. He let out a long breath and cleared his throat. Grover checked his watch. "Unfortunately, Kyra, I have to take a call right now. I've asked Sara to give you a tour of the farm. I don't think my call will take too long, and I can meet you for a drink at L'Huître, Margot's restaurant, in about an hour, if that's okay with you?"

"Yes, of course. Thank you."

"Excellent." He smiled, and Kyra thought he looked relieved. "I'll show you to the back door, and you can walk down to the farm stand. Sara will meet you there."

The farm stand was little more than a shed. Crates of produce were stacked in makeshift rows with handwritten chalkboard signs identifying the items and their prices. A few scales hung from the ceiling for shoppers to weigh their selections. Three industrial-sized, glass-front refrigerators lined one wall and contained artisanal cheeses and meats. Kyra noticed a pile of textiles in one corner—blankets, hats, mittens, and skeins of yarn.

"Good afternoon." Sara entered the store. "I'm Sara. I'm here to give you a tour of Mander Lane Farm." Her face made it crystal clear how little she thought of her assigned task.

"Hi. We met briefly last night. I'm Tarek Collins, and this is Kyra Gibson."

"Nice to meet you. Well, let's get going." She waved to the shop. "Nearly everything we sell here has been produced on the farm. We have sheep and goats for milk and wool. We also have a small herd of cows, a few horses, and, of course, the famous silkie chickens. All of our products are produced incorporating state-of-the-art sustainability practices." She recited the information without emotion, her voice flat, her eyes dull and unfocused. "We grow a wide variety of produce and grain, including…"

Tarek gave Kyra a doubtful look. She recognized his silent plea for escape. It mirrored her own.

"You know, Sara, umm, thanks for the offer, but honestly, I'm not sure we need the official tour," Kyra interrupted, hoping she sounded grateful. "We're just killing some time before we can visit with my father's friend, Mr. Grover, so, if it's all right with you, maybe we can just wander around?"

"Oh." Sara ran her hand through her short hair. "Really?"

"Oh, definitely. If you can point out the highlights, we'll be fine on our own." Kyra hoped her smile was encouraging.

"Okay, sure." Sara's rigid posture relaxed. "Thanks, that would be great. I've loads of work." She didn't even try to conceal her relief. "The site of the new barn is directly behind us, and the paddocks are down that way. You'll see the temporary structures where we shelter the livestock over there, and the fields are back there. The chicken coops are down the path and to the left." She pointed in various directions.

Kyra hoped Tarek was paying attention, because she certainly wouldn't remember everything Sara had said.

"The farm is about eighty acres, and it's all connected by paths with signs, so you really can't get lost. If you need me, I'll be in the office above L'Huître. Enjoy." Before they could react, Sara disappeared from the shop.

"She seems stressed." Kyra turned to Tarek.

"Yeah, *stressed* is the word I'd use." He glanced toward the exit, then grinned at her. "Want to check out the old barn?"

They left the farm stand and followed the paved path curving away from the house. As they wandered closer to the blackened structure, the acrid smell of the fire's aftermath tainted the fresh air. Up close, the damage was shocking.

"Jesus," Kyra whispered.

"Yeah, the fire marshal said it probably burned at nearly fifteen hundred degrees." Tarek pointed. "Back there was a room. Probably an office or a tack room. The fire started there, but the accelerant had been poured all over the floors of the building, which is why they're sure it was set deliberately. The main barn doors were bolted from the inside. We think whoever started the fire exited via that egress off to the side, closest to the office. The fire was started sometime after ten p.m. and was raging through the structure not long after igniting."

"Where was the body found?"

"In the office. The fire did a thorough job of cleansing the site of any useful evidence. But it's a barn. It's going to be covered in so much DNA and other physical evidence it would be difficult to make a case based on that alone." He turned to Kyra. "You ready?"

She nodded, pulling her eyes from the destruction, glad to leave it behind.

"Let's go see the paddocks. What the hell is a famous silkie chicken anyway?"

Kyra huffed a laugh and contemplated how to answer. They turned toward the fields that sat on the far side of the barn and the large temporary structures erected there. A young man exited one of the larger shelters leading a chestnut horse.

"Hi. L'Huître is actually back that way," he said, and pointed behind them.

"Oh, thanks, we're just looking around a bit," Kyra replied. "Who's this?" She offered a flat hand to the horse, who gave her a few sniffs before losing interest in her and rubbed her nose against the boy's back.

"This is Gale. She's one of Sara's eight, oh, uh, six horses. The other two were lost in the fire." He jerked his chin toward the ruined barn.

"I'm so sorry." Kyra patted Gale's neck.

"Yeah, thanks. Sara collects them after they're too old, lame, or unwanted by the other farms or stables on the island. She gives them a good home to live out their retirement." He gave Gale a pat. "This old girl is probably in her twenties."

"That's kind of her." Tarek eyed the horse and stepped back putting distance between him and the animal. Kyra bit back a smile. "She buys and sells all the animals?"

"Yeah, she runs the farm for the Hawthorns pretty much." The horse nuzzled his pockets, and he nudged her away. "I don't have anything, old girl." He scratched her chin.

"How long have you worked here?" Tarek asked.

The boy's eyes snapped up his brow furrowed in suspicion. "Why?"

"Oh, no reason. Sorry." Tarek held his hands up in mock surrender.

"I gotta get her back to her paddock." The boy made a clicking sound and led Gale off.

"Smooth," Kyra teased.

"I tried." He shrugged, unfazed.

They continued following the path along the green post and rail fence. Eventually, they came across an outbuilding with a small enclosure.

"This must be where they keep the silkie chickens," Kyra said, pointing to a sign with the silhouette of a chicken. She peeked through the fence, looking for the strange little creatures. Sure enough, a black, feathery-fur-covered Muppet ran across the enclosure. Kyra heard Tarek gasp, and she stifled a giggle.

"What even is that?" he asked, his eyes wide.

"Right? Odd things, but he's cute."

"But … why?" he asked, sounding so bewildered.

Kyra couldn't help laughing.

"Why is that funny?" he demanded.

But when the strange chicken started scratching the ground and bobbing its head to music only it could hear, Tarek let loose a deep laugh. His shoulders shook, and he held his hand to his mouth. He caught his breath. His green eyes sparkled, and his cheeks were flushed. If the aloof man from the police website was handsome, this Tarek, the relaxed and carefree version, was striking. Kyra's heart skipped.

They were interrupted by the sound of an engine and wheels crunching on gravel. Long fingers wrapped around her elbow, and Tarek guided her to the side of the path.

A vehicle came toward them. It was sort of like a four-by-four golfcart and was clearly used as transportation on the farm. It slid to a stop in front of them, and the driver cut the engine. Kyra recognized him from the party.

"Afternoon." Dr. Brian Lee gave her a lazy smile, his eyes traveling the length of her body. Kyra suppressed a shudder. *Gross.* "What are you doing here?"

"Just visiting. We're meeting Mr. Grover."

"Grover? At L'Huître?"

Kyra nodded.

"Get in." He gestured to the vehicle. "I'll give you the fast tour. I'm heading that way." Kyra glanced at Tarek, who shrugged and gave a nod.

"Thanks."

Brian pressed a button on the cart's dashboard. The engine sputtered to life, and he revved it to a loud, keening growl.

"Tarek," the detective shouted over the engine noise and pointed to himself. He helped Kyra climb into the back before hopping into the passenger seat.

"Brian!" Brian pointed his thumb at his chest and turned the cart around. He gave them a speedy tour of the farm, shouting out various points of interest that could be described in one word—field, dairy, stable, orchard.

He slowed the cart to a stop next to a row of similar vehicles and cut the engine. Turning around to face Kyra, he pointed. "Over there is where the new barn is being built. It'll be one hundred percent carbon neutral, powered on solar and temperature controlled from geothermal. Phil and Margot are committed to giving back to the community, and we're only using local companies to build it. Some company, Green Forest, or whatever."

"Sounds like you're really involved in the effort." Kyra smiled, encouraging him to share more about the farm and the Hawthorns. She caught Tarek's smirk and clasped her hands together so she wouldn't pinch him.

"Oh yeah, well, Phil and Margot need the help, and I'm happy to throw my hand in."

"Do you live here? On the farm?"

"No, DC, but I'm here as often as I can get away. I'm a doctor, you know."

Yes, Brian, we know. She glanced at Tarek. He wasn't smiling anymore but was watching Brian through narrowed eyes.

"It certainly is beautiful," Kyra said, and she meant it.

"That's L'Huître. It means the oyster. Margot's wine

bar." He pointed to the building Kyra had spotted from the solarium. The fresh yellow-brown cedar shingles had not yet weathered to Cape Cod's signature gray. "I've gotta get inside. I'll catch you later." He climbed out of the cart and strode toward the restaurant.

"Nice guy, even sober," Tarek muttered as he helped Kyra out of the back seat.

Tarek pulled the door to L'Huître open, letting Kyra step inside. She stumbled back, narrowly avoiding being struck in the face.

"Oh my god, I'm so sorry," cried a woman carrying photography lighting.

Without stopping, she threw them an apologetic look and scurried off clutching a lamp and reflectors. Kyra straightened and cautiously stepped through the door, Tarek behind her.

Margot Hawthorn stood in the center of the room, a sun around which everything whirled. The senator's wife was dressed like she had stepped out of *Country Life* magazine in an editorial spread for the genteel farmer—wellies, a Maquien riding jacket, and a Burberry scarf tied at her neck. Her hair had been pulled back into a severe chignon, showing off gargantuan pearl earrings. Margot was talking to a photographer while another assistant scrambled around, taking down lighting.

"Sara, where is my husband?" Margot stamped her rubber boot. Sara stood off to the side looking pained, like she'd rather be anywhere else, even giving a farm tour.

"I'm not sure, Margot," she said. "I can call up to the house." Before Margot could answer, Sara slipped behind the counter and grabbed the phone receiver.

"Call Chase as well," Margot commanded, and then to the photographer, "I want a photo of the family outside for the article."

"Yes, Mrs. Hawthorn."

The photographer turned around, his shoulders slumped, his expression defeated. He gave Tarek and Kyra a tired smile.

"Hi," Kyra said to the photographer. "We were supposed to meet our friend, but we can come back later."

"What?" Margot's head snapped around, and she noticed Kyra and Tarek. She frowned. "L'Huître is closed," she said, looking down her nose.

"So sorry, Margot. Tarek and I were meeting Grover. We can wait outside."

"Obviously, not. We're taking photos of the family out there." She sighed. "Just stay in here. Take a table in the back. Just stay out of the way." She waved to the other side of the room. "Sara. Tell Grover to get here immediately. And you"—she glared at the photographer—"do you need more interior shots?"

"No, Mrs. Hawthorn." The photographer checked his digital-camera display. "I got everything I need. We just need the portraits you want of you and the family."

Margot stomped outside. The photographer and his assistants scrambled after her.

Kyra followed Tarek to the table at the far side of the room. A small bud vase held a few stems of daisies. Kyra brushed her fingertips along the petals. Fake.

Sara appeared seemingly out of nowhere, with a bottle of

wine and four glasses.

"Grover will be right down. Here." She set everything on the table and handed Tarek a corkscrew. "I had no idea she had a photoshoot. It wasn't on the schedule. Grover wouldn't have invited you if we'd known." Kyra began to apologize, but Sarah shook her head. "No, don't worry about it. Help yourself. Grover likes this one." Sara rubbed the back of her neck and followed Margot outside.

"Thanks?" Tarek called after her, then reached for the bottle to study the label.

"Is that one any good?" Kyra craned her neck, trying to see out the window, but couldn't see the photoshoot.

"No clue." He opened the bottle and poured them each a glass.

Brian appeared from a hallway. He had changed into a casual linen-blend suit in a mossy-green color and an off-white T-shirt, for a look that was more Miami beach than New England farm. He spotted them and strode over.

"Oh, good. Pour me one?" He poured himself a generous glass of wine. "Have you seen Adele?" he asked, his lip curled.

He glanced around the restaurant.

"No." Tarek shook his head.

"Figures. She made a tremendous deal about this family photograph, and then she's not even here." He finished the glass in a single gulp, grimaced, and poured another.

As Brian set the bottle back down on the table, a woman appeared in the doorway. She strode in, heels *clicking* on the hardwood. Her pastel-green chiffon dress billowed around her. Her hair had been pulled into a chignon matching

Margot's. When Adele's gaze latched onto Brian, Kyra got her first good look at Margot's daughter. She resembled Margot but taller and wider. Wisps of dark hair had escaped from her bun, and her eyes were rimmed red, her cheeks splotchy, like she'd been crying.

"Where the fuck have you been?" she shrieked at her husband, her eyes daggers.

"Here, as we discussed this morning." Brian's voice, though calm, bristled with irritation. "Are they ready for us?" He smoothed his shirt, dismissing his wife's hysterics.

"No!" Adele's voice was shrill. "Mother"—she sneered— "doesn't want us in the photograph. 'The editorial is for the promotion of Mander Lane and L'Huître, to help Philip's campaign, Adele. It doesn't concern the Lees,'" she mimicked Margot.

Kyra wished she could melt into the wall. Adele hadn't seemed to notice them yet. Kyra glanced at Tarek, who was observing the unfolding drama, his expression unreadable.

"Fine." He left his wineglass on the counter and strode toward the door.

"Where do you think you're going?" Adele screeched and blocked his path.

"What's it to you?" he snapped.

"You have to get us into that photoshoot, Brian. We can't be excluded from the article. I'm a part of this family." She stomped her foot. Her hands fisted at her sides. "She cannot keep doing this." Adele sucked in a breath that sounded like a sob. "She *can't!*"

"Keep your voice down," Brian snarled, his voice like gravel. He glanced at Kyra and Tarek. "You're making a scene. Again. You're unhinged." He stepped closer and got in her face. "You insisted Margot wanted us here for Phil's campaign party, but we weren't invited, and now this." He waved his hands toward the front of the building. "All lies. I have better things to do than deal with your insanity and family drama." He brushed past her and stormed toward the door.

"Rot in hell, Brian," Adele screeched.

Kyra winced.

"Shut up." Brian whirled around and Adele stumbled back. "Have you no pride? Begging and pleading to be a part of a family that doesn't *want* you! You're pathetic. Go back to your sailor. You're his problem now." Before Adele could respond, Brian marched out, the door slamming behind him. Only then did Kyra realize Tarek had stood up, ready to intervene if the argument had escalated.

Adele turned to them. Surprise flickered across her features like she only just now realized they were there. She glared at them her chin raised like she was challenging them to say something. With a scowl, she flounced out the door.

"Sounds like you may have been right about who else was on that boat," Tarek said, sitting back down.

"I guess so." She frowned, feeling bad for Adele. "Poor woman. I wonder why Margot doesn't want her in the article."

"Margot and the senator don't acknowledge her in public," Tarek said, spinning his empty wineglass. "It took a fair bit of research to find out she was even related to Margot. Apparently, Margot changed her name shortly after Adele was born."

"Really? What was her name?"

"Penny Wolkowyski. She changed it to Margot Moulin. Claims she was born in France."

Kyra frowned, working the name over in her mind. "Margot doesn't look like a Penny, but why not change Adele's last name, too?"

"Maybe an illegitimate daughter didn't fit with the senator's narrative? But it sounds like she'd distanced herself from her daughter long before she met her husband." Tarek shrugged.

My father hadn't wanted to be tied down, but he was never ashamed of me.

"How long do you think Grover will be?" Tarek asked, leaning back in his chair. His cell phone rang, and he fished it from his pocket. Sitting up straight, he answered. "This is Collins. Yes. Okay. Are you sure? No, I'm still on the island. Have you notified the senator? Yes. I'm here now. I'll take care of it." He hung up and turned to Kyra, his mouth set in a thin line, his expression grim. "Drinks will have to wait. The body has been identified."

Chapter Twelve

KYRA FOLLOWED TAREK up to the house. He knocked on the front door. The same woman who'd answered earlier opened it, clearly expecting him. She looked even more frazzled than before.

"This way, please." She ushered them in and led them to a sitting room.

Kyra sat in an armchair, but Tarek prowled around, taking in his surroundings.

Mr. Grover joined them a few minutes later. He looked pale, worried. "I understand that the body has been identified."

"Yes, sir." Tarek nodded. "Did you want to wait for the senator and Mrs. Hawthorn?"

"No, I'll represent Senator Hawthorn and his office for now. If we need Phil, he's in his office, but I'd prefer not to bother the family. Please, go ahead."

Kyra thought it strange the family wasn't interested in learning more about the person who'd died on their property. *Maybe they're trying to distance themselves from a scandal?*

Tarek cleared his throat. "The ME used dental records and has identified the victim as Brendan Delaney of Framingham and lately DC. His death is being ruled a homicide."

"A homicide?" Grover repeated. His eyes went wide, and he collapsed on the couch. "My god. Brendan? Do they know what happened?"

"Yes, sir. There was damage to the victim's chest consistent with a close-range gunshot wound. The ME also found what she believes are bullet fragments. She has submitted those for additional testing. Dr. Khaleng found no evidence of smoke in the victim's lungs and believes that Mr. Delaney was deceased before the fire was set. Based on the evidence, she has made the reasonable deduction that the victim died from a gunshot wound to the chest. Forensics will return to the scene to search for blood and casings."

"Fucking hell." Grover's brow furrowed.

He ran his hands through his hair, making it stick up. He turned to the woman standing just inside the door, ghostly pale. She must have returned, unnoticed.

"Beth, get Phil. Now. And call an emergency meeting with the public relations and campaign teams. We need to get in front of this."

Beth gave a nod and slipped out of the room.

Grover ran his hands through his hair again and stood up. He started pacing. "We need to notify his family."

"An officer from my department has already spoken to Mrs. Delaney, sir. I'm returning to the mainland to follow up there in the morning." Tarek caught Kyra's eye, then looked back at Grover. "It would be helpful to know the activities of everyone who was home Sunday evening."

"Yes, of course." Grover walked over to a desk and pulled out a calendar. He studied it for a moment. "That evening I was here all night." He ran his finger down the book. "When

I'm needed on the island, I often stay here at the house. Obviously, Phil and Margot were here. The Hawthorns' PA, Beth"—he jerked his chin toward the door—"stays with the family, so she was here." He rubbed his eyes. "I don't think Chase was in town, and I'm not sure if Margot's daughter and son-in-law had already arrived. Their visit wasn't scheduled."

"Bill." Phil Hawthorn stormed into the room, his wife right behind him. "What's going on?" He stopped short when he saw Tarek. "Bill?" he repeated, turning to his chief of staff.

"Phil, Margot, this is Detective Collins with the Massachusetts State Police. They've identified the body found in the barn. It's Brendan."

"Brendan?" Margot repeated, her lips pursed. "Do we know a Brendan, darling?"

"Yes, ma'am, Brendan Delaney," Grover said without looking at her.

"What!?" A strangled cry came from the hall, and a man Kyra would have placed in his mid-twenties burst into the room. "Brendan?"

"Chase. Calm yourself," Margot hissed. "Beth, take my son."

"Shut up, Mother." He turned to his father, then to Tarek, his eyes wide, looking distraught. "What happened? Please?"

Beth corralled Chase toward the door. He looked like he was going to protest. His eyes jumped between his parents. Then his shoulders sagged, and he let Beth lead him from the room.

"Please, take a seat. Senator, Mrs. Hawthorn." Tarek caught Kyra's eye and glanced toward the door, dismissing her.

She snuck from the room and wandered down the hall. Kyra found the kitchen and sat at an enormous granite island to wait for Tarek. She pulled her phone from her purse and scrolled through work emails. The pale woman from earlier entered.

"Beth?"

She started, as if she hadn't noticed Kyra. "Yes?"

"Sorry, I'm Kyra Gibson. We met earlier, but I didn't get your name. I'm here with Tarek, um, Detective Collins?"

"Oh, yes. Bill's guest." Beth nodded and wrung her hands.

"Here, sit down." Kyra guided Beth to a stool, and the poor woman all but collapsed onto the chair.

Her head dropped into her hands. Kyra placed a hand on the woman's shoulder. She was trembling.

"Let me get you some water." Kyra filled a glass at the tap and handed it to her.

"Thank you," she said and took a sip. "This is all so horrible." Her voice caught. Beth's eyes glistened, holding back tears, disbelief written all over her face.

"Did you know Brendan?" Kyra asked.

"No, not really." Beth stared into her glass. "We'd run into each other from time to time at the house in DC and, of course, at the office. He and Chase were close … friends." The way Beth lingered on the word caught Kyra's attention.

"What about here?"

"None of the aides come to the island. Not to Mander

Lane." Beth shook her head.

"So, you don't know why he was here on Sunday?"

Beth pressed her lips together, thinking. "No. Chase was in Boston. No one was expecting him."

"It'll be okay, Beth. Detective Collins will figure it out." Kyra tried to soothe the frightened woman. "Who else was at the house that night?" she asked, trying to keep the conversation going.

Beth looked like she was about to burst into tears. "The senator and Margot. Of course, Bill. He's almost always here when we're at the farm. Sara and her staff." Beth shrugged. "Just the regular people."

Kyra poured herself a glass of water and sat next to Beth. "Sara? The farm manager?"

"Yes, she lives on the property. She has an apartment above L'Huître. Oh, and I think Adele arrived Sunday or the night before. She was staying with a friend for a few days, though. She came to stay at the house with Dr. Lee yesterday." Beth sniffled. Her eyes were lined with tears. "But no one would do something like that to Brendan." A few tears slid down her cheeks. "He was nice."

"They'll figure out who did this," Kyra said with more confidence than she felt.

Beth's breathing was shaky. She sipped her water.

"You must have known my father?" Kyra blurted and immediately wished she hadn't.

Beth blinked, confusion creasing her brow. "Your father?"

"Ed Gibson? He was friends with Mr. Grover?"

"Ed Gib ... Mr. Gibson was your father?" Beth's mouth

formed an *O*. She reached for Kyra's hand. "I didn't know. I'm so sorry. Yes, I knew him, of course. He's been a guest here, many times."

"Do you know why?"

"Why he visited?" she asked, frowning.

Kyra nodded.

"Recently, social visits, I think. With Bill and sometimes the senator or his colleagues. Margot hosts large cocktail parties during the off-season. He was often included on the guest list. And before that, we'd see him in Washington from time-to-time." A bell rang from somewhere deep in the house. Beth jumped to her feet, almost knocking over her glass. "Excuse me. That's Margot." She paused on her way out. "Thank you."

Kyra felt restless and a little bored sitting alone in the kitchen. Her stomach growled reminding her she hadn't eaten, but she didn't want to leave Tarek without a ride. *Maybe I can grab a snack at the farm stand?*

She left the kitchen and walked down to the farm stand. It was deserted and the produce shelves had been covered. The shop was closed for the day. Kyra tried the restaurant. She opened the door and found Sara sitting at one of the tables.

She looked up from the laptop in front of her. "Yes?" she asked, sounding annoyed. "Can I help you?"

"Oh, are you closed?"

Sara's eyes narrowed, and she stood up. "Where's your friend?"

Kyra explained Tarek was at the house with the family, that the body had been identified.

"Oh." Sara closed her eyes and pinched the bridge of her nose. She snapped her laptop shut and tucked it under her arm. "I'll be needed at the house, but I have to grab some things from upstairs. Come on in." Sara shut the door behind Kyra. "This way." She led her down a back hallway and up a staircase to a landing. Sara pushed open the door, and Kyra followed her into the apartment. Sara dropped her laptop on a table. "I'll just be a minute," she said and disappeared through another doorway.

Mander Lane's farm manager was using her living room as her office. Stands of files and other papers covered the tiny dining table. A whiteboard with the month's feeding and planting schedules, along with the names of people who'd been assigned those tasks, hung on a wall. Kyra stepped closer. Nearly all the responsibilities had been assigned to a circled "S." She wandered into the kitchenette. Sara had a microwave and a glass-front mini-fridge full of vials and bottles of supplements and medications. Similar bottles sat in labeled baskets on the counter.

Kyra scanned the labels. The baskets' contents included bottles of iodine and copper, some prescription bottles of antibiotics, dewormer medications, and a bottle of ammonium nitrate. *Wait. Ammonium nitrate?* Kyra picked it up and looked at it more closely. She thought she'd read somewhere ammonium nitrate was often used as a fertilizer. *But isn't it explosive? Didn't Tarek say that the accelerant used in the fire was a type of fertilizer?* A noise came from the bedroom, and Kyra quickly, but very, very carefully, replaced the bottle. The door to Sara's bedroom opened. She'd changed into a pair of jeans and a worn sweatshirt.

"Thanks for waiting." Her eyes fell to the supplements on the counter next to Kyra. "The Hawthorns want the prestige of running a fully organic, sustainable farm with no idea of the extra work it requires. I try to hire local kids who need jobs, but many of them don't have the experience, so a lot of it falls to me." She squared her shoulders as if preparing for Kyra's disapproval. When she didn't, when Kyra just gave her a blank look, Sara's chin dipped in a curt nod and she followed Kyra out the door.

Sara rapped on the open door before entering the sitting room.

"Oh, Sara. I was just going to ask Beth to call for you," Mr. Grover greeted them. He was still pale, his features drawn. Tarek was sitting in the same place, notebook in hand. "Detective Collins needs the names of all the hands you had on the property on the night of the fire."

"Yes, of course." She pulled out her phone and sat down next to Grover.

Kyra gave Tarek a nod and left the room. She wandered back to the kitchen to find Chase sitting at the island. In front of him was a half-empty bottle of bourbon and a glass.

"I'm sorry," Kyra stuttered while backing up.

Chase turned his head. His bloodshot eyes zeroed in on her face. "You're with the police." It was a statement. He pushed his greasy blond hair away from his face, his unfocused eyes never leaving her.

"Sort of," she replied and shrugged. "Are you okay?"

"Brendan." He gulped down the rest of the contents of his glass and poured another. "He's dead."

"I know. I'm so sorry."

"I didn't know he was coming to see me. I was in Boston." He wasn't listening to her, she realized. He was grieving, needing someone, anyone to listen to him. "Maybe if I'd been here…" His voice cracked. He gulped down half his drink.

"You think he was coming to visit you?"

"Why else would he come here?" His expression turned accusatory, then melted away, replaced by sorrow. "He only came to the Vineyard to see me. He didn't know anyone else here."

"He visited you here often?"

"No." Chase shook his head. "He's been a few times. When the family—"

"Chase," a shrill voice snapped.

Kyra spun around and came face-to-face with Margot Hawthorn.

"What are you doing in here?" Margot demanded, her tone as scornful as her stare.

"Oh, I'm sorry, I was just waiting for the detective."

"Yes, as I've already told your *colleague*, my son won't be answering questions without our attorney. Nothing you've coerced him into saying will be admissible, and the behavior by the state police is appalling. I've every intention of filing a formal complaint about you." Margot positioned herself between Kyra and her son. She straightened to her full height. Chase barely acknowledged his mother.

Kyra stepped back, shrinking under Margot's hostility.

"I'm not the police," Kyra said, trying to explain.

Margot glared at her, and Kyra gave up. *She's just protecting her son.*

"I'll go." Kyra peered around Margot's body to speak to Chase. "It was nice to meet you, Chase. I wish it'd been under better circumstances. I'm very sorry about Brendan."

Chase gave a nearly imperceptible nod, his eyes on his glass.

Kyra felt the burn of Margot's stare as she left the kitchen and continued out the front door.

Chapter Thirteen

KYRA KEYED IN the code Tarek's locksmith had texted her to open the front door. He had also installed a deadbolt on the interior. She turned it, already feeling more secure. Cronkite was awaiting Kyra's return, sitting on the kitchen island. He greeted her with an impatient meow.

"Sorry. I'm home now, Cronker." She gave the cat's ears a scratch and tossed him a few treats. She had driven back on her own after texting Tarek that she was going home. Hopefully, he'd find a ride back.

Kyra still hadn't eaten. She stood in front of her fridge. She surveyed its meager contents before letting the door close. The emptiness of the house felt stifling. She packed up her laptop and grabbed the car keys. *I'll grab food in town.*

She drove into Edgartown and parked. She wandered the streets before finding herself in front of Gully's place. Smiling, she pushed open the door and entered the warm, musty pub. The hostess waved at her to sit anywhere, and she chose a small table near the fireplace. The heat from the flames warmed her back, and the tightness across her shoulders melted. Her interactions with Margot Hawthorn had stung more than she realized. *She'd looked at me like I was some foul insect or gum stuck to her shoe.* Kyra shivered. She ordered a glass of wine and a cup of clam chowder. When the server left, she set up her computer.

Kyra tried to concentrate on work, but the warmth and familiarity of the pub, along with the guests' soft chatter, made it impossible. Her soup and drink arrived and, accepting defeat, she let her attention wander and people-watched from behind her computer screen.

A man sat alone at a nearby table. He looked familiar. Recognition dawned on her. *It's the man from last night, the one from* The Island Pearl. *Adele's Coast Guard officer. What was his name?* Kyra racked her brain, trying to remember. He was nursing a beer, scrolling through his phone. *Tarek had said he'd been the one who'd found my father.*

"Hey," she called, and when he looked up, she gave him a big smile and wiggled her fingers. "Hi, we met last night. Want to join me?" She pointed to the empty seat at her table.

He stared at her for a second, shrugged, and shuffled over. By his sluggish movements, Kyra guessed he'd been at the pub for a while.

"Hi," she said again, forcing a cheerful smile, and extended her hand. "I'm Kyra." His hand was hot and rough in hers.

"Hey," he grunted. "Brody."

"It's a pleasure to officially meet you." Kyra exaggerated her accent. "You were on that fancy boat in the harbor last night. Is it yours?"

"Basically." He shrugged. "It's my friend's, but I can use it anytime I want."

Is that so? Were you using it last winter?

"Oh, really? Are you a captain?" She tried to look impressed, widening her eyes, feigning interest. She pushed her hair behind her ear and tried not to cringe at her awkward flirting.

"Oh. No." He shook his head, and a smug smile crept across his face. "But I know boats. I'm Coast Guard." His eyes traveled down her chest, and he licked his lips.

Ick. "Oh, so you must spend a lot of time here on the island." *This. Is. Humiliating.*

"I'm stationed in Falmouth, just on the mainland."

He finished his beer, and Kyra ordered another round, although she'd barely touched her drink.

"I spend a lot of time on the island, so yeah." He waved at the harbor. "Helping rich people who've grounded their expensive toys." His tone had gone bitter, and his lips curled into a sneer. Brody slugged back a third of his pint.

"Really? My, that must be dangerous."

"Not in the summer so much." He shrugged and leaned back. "They just have to wait for the tide to come back in. But in the winter, when we get the nor'easters—these big storms that blow northeast with snow and rain, sort of like a hurricane—the waves can engulf houses." He gestured around him. "The harbor, even this bar, has all been underwater. The storms throw the boats onto the shore, or sometimes people go out in the storms and get stranded, or worse."

"I heard there was a dreadful storm this past winter in January?" Kyra sipped her wine.

"Oh, yeah. A real bad one." Brody nodded. "It damaged a bunch of rich people's houses. I had leave that week, so I was visiting my friend here on the island, but they dispatched my crew on two rescue missions."

"Did the storm impact you and your friend? Were you on your boat?"

Brody frowned. *Shit.* She'd asked the wrong question.

She scrambled to recover. "I mean, it would have been terrifying to be on the water during a storm." She ran her finger around the rim of her wineglass. He watched her movements and glanced at her mouth. She tried not to roll her eyes. *Just. Fucking. Shoot. Me.*

"Yeah." He stretched his hands over his head. "I, uh…" A blast of cold air hit them from the open door. His eyes went wide, and he sucked in his cheeks.

Kyra turned to see who had caught his attention. Adele Lee was standing at the entrance, her eyes locked on Brody. Her face and neck were red and blotchy with rage. She marched to their table, her boots *thunking* on the floorboards.

She sat. "What the fuck is going on, Brody?" Adele hissed, her eyes boring into him.

"Oh. Hi, babe," he said. *Guess that confirms that.* "This is uh…" He turned to Kyra. "What was your name again?"

"Kyra." *What a dipshit.*

"Yeah, Kyra. She's from England. She was just asking me about the island," he slurred.

Adele's eyes fell on Kyra, and she tried not to flinch under her glare, so much like Margot's. "You're that nosy off islander who was snooping around my house today. With that cop." She whipped her head back to Brody. "What the fuck have you been saying to her? Mother caught her and threw her out. We're suing the police department for harassment." She lifted her chin and eyed Kyra as if challenging her to contradict her.

Kyra pushed her chair back and stood up. She wasn't in the mood to be attacked by another Hawthorn woman. "Not that I owe you an explanation, but I'm not with the police. Detective Collins is the one investigating the death of your brother's friend." Kyra tossed some money down and yanked on her jacket.

"Wait," Adele shouted.

Kyra froze. The room fell silent. Heads swiveled in their direction.

"That degenerate is *not* my brother. He is *nothing* to me."

Feeling eyes on her, Kyra shrugged, hoping she looked bored, and left the bar.

Outside her composure crumbled. She breathed in. *One, two, three.* And out. *One, two, three.* The pounding in her chest subsided. She pressed her hands to her cheeks, hot with embarrassment. *She is totally unhinged.*

Kyra was still queasy when she pulled into her father's driveway. Tarek's state-issued SUV still sat in front of her garage. She entered the house and through the living room's wall of windows saw Tarek standing down by the cove, holding his cell phone up to the sky. She walked out onto the patio.

"Hello?"

He jumped and whirled around. "Oh, hey." A smile spread across his face.

A pleasant fizz ran through her body, and she grinned

back.

"You startled me." He gestured to the phone. "One bar."

"Come in. You can use the landline. I swear, this island is still in the Dark Ages."

Tarek followed her inside and disappeared into the office.

Kyra turned on the fireplace, yanked off her boots, and curled up on the couch. She tucked the throw blanket around her legs.

Soon, Tarek came back. He gave her a tired smile. Kyra saw the strain behind his eyes as he sat next to her and let out a long sigh.

"How did the rest of the interviews go?"

"Standard." He leaned back and stretched out his long legs. "We don't have much more information than we had this morning."

"There's something off about that family." Kyra frowned and told him about her interactions with Margot at the house and then Adele at the pub.

"The way she spat at me." Kyra shivered at the memory. "She was so *angry*. She said Chase wasn't her brother. What do you think that means?"

"I got the impression that Adele is a bit of a loose cannon. Was she implying that he's not Margot's son? Or she doesn't consider them siblings?"

"I don't know." Kyra shook her head.

"It's strange that she's so ostracized in public but still welcome at the house."

"I'm not sure she *is* welcome." Kyra propped her feet up on the coffee table and rested her head against the couch cushions. "She said there was a mix-up with their invitation to the senator's party." Kyra chewed on her bottom lip, trying to remember the argument she'd overheard at the fundraiser. "But both Beth and Mr. Grover claim she wasn't expected at the party. Then there was that argument with her husband today. I don't think the family knew she was coming, or at least they hadn't asked her to come. She could have been staying elsewhere until last night." She turned to look at Tarek.

He was watching her, his eyes dark. Tarek sat up.

He cleared his throat and ran a hand through his hair, making it stand in every direction. "We're working on tracking down when the Lees got on the island." He pulled out his phone and scrolled through his messages. "I got the information on the burner phone. That's why I came over. To show you. The number your father was texting was registered to Senator Hawthorn's office."

"What? Seriously?" Kyra sat forward. "Do you think it was the senator or Mr. Grover?"

"I doubt either would be foolish enough to use their office phones. The senator wouldn't want to implicate himself in a scandal, but it looks like your dad was meeting with someone close to Phil Hawthorn."

"You said the number was from the Boston suburbs?"

Tarek nodded and he looked away.

"Didn't Grover say that was where Brendan was from?" Kyra felt her excitement building, like when she figured out the bits to a complex deal. "Frameham or something?"

Tarek pursed his lips and gave her a strange look. "Framingham," he said after a long pause. "He grew up there."

"Did you check if it was his phone?" Tarek was looking out at the cove. *Why is he being strange? Does he know something that he isn't telling me?* She crossed her arms over her chest.

"You think the two incidents are related?"

Kyra started. *Wait, what?* "Don't you?"

Tarek cocked his head to the side and raised an eyebrow. Kyra felt a surge of irritation. She pushed her hair away from her face and counted the facts off on her fingers. "My father died on the senator's boat. He was talking with someone in the senator's office. Brendan, the senator's aide, ends up shot. The contact number in my father's phone is from the same area where Brendan grew up." Kyra glared at him. "Aren't you the one paid to make connections? I thought you didn't believe in coincidences." She threw his words back at him and stood up.

She was fed up with his caginess. It was infuriating.

Tarek stood up, too. He slid his hands in his pockets and studied her for a moment.

"No, I don't." He broke eye contact. "But, Kyra, you need to understand."

No! His placating tone only pissed her off more. Kyra stomped off into the kitchen, pulling her phone from her pocket. Her fingers flew over the screen.

"Wait, what are you doing?" Tarek cursed under his breath, and she heard his footsteps as he followed her.

"Grover will have Brendan's phone number." She poured herself a glass of water.

Grover responded almost immediately, and she pulled up the text. She tossed the phone at Tarek with a little more force than necessary. He caught it easily.

"Well?" She raised her chin in a challenge.

He set her phone down without looking and sighed. "It's the same number."

Kyra huffed an incredulous laugh. *You've got to be kidding me. What game is he playing at?* There was only one reason he'd act this way. He didn't trust her. *Does he think I'm somehow involved?* Her stomach dropped.

Tarek's eyes closed, and he sucked in a breath. When they reopened, something in his demeanor had changed.

"Recent findings should provide sufficient grounds to reopen the inquest into Mr. Gibson's death."

Kyra flinched at his renewed formality.

"Fine. Do it," she snapped at him.

She was hurt. After the charity party, the pub, the farm, she'd thought they were friends, or at the very least, on the same team. Now he was relegating her to *family member of murder victim.* It stung.

"I'll make the official recommendation tomorrow, before I head off Island." Tarek nodded. "Goodnight, Ms. Gibson." He turned to leave.

"You're going somewhere?" She hated that her voice wavered.

Tarek turned back, and something in his expression softened. "Yes. I'm returning to the city to meet with Brendan's mother."

Kyra looked away. "What about the ping locations from my father's phone?"

"Cyber forensics are unable to pinpoint a specific address, but they have isolated the areas within a few blocks.

When I'm in Boston, I'll visit the locations, try to narrow it down."

"I can go. I can help."

"What?" He stared at her. "No."

"I'll know the meeting places. And I know how he worked with his sources."

"Respectfully, you haven't had a relationship with your father in over twenty years." His voice was cold, dismissive.

Kyra flushed, embarrassed. *He's not wrong. I did hardly know him. And that's my fault. What does that say about me?*

Tarek made a frustrated noise and stepped closer. "You can't be a part of the investigation, Kyra. This is official police business now." He ran his hands through his hair and gave her an imploring look, like he was searching for the right thing to say. "Look, I'll email you the information on the pings. If you see anything, let me know. I'll call you when I'm back on the island."

Kyra stood staring at her kitchen floor long after Tarek had left.

Chapter Fourteen

Friday

K YRA PARKED HER Range Rover at the small Martha's
Vineyard Airport and grabbed her overnight bag from
the backseat. She made her way through check-in and
security. After Tarek had left the house last night, she'd gone
through their conversation over and over and, needing a
third-party perspective from someone who knew Ed, she'd
dialed Grace and Charlie. Grace encouraged her to go to
Boston. Even if Detective Collins was being a *stubborn
jackass.* Charlie's words. Kyra knew Ed better than he did
and would know more about his activities. She'd laughed at
Charlie's increasingly colorful language for the detective.
There was no way in hell she was going to get caught stuck
on the ferry with that *stuffed-shirt, little shit* though, and at
Charlie's recommendation, she'd decided to fly. Grace
offered to make hotel arrangements once Kyra had the map
of the cell phone pings, and they promised to check in on
Cronkite while she was away.

After the rush of buying tickets, packing, and getting to
the airport, now sitting at the gate waiting to board, her
righteous indignation had waned. She felt stupid and
impulsive. She was debating going back to the house. Then

she thought of the codes on the phone. Ed could have deleted them, especially the meetings that had occurred. And what about the cloud storage company? Finding these things, these clues, it felt like they'd been left for someone. For her. She pressed her fingers to her temples, trying to rub away some of her tension.

If I'd answered his texts. If I'd come for Christmas, he might still be alive. I owe this to him to find out what happened.

Kyra bit her bottom lip and let her hand fall to her bag.

Worst-case scenario, I find nothing and spend a few days walking around Boston.

She brushed her fingers across the manilla folder containing the cell phone triangulation data. Her flight was called, and before she could talk herself out of it, Kyra boarded the plane.

Within minutes, Kyra wished she'd talked herself out of it. She white-knuckled the armrests of her seat as the tiny propeller plane dipped and swayed over the Atlantic. It rattled like it was coming apart at the seams. She glanced at the man sitting across the aisle. He clung to his golf clubs; his expression strained. If she hadn't been petrified of plummeting into the sea, she'd have laughed. The poor man looked as terrified—and ill—as she felt.

"Don't worry. We'll be fine. This isn't even bad." The flight attendant failed to comfort the passengers from her seat at the front of the plane. "We'll be on the ground in no time." She gave an encouraging smile.

Kyra swallowed the urge to vomit and tried to focus on the horizon.

Not soon enough, the plane landed, and she made her

way through Logan Airport. She'd beelined from the plane to the restroom to splash cold water on her face. Her neck and chest were sticky with nervous sweat. She caught her reflection in the mirror. Her cheeks tinged a sickly green. *Never again. Never. I'd rather swim than fly like that.*

She followed the signs for ground transportation to find a taxi. To her astonishment, she saw a man in a blue blazer holding a sign with her name. Kyra grinned. *Grace.*

"Hi, I'm Kyra Gibson," she said, stopping in front of him.

"Good morning!" he boomed in a deep timbre. His eyes crinkled with a wide smile. "Joel Riordan, pleased to meet you." He shook her hand. "The Ms. Chamberses arranged for me to drive you around," he said, handing her a business card. "I'm right outside." He pulled her bag from her shoulder and led her to the car.

"How do you know the Chamberses?" Kyra asked once settled in the backseat of the SUV.

Joel pulled onto the serpentine highway that snaked around Logan Airport. "I've known them ladies for years and years now," Joel responded, his accent a strange combination of Boston and New York. "I drove Grace when she was working in the Big Apple. That's what we Yanks call New York City, you know."

Do you, really? Kyra highly doubted it.

"I moved back home fifteen years ago to be closer to Boston Children's, but we stayed in touch. Grace always checked in on me and my Alice whenever she was in the Hub. And when she needed a driver, she'd call." Joel gave her a proud smile in the rearview mirror. "Since they moved to the Cape, I pick them up at the ferry for Charlie's appointments at Mass General."

"Boston Children's?"

"Best children's hospital in the world." He tapped a picture of a teenage girl with a wide, toothy smile stuck to his dashboard. Joel's voice went soft. "My Alice has cystic fibrosis." His eyes met hers through the mirror again. "Grace and Charlie have been very kind to us."

"They've been very kind to me, too."

THEY TRAVELED THE route Kyra had taken just days earlier, driving under the city on a submerged highway; however, unlike her previous trip, Joel emerged from the tunnel and into the city itself. Boston was unlike any city she'd visited. It wasn't as loud or shiny as New York or London, and it wasn't nearly as big. Boston wasn't Gothic or romantic like Paris or Rome, and where Lima and Singapore were tropically colorful, Boston was a rainbow of grays and greens. It was unique, with a casual solemness of a city trying to prove itself to the world. It had a slight resemblance to the small medieval European cities she'd visited, with its random streets and spidering intersections, but its Americanness was on full display. Every corner seemed to celebrate a rich history of resistance. Joel good-naturedly pointed out landmarks like they should have meant something to her. Copley Square, Beacon Hill, the Public Garden, which was different from the Boston Common, apparently.

When they finally turned off the main street and stopped

in front of a hotel, she was relieved the tour was over. "This is your hotel. It actually has a very interesting history, you know."

Oh, for the love of god, no.

"It used to be the site of a mansion for a Revolutionary War patriot, Edward Bromfield. The current building was built in the mid-1800s."

"Interesting," Kyra lied. "Thanks for the ride." She pushed the door open and stumbled out.

Joel rolled down the window, his expression unfazed. "I'll park in the garage, but if you need me, text me, and I'll meet you here."

"Oh, that's not necessary."

"It's all set. I grew up in Boston, so you couldn't have a better guide." He gave her a wide grin. She didn't doubt his claim. "And Ms. Chambers made me promise to keep an eye on you." He winked.

"Thanks, I'll text you in a bit." Kyra sighed, half annoyed with Grace and half thankful.

Kyra entered the lobby. It was decorated in contemporary luxury, with lots of sparkling gold accents and navy-blue suede. She checked herself in and asked the concierge for a tourist map, hoping to get her bearings. She circled the location of the hotel and recommended a few local restaurants within walking distance.

Kyra unlocked her door and dropped her bags on the bed. She texted a thank-you to Grace and Charlie for making the arrangements.

"Enjoy it, dear! I recommend it to everyone." Charlie added a few heart emojis and told her not to skip the North End

for Italian.

"Oh, and thank you for sending Joel."

"I've worked with him for years. He knows Boston better than anyone. If anyone can help you find Ed's spots, it's him."

Kyra glanced at her bag and the folder of maps. She could use the help of a local. *Right, Joel.* With some resignation, she fished out the card he'd given her.

"Hi, Joel, it's Kyra. I could use your expertise finding some places in the city. Can I buy you a coffee?"

"I'll meet you in the lobby."

She gathered her things and rushed down.

Joel was waiting for her next to the doors. He gave her an affable grin and motioned for her to follow. "One of my favorite coffee shops is just down the street."

"Perfect."

Joel led her out of the hotel and down Beacon Street. As they walked, he pointed out historic buildings and monuments and told her which restaurants and bars certain state-government representatives frequented. He told her about the history of anesthesia and some commemorative statue that was, in his words, a "don't miss."

They stopped at a pretty European-style café. They ordered at the counter and while Joel waited for their drinks, Kyra staked out a table. She spread out the printouts of the files Tarek had sent—maps of the Massachusetts coastline and a more detailed one of Boston. Both were marked with translucent circles showing where her father's phone had been used, correlating to the time-and-date clues from his texts. Kyra was comparing the Boston map to the tourist map from the concierge when Joel placed a coffee in front of her and slid into the other empty chair.

"Grace said you were looking for something in Boston?" he asked, eyeing the maps.

Kyra hesitated, wondering how much she should share with him.

Joel leaned forward and, shifting his eyes back and forth, said in a stage whisper, "I'm a wealth of local knowledge and excellent at *seecrets.*"

"Okay." She chuckled. Grace said she could trust him. "I'm trying to find places," she explained and pushed the maps toward him. "Before he died, my dad was meeting people; well, at least one person, Brendan Delaney, in the area, and I'm trying to figure out where they were meeting based on his cell phone usage."

"The dead congressional aide?" Joel frowned.

"Yeah, you've heard?"

"It's one of the biggest news stories right now. That and the Sox, obviously."

Obviously.

"Are you sure you still want to help?" She wouldn't blame him if he got up and ran. This was something out of a mobster movie.

"I didn't vote for his guy." He grinned. "Show me."

"Look here, at this text." She pointed to the first one, *1311-730-5.* "He was meeting his source on the first Tuesday of November at 7:30 a.m." She pointed to the map of Boston. There were several early morning pings in a neighborhood called Beacon Hill. "Where would someone meet early in the morning in this area?"

"There are a few places that open early for breakfast on

this street." Joel thought for a moment. "Over here is a bakery and a few bodegas. Here's a well-known greasy spoon called the Theatre Café. It's a favorite of state house workers and reporters." The concierge had circled the same place on her tourist map.

"That could be it." She marked it on the map. "I'll go by tomorrow to see if he's been there."

They studied the other clusters of pings locating areas where her father had used his burner phone. Kyra pointed to a circled area from late on the third Wednesday in November.

"That's South Station." Joel squinted at the map. "It's the train and bus depot."

"I guess it makes sense they'd meet near the train station, if he had been calling someone at the senator's office and they were traveling by train to and from DC. What do you think about these?" She pointed to a few other evening pings.

"That's the Seaport District. It's not far from South Station. Over here's the federal courthouse and the Institute of Contemporary Art, then these blocks here are mostly office buildings, condos, a few restaurants."

"What kind of offices?"

"Law offices, insurance companies, technology and energy companies."

Wetun Energy. She pulled out her phone and searched for Wetun's corporate headquarters. It was located at 1001 Seaport Boulevard, dead center for one of the circles. *Could my father have been meeting Brendan at Wetun Energy?*

"My dad was investigating the Cape Cod wind-farm project. Do you know anything about it?"

"Yeah. It's been on and off for years. It's been ... controversial."

"What do you mean?"

"The nuclear power plants that power the coastal towns are old and in need of replacement or repair. There's been a lot of political, er ... back and forth on whether to continue to invest in nuclear or go to wind. The environmental impact and sufficiency of an offshore wind farm to power the entire Cape changes depending on who's making the arguments. And all those people with homes along the coast will have obstructed views from their mansions." Joel's scowl revealed how he felt about that particular objection.

"Wherever they were meeting in the South Station area, they met there again in December." She pointed to the second-to-last text, *3212-20-04*, the third Monday in December at eight p.m. at the fourth place. She cross-referenced the date of the last text *!!2601-13-08!!*. Her father had sent it the night he'd died. The last meeting hadn't taken place. Kyra sat back and drank the dregs of her coffee.

Joel scanned through what they'd found. "You need to speak to someone at Wetun."

"I do." Kyra sighed, frustrated. "I think I have to call the detective." She rubbed away the start of a headache.

Chapter Fifteen

"COLLINS." HE ANSWERED his cell phone after the third ring.

Kyra gritted her teeth. He had caller ID, so of course he knew it was her.

"It's Kyra." She was lounging on the hotel bed. After Joel had walked her back to her hotel, she'd tried to think of any way she could get a quick appointment with the Wetun CEO without Detective Collins's help. At a loss, she had to admit she needed him.

He didn't say anything.

"I'm in Boston."

He still didn't respond.

"I came to see if I could figure out where Ed was meeting his source." *You know, Brendan, the second murder victim.* "I think I've found two of the three places." She waited for a reaction and when nothing came, "Tarek?"

"I'm listening." His tone wasn't encouraging.

"He met with his source at, or near, Wetun Energy's headquarters at least twice. His first meeting, I'm pretty sure, was at a diner in Beacon Hill."

"Okay."

Oh, for fuck's sake. Her temper flared. He was going to

make her ask for his help.

She ground her teeth. "I need your help to talk to someone at Wetun, and you already know the CEO." She didn't mention that it was her party invitation that allowed for the introduction. She didn't think Tarek would appreciate the reminder. When he didn't say anything, she tried a different approach. "Please?"

"I'll see what I can do."

"Have you talked to Brendan Delaney's family yet?"

"I'm heading there now."

"Ask them if Brendan gave them a folder to hold for him," she said, thinking of the folder her father had given Grace and Charlie.

"I'll call you when I'm done."

The line went dead.

Kyra threw her phone down with a frustrated cry. She turned the TV on, trying to drown out her thoughts and irritation. She glanced at the clock. It was barely eleven. She slumped back against the pillows. Tomorrow morning was the best time to go to the diner because it was more likely she'd run into the people who would have seen her father. It was too early to go to a pub and wallow in self-pity. She could call Joel for a tour of the city, but the thought of more of Joel's information torture made her recoil.

What am I even doing here?

She turned her face into her pillow.

"*Arrrgghhhh.*"

Her phone rang. She sat up and scrambled to collect it from the edge of the bed. Tarek. Kyra smoothed her shirt.

"Hello?"

"Where are you staying?" Tarek sniped, his voice harsh.

She winced. "P … pardon?" she stammered but recovered before he repeated himself and gave him the name of the hotel.

"I'll be out front in fifteen minutes."

The line went dead again.

Kyra stared at her phone and blinked, stunned for a few heartbeats, before jumping up, spurred into action. She wasn't sure why Tarek had changed his mind, but she would take it. Grabbing her shoes and jacket, she hurried for the elevator, unable to suppress her excitement. Once inside, using the mirrored walls, she tried to school her features, so she appeared aloof, properly bored and professional, but only succeeded in looking a bit constipated. She made a frustrated sound in the back of her throat as the doors opened. Grabbing a newspaper from the lobby, Kyra went outside to wait for the detective. She was pretending to scan the headlines when his police SUV stopped at the curb.

"Get in," he called to her through the window.

She climbed into the front seat, trying not to smile. "Hi," she said, folding her paper.

His eyebrow rose over the frame of his aviators. He put the car in drive and pulled away.

"Right, so where are we going?"

"To the Delaney house." She got the impression that any further questions would get her kicked out of the car, so she sat back and stared out the window.

Detective Collins steered the SUV onto the motorway, driving west on I-90. After what felt like hours of sitting in strained silence, but was probably less than twenty minutes, they exited the interstate and pulled to a stop in front of a neat duplex on a tree-lined street of two-family homes.

Kyra opened her mouth to ask why he'd changed his mind. Why he'd let her come with him, but the detective cut her off, his eyes on the house.

"This is Brendan Delaney's mother's house. He grew up here." He gave her a pointed look. "Keep quiet."

She schooled her face into an impassive mask. *Fine.*

Mrs. Delaney's yard was well kept. Tulips, daffodils, and hyacinths of every color were springing up in tidy flowerbeds. Tarek rang the doorbell, and a woman in her late forties opened the door. She was heavyset, and her pale face was drawn with grief. Her short, gray-streaked hair was pulled back with a headband.

"Yes?" she croaked.

"Mrs. Delaney? My name is Detective Collins with the Massachusetts State Police, and this is my ... associate, Ms. Gibson. My department arranged a meeting with you to inquire about your son." Tarek flashed his badge.

"Yes. Come in." She left the front door open and shuffled into the kitchen.

Kyra shut the door behind her and followed. The kitchen was bright, painted pale yellow with white cabinets and countertops. Its cheerfulness was abrasive, dismissive of its inhabitant's obvious sorrow. Tarek and Kyra sat across from Mrs. Delaney at a small kitchen table.

"As I said before, Mrs. Delaney, I'm investigating the circumstances of your son's death." Tarek's tone was deliberate, his voice soft.

"You mean his murder." She choked back a sob.

Kyra winced.

"Yes, ma'am. I'm sorry." Tarek nodded, then repeated, "Your son's murder."

"What do you want to know? I told the other officers everything."

"I understand, but sometimes it's helpful to go over it again." Tarek pulled out his notebook. "Do you know why Brendan was on Martha's Vineyard?"

"No." She shook her head.

"Did he go there often?"

"I really don't know. He was often traveling places with the senator's team, but I didn't always know where he was going. He might have mentioned Martha's Vineyard once or twice last fall."

"Do you know anyone who would have wanted to hurt him?" Tarek asked.

"No. Brendan was a good man." Tears gathered in her eyes. "He worked hard. He was kind."

"What about a social life?"

"He has friends here that he kept in touch with, and there were young people in Washington, mostly from work, I think. I knew he was seeing someone. He was very happy, but he wasn't ready to tell me too much yet. He said it was still new." She dabbed at her eyes with a raggedy dishtowel.

"When was the last time he was home?"

"During the holidays. This year he came for Thanksgiving, then again for Christmas." She frowned. "Actually, he was home a lot last winter. Almost every other week he'd stay for a night or two. He came for Christmas and left after New Year's. He hasn't been here since."

What day did he leave? Kyra tried to get Tarek's attention. *Does she know about my father?*

"Was it unusual for him to visit so frequently?" Tarek asked.

Kyra sat back against her seat, frustrated. Tarek was ignoring her. Again, she wondered why she was here.

"Maybe not. He often had meetings in the city." Mrs. Delaney fidgeted with the dishtowel. "He could have stayed in a hotel, but Brendan said he preferred to stay here, and…" She sucked in a haggard breath. "I wanted him home." Her eyes met Kyra's, and Kyra's heart went out to her.

"How long has your son been working for Senator Hawthorn?"

"Oh." Mrs. Delaney shifted and thought. "He started there maybe two years ago?"

"And before that, where did he work?"

"At a green-energy company in Boston, Wetun Energy."

Kyra froze. She glanced at Tarek, but he didn't give away that he'd ever heard of Wetun.

"He was very passionate about environmentalism. That's why he went into politics. He said he could do more working for change inside the system."

"What was his position at the energy company?"

"He was in government affairs. I don't remember his exact title."

Tarek closed his notebook. "Thank you, Mrs. Delaney. You've been very helpful. I don't think I have any more questions right now, but do you think we could look at Brendan's room?"

"This way." She nodded and pushed back her chair.

They followed her up a narrow staircase to a small bedroom. On the walls, he'd hung posters of Italian cars and pennants from Framingham High School. "I never changed it, even after he moved out," Mrs. Delaney explained, standing in the doorway.

Tarek walked over to the desk and shuffled through the papers there. He opened the drawers, glancing at the contents. "Did you find a laptop or a phone?" he asked.

"No."

Kyra blurted, "Did he ask you to hold a file or a folder for him?"

Tarek glared at her, and she shrugged. *If you weren't going to ask...*

Mrs. Delaney startled. "Actually, yes. How did you know?"

Kyra wasn't sure how to answer.

"Can we see it, please?" Tarek asked.

"Wait here. I'll get it." Mrs. Delaney left and returned with a sealed FedEx envelope. "He sent this to me after the New Year. Told me to hold on to it for him and he'd pick it up when he came home." She shrugged and held out the envelope to Tarek.

"Do you mind?" When Mrs. Delaney didn't protest, he opened the envelope and emptied its contents onto the bedspread. It contained a manila folder with some handwritten notes.

Kyra's heart skipped, but she kept her face neutral.

"Can we take this?" he asked.

"Yes, of course." She peered at it. "What is it? Will it be helpful?"

"I'm not sure yet." Tarek handed the folder to Kyra, who gave it a quick scan.

She recognized the same articles Grace had been holding. She gave Tarek a nod and tucked the folder under her arm.

"Thank you, Mrs. Delaney. We won't impose on your time any longer."

Brendan's mother led them to the front door and held it open.

"If you think of anything at all, even something that seems irrelevant, please let me know." He handed her his business card.

"You'll find who did this?" she asked, her eyes wide.

"You have my word that I'll do my best," he said and walked back to the car.

Kyra said goodbye and followed him.

As Tarek pulled the car away from the curb, Kyra turned back to see Mrs. Delaney watching them from her front porch, clutching that towel to her face.

"What's in there?" Tarek asked, nodding toward the papers in Kyra's lap.

"I'm allowed to speak now?"

"Yes." He let out an audible sigh. "What's in the folder, Kyra?"

She flipped through the pages. "Articles about Wetun and the other energy companies, the same ones my dad had, and another one of these notebook pages with handwritten phone numbers." She held it up to Tarek, who glanced her way. "Keep your eyes on the road!" She yanked back the page.

"Then don't show it to me," he sniped, sounding more

amused than angry. His lips twitched like he was trying not to laugh.

Kyra studied the paper. "It's the same as Ed's. A bunch of phone numbers and a random extension." Something was nagging at the back of her mind.

"Is the extension the same as the one your dad recorded?"

"I don't remember, but one of these phone numbers is his old editor at the *Times*."

"That makes sense. Wouldn't they be in contact with someone still at the paper if they're doing an exposé?"

"Maybe…" She wasn't convinced. "If the paper knew about their investigation, wouldn't someone have contacted the police when they both died?" Then it clicked. "Wait." She pulled out her phone and found the website for her father's cloud-storage service. "Look, Tarek, SkyCloud takes a password *or* a pin number." She entered the six digits from Brendan's folder as the pin.

Access Denied. Incorrect account number or pin. "Goddammit." *I'd have sworn that was it.*

"Could Brendan have an account, too?"

"Maybe? You think this is his pin? My father's account number was in a sealed envelope addressed to me."

Could Brendan have an envelope addressed to someone somewhere?

"And the extension in your dad's files is his pin number?"

She let out a curse. "Could that be it? Did I have it the whole time?"

"Hey, it's okay." He gave her a crooked smile. "We'll get it tomorrow."

The console's screen lit up with a call from headquarters. Tarek gave her a look. A silent command to keep quiet. "Collins." The office had received the DCPD's report on Brendan's apartment search but hadn't found anything useful. Brendan's laptop and phone were still missing. "What about documents or files?" Tarek asked.

"I'll email you the full report, but they didn't find anything, Collins. I have it here, and it's pretty uninteresting."

"What about a calendar or a datebook?"

"No, sir."

"Ask about a sealed envelope," Kyra whispered.

"Did they find a sealed envelope containing an account number for a cloud-storage company?" He made a pained face at her.

"Sir?"

"Seriously." He ran his hand through his hair. He glanced at Kyra with an are-you-happy-now look. "Anything in the report?"

"No, nothing like that, but we can double-check."

"Ask DC to check with the senator's office. Check Brendan's desk there and ask after his schedule over the past twelve months. Also, subpoena his credit card and bank records."

"Yes, sir, I'll submit the inquiries and send that over as soon as I get it."

Tarek thanked the voice and disconnected. "They'll look again, but I'm not optimistic. Didn't you say your dad hid that envelope where no one but you would find it?"

Kyra's stomach hollowed out and she turned away to stare out the window. *Yes, he did.*

"You're not going to ask me about Wetun Energy?" Tarek asked as they entered the city.

"Pardon?" She jolted in her seat. They'd been sitting in traffic, in silence, for forty minutes.

"I scheduled a meeting with Dr. Alonda at Wetun Energy this afternoon." Tarek waited for her reply, but Kyra stayed silent, unsure what he wanted from her. "Will you come with me?"

"I … I can. When is it?"

"We have to go straight there."

The SUV emerged from the underground highway. Tarek snaked through city streets that twisted, turned, and changed names at random. With the unique confidence gained from having done something hundreds of times, he navigated one-ways and back-alley cut-throughs until he pulled up in front of a high-rise building on Seaport Boulevard. He didn't bother to find parking; he just left the car in front, in a no-parking zone.

"Ready?" he asked, turning to her. "I'll do most of the talking, but if anything catches your attention, let me know."

Kyra gritted her teeth in annoyance. She wasn't used to taking orders or being relegated to the assistant, but she nodded.

They entered a sterile lobby. Tarek spoke with the security guard who issued them temporary badges and instructed them to take the elevator to the fourteenth floor. The elevator opened into Wetun's office lobby with white marble floors and lots of glass. At one end of the elevator bay was a security door and at the other, a large reception desk made of more marble. Behind the desk stood an impeccably dressed young man wearing a headset. He was speaking in Spanish to whomever was on the other line. He held up a hand and pointed to a bench, signaling they were to take a seat. After a few moments, he tapped the side of the headset and turned to them.

"Welcome to Wetun Energy. Can I help you?"

"Yes, I'm Detective Collins, and this is my associate, Ms. Gibson." Tarek flashed his badge. "We have an appointment with Dr. Alonda."

"Yes, sir. Let me check." The man picked up a tablet and tapped something out. He clicked his tongue. "Ah, I see. Please follow me."

They followed him through the security doors and down a hallway to a large boardroom. "Please take a seat." He gestured to the empty chairs pushed in under the huge white marble-topped table. "I've alerted Dr. Alonda's assistant, and she'll be with you momentarily."

The receptionist opened a mini-fridge in the corner of the room and pulled out four bottles of San Pellegrino. He handed one each to Tarek and Kyra and placed the other two at seats at the end of the table before disappearing. Tarek chose a seat a few down from the table head, and Kyra sat next to him. She was studying the garish corporate art taking up an entire wall when two women entered the boardroom. Kyra estimated they were in their early fifties but one, whom Kyra surmised was Dr. Alonda, was dressed in a finely tailored navy business suit so complementary to the décor's color scheme, it must have been intentional.

"Detective Collins?" the woman in the blue suit addressed Tarek. "It's a pleasure to see you again. This is my assistant, Bea." Dr. Alonda sat in the chair at the end of the long table. Bea took the empty one to her right and pulled out a notebook. "Now, how can I help you?" Dr. Alonda asked, clasping her hands together and resting them in front of her.

"Yes, thank you for your time. I'm investigating a series of suspicious incidents that have occurred on Martha's Vineyard over the past few months. Your company's name keeps coming up in the investigation, and we have a few questions. I was wondering, how well are you acquainted with Senator Hawthorn?"

"Well, as the head of the energy committee, I'm fairly well acquainted with him and his colleagues. Their policies directly impact my company."

"Can you tell me more?"

"Of course. We're submitting RFPs for an offshore wind farm off the coast of southern Massachusetts." Dr. Alonda stood up and began walking back and forth. "This wind farm would provide enough green, low-carbon energy to power the Cape Cod population. It's a wonderful opportunity to advance the senator's initiative for long-term, sustainable energy."

"That sounds like an opportunity that could have a net-positive impact on the region and is in line with the senator's platform, as I understand it," Kyra said, ignoring Tarek's side-eye.

"Yes, exactly." The CEO almost smiled at her new ally.

See? She knew how to flatter and manipulate C-suite egos.

"But we're competing against at least four other corporations who have similar proposals for different regions and are facing significantly less hostility from local wealthy constituents."

"I'm sorry?" Tarek asked. "What do you mean?"

"We're proposing to install one hundred and thirty wind turbines five miles off the shoreline in the Nantucket Sound. It's possible that on clear days a person could see the turbines from the southern coast of the lower cape in towns like Hyannis or parts of the northeastern side of Martha's Vineyard. The senator and his committee were very much in favor of our proposal because the site we've chosen has been thoroughly vetted by ecologists and environmentalists, and its negative impact on the local plant and wildlife would be minimal and contained; however, after the height of the turbines was disclosed in the press with claims that views from people's homes would be obstructed, we've received a lot of pushback from the senator's colleagues. Especially those who have real estate investments in the area. It doesn't matter that our research shows that during the high season in the summer, It's so naturally hazy in the area it would be a rare occurrence to see the turbines from land."

Dr. Alonda stopped walking and turned to Tarek and Kyra. "In the winter, it could be more often," she conceded and straightened her jacket. She retook her seat and sipped her water. "We've also received significant pressure from the local business communities. The building and construction industries are concerned that easy, inexpensive access to green energy would de-incentivize homeowners and new construction from investing in other energy-efficient options that are more expensive, such as solar and geothermal.

Laughably, our opponents have suggested that the energy savings would dissuade consumers from other conservation efforts, like purchasing energy-efficient appliances, windows, sustainable building materials, and so on, even when inefficient alternatives are hardly available."

Dr. Alonda sucked on her teeth.

"All of this pushback has meant we've had to invest significantly in lobbying and marketing efforts to offset the negative campaign by our opponents and subsequent bad press the project is receiving. We've been working closely with Senator Hawthorn and the energy committee to advance the project."

Dr. Alonda paused and shared a look with Bea.

She turned back to Tarek and shook her head, disappointment written on her face. "Recently, however, Senator Hawthorn appears to be distancing himself from the project because of the optics of his familial involvement, making it more difficult for my company to make headway."

"What do you mean, optics of his familial involvement?" Tarek asked.

"Yes, apparently a son-in-law has bought a large amount of Wetun Energy stock, and given the timing of his purchase, opponents to the project have suggested that he may have been privy to information about the award of the contract. Of course, that's all bullshit." Her nose wrinkled in distaste. "We've not been awarded the contract, but our opponents and the investors of the other energy projects have been quick to take up this fiction to discredit the senator and suggest that Wetun is involved in a scandal. The SEC and the DOJ ran preliminary investigations and found no evidence of any inappropriate behavior." She shifted in her seat and leveled a look at the detective. "I'd never heard of Dr. Brian Lee before the investigation."

Dr. Brian bought Wetun stock? Kyra wondered when. Why?

Dr. Alonda threw her hands up. Kyra glanced at Tarek, but he didn't give away that he knew Brian Lee.

"Do you know Edward Gibson?" Kyra asked.

"No, should I?" Dr. Alonda pursed her lips.

"Mr. Gibson was a reporter. He died earlier this year but may have reached out to you about the wind farm?" Tarek clarified.

"No. Not that I'm aware of. Bea?"

Bea checked her phone before shaking her head. "I don't see any meeting with anyone with that name." She thought for a moment. "If he was calling from a paper, he would have been put in direct contact with public relations. I'll ask Rachel." She typed on the tiny screen.

"What about Brendan Delaney?" Tarek inquired.

Did Dr. Alonda stiffen? Kyra narrowed her eyes, but if she had recognized the name, the CEO recovered quickly.

"I'm not sure." Dr. Alonda shook her head. "Is that name familiar to you?" she asked Bea. "Do we know a Mr. Delaney?"

"I don't see anything in your recent calendar with anyone with that name either." Bea answered. She continued scrolling through her phone.

"Brendan used to work for you before taking a position as an aide in the senator's office," Tarek prompted. "In government affairs?"

"I'll check with HR, but Wetun has over a thousand employees. Dr. Alonda certainly wouldn't be expected to know them all by name," Bea said and placed her phone on the table facedown. She straightened a tidy stack of papers.

"How many people work in this office, Bea?" Kyra asked. Bea started and shifted a nervous glance to Dr. Alonda, who was checking her own phone.

"We have fifty full-time employees in the corporate headquarters." Bea swallowed.

Dr. Alonda cleared her throat and stood up.

"Yes, if that's all, I'm afraid Dr. Alonda has another meeting." Bea stood as well.

"Just one more question." Tarek raised his hand. "Where were you on the night of January third?"

"Why?" Dr. Alonda froze, a frown creasing her brow.

"Just being thorough." Tarek shrugged.

"The third? I believe I was still skiing with my family in Vermont." She turned to her assistant. "Is that right?"

"Yes, ma'am. You returned on the fifth."

"Can anyone corroborate that?" Tarek asked, standing up.

"Of course. My husband and children. Probably the staff at the lodge."

"How about last Sunday evening?"

She blinked. "Home, with my family."

"Dr. Alonda," Bea interrupted. "At seven p.m. you were on a scheduled video conference with the board."

"Oh, right. I did take that call." Dr. Alonda nodded. "Bea, can you provide names from the lodge and the board members to the detective so they can confirm?"

"Right away." Bea nodded. "Will that be all?" she asked Tarek.

"Yes. Thank you for your time."

As if by magic, the receptionist appeared and ushered them back to the elevator bays.

"They're lying about Brendan," Kyra said once the elevator doors closed.

"You caught that, too?"

"Even if they hadn't given it away by acting strange, there's no way you don't know everyone in such a small office, at least by name. You especially know the people in charge of your government contacts."

The elevator doors opened, and they exited the building. Tarek headed for the car, but Kyra stopped. She placed her hand on his forearm. "One second." Taking up the ground floor of a building on the corner was a restaurant. Its tinted front windows so dark they were almost opaque. She walked over to the intricately carved wooden doors and entered. Inside, it was more like a lounge, with velvet seating and dim lighting from electric lanterns. Its few patrons sipped afternoon cocktails. The air was heavy with exotic spices. *Moroccan.*

"Two?" the hostess asked, picking up menus.

"Actually, I was wondering if you've ever seen this man here?" Kyra pulled out her phone and showed the hostess a picture of her father. The hostess glanced at the phone and shifted her weight.

"I'm Detective Collins with the Massachusetts State Police." Tarek reached around Kyra to show the hostess his credentials. "Have you ever seen that man?"

The hostess looked more closely, then shook her head. "No, but I'm new. You may want to ask at the bar."

They made their way to the back of the restaurant. The bartender greeted them, and they showed him the photo. He squinted at it, tilting the phone for more light.

"Sure," he said. "He came in a few times last winter, but I haven't seen him in a while."

"You recognize him, then?" Kyra asked.

"Yeah. He and his buddy came late for our dinner crowd on weeknights. They were working on something. Always had their laptops and notebooks." He gestured around the room. "Figured they were writers or something. We get a lot of the artsy types here. He was polite and always ordered single malts. Our normal crowd is more Manhattans and Negronis."

"Was this his companion?" Tarek pulled up a photo of Brendan from Senator Hawthorn's website.

The bartender studied it for a moment and shrugged. "Could be. I'm not sure."

"Thank you." Kyra walked outside, her brain whirling.

Tarek touched her elbow before unlocking the car. "Well?"

"I didn't think it made sense that they'd meet at the Wetun offices." She chewed on her bottom lip and opened the door. Tarek walked round the SUV and slid into the driver's seat. "My dad loved Moroccan food. Maybe they were meeting there to discuss whatever they were … discussing." Kyra tapped her fingers against her thigh. "I'm missing something. I wish I knew what he was doing. Why he was meeting with Brendan." Kyra pinched the bridge of her nose and rested her head against the seatback. "I'm pretty sure they also met at a diner, or at least Ed went. The Theatre Café, close to my hotel. I'm going to check there in the morning."

"I know the place." Tarek started the car. "I'll come with you."

Chapter Sixteen

Saturday

K YRA JERKED AWAKE. It took a moment for her sleep-addled brain to process that she was in a hotel in Boston, not her room on Martha's Vineyard, not her office, and certainly not her flat in London. She rubbed her eyes. There'd been a lot of change in the past few days. Her phone pinged. It was Tarek texting that he'd meet her outside in an hour. She checked her flight itinerary. She'd have enough time to go to the diner, then head to the airport for her flight back. Her stomach churned at the thought of getting back on one of those propeller planes. Maybe she'd ask Joel to drive her to Woods Hole. Kyra didn't know what would be worse—thirty minutes of blinding terror or two hours of mind-numbing boredom.

Showered and dressed, Kyra sipped on her coffee while watching the hustle and bustle on the street below. It reminded her of her street back in London. Her flat was in a busy part of town, a short walk from her office. She'd rented it years ago for its proximity to work but had never gotten around to really moving in. It'd never felt like a home.

If I go back, I really need to find a new place to live.

"If I go back?" Kyra sat down on the edge of the bed. *Of*

course, I'm going back. She felt like she was scolding herself, but the thought of returning to solitary life in London left her feeling cold and empty.

Her phone buzzed, and she grabbed for it, fumbling as she pulled the cord from the wall. The detective was downstairs.

Tarek strolled up to the front of the hotel, just as Kyra was exiting. He seemed more relaxed today. He greeted her with a smile that Kyra couldn't help but return it.

"Good morning."

"How was it?" he asked, tilting his head toward the hotel.

"Great. Grace set me up."

"Hungry?"

"Famished."

"Come on. It's just up the street."

Despite the chill, the Boston Common was full of people in the middle of their morning routines—jogging, hurrying to work, walking their dogs.

Kyra followed Tarek to an old-fashioned, cafeteria-style breakfast place, the kind with retro plastic tables and mismatched chrome-and-vinyl chairs, the varying colors, all slightly faded. The laminate tiles in front of the counter were so worn through Kyra could make out the subfloor beneath.

The Theatre Café was busy with the late-morning crowd. She studied the menu posted above the counter while they waited their turn.

"Tarek Collins!" A voice pierced the busy din.

Kyra turned to see a grinning gray-haired woman walking toward them. She wore an apron with the restaurant's name screen printed across the front.

"Donna," Tarek said.

Kyra's mouth fell open when he wrapped his arms around the woman.

Barely recovered, Kyra shut her mouth and plastered on a polite smile.

"How are you?" Donna held him at arm's length and looked him up and down, assessing him with motherly concern.

"I'm fine, Donna." Tarek's eyes shone with affection.

She gripped his forearm, pulling him to her side. Her eyes flicked to Kyra, then back to Tarek.

"This is Kyra."

"So nice to meet you." Donna beamed and clasped Kyra's hands. "I have a table for you." She ushered them to a table in the corner, then called back over her shoulder, "Antonio! Tarek is here. He brought a friend." She pointed to a chair. "Sit."

"You said you knew this place, not that you were a regular," Kyra hissed through her teeth as she dropped into her seat.

"I haven't been a regular in a while." Tarek shrugged. "I hope you really are hungry. Donna's going to bring whatever she wants us to eat."

A server brought over two thick ceramic mugs of hot coffee. Kyra wrapped her hands around the cup, snaking her fingers through the handle. Donna joined them, gripping her own coffee mug with faded lettering that read WORLD'S GREATEST GRANDMA.

"Tarek. We didn't know you were in town. How long has it been? When was the last time you were here?"

"I stopped by last month, remember? We set up your new router?"

"Oh, yes. That's right. That feels like so long ago, but it works." She pointed to a television playing a staticky local news show. Kyra felt Tarek sag next to her and bit back a laugh.

"I'll come back and set up the TV for you, but I'm actually here on business today."

"You work too hard." Donna tsked, but she smiled with unabashed pride. "You'll eat first." She turned to Kyra. "When he was attending school, he spent all his time here. He worked during the day and studied all night. We couldn't get rid of him." Donna's smile widened.

"You worked here?" Kyra asked, trying to picture a young, stern Detective Collins serving coffee and wearing an apron.

"I did." His eyes sparked, daring her to laugh. "I cooked. Antonio, Donna's husband, taught me." Tarek pointed to the kitchen.

"You can cook?"

"Of course he can," Donna scoffed. "But he spent more time studying than cooking."

"You went to school near here?" Kyra asked.

"Up the road, at Boston University." He pointed behind them.

"Yes. He's a doctor."

"No, Donna, I only have a Master's."

Donna bit the inside of her cheek, and her eyebrows hitched together.

Tarek turned to Kyra, his cheeks pink, and shifted in his

seat. The stoic detective had morphed into something else under Donna's boasting. His embarrassment was charming. Kyra tipped her head to the side, a silent question.

"Psychology," he muttered, and she grinned at his discomfort. "But, Donna, actually, I really do have a few questions for you, if you don't mind?"

"For me? Antonio!" she bellowed toward the kitchen. "Tarek needs us."

A member of Donna's staff, followed by two more, appeared bearing plates of food—eggs, bacon, sausage, pancakes, fruit, three different types of toast. Kyra's eyes widened watching the parade of breakfast. She met Tarek's eyes. He smiled apologetically and shrugged as if to say, *I told you*. Donna directed her staff and organized the table, her rings clinking on the Fiestaware plates.

"More coffee?" Tarek asked.

Kyra nodded.

Donna scooted back in her chair.

"No, sit. I'll get it." Tarek went behind the counter and returned with a carafe and a carton of almond milk. He handed Kyra the carton and topped them all off and filled a fourth mug. He handed the carafe back over the counter as a man shuffled over. The man must have been in his seventies, slightly stooped. He was dressed in thin, stained jeans at least two sizes too large, held up with clip-on suspenders.

"Tarek!" He clasped Tarek's hand in both of his and gave him a wide, toothy grin. "Sit! Sit! You need my help?" he asked in a thick Italian accent.

"Have you ever seen this man?" Tarek showed them a photo of Ed Gibson on his phone.

Antonio pulled his glasses from his breast pocket and peered at the screen. "Yes, of course. Edoardo. Such a nice man. So sad."

Donna pulled the phone close to her face, her nose nearly touching the screen. "Yes, that's Edward." She confirmed with a chin dip, her expression serious.

"You knew him?" Kyra asked.

"Mmmhmm. Why?"

"How did you know him?" Tarek asked.

"Edoardo was a good customer for many years. He came first alone, like you, always studying, then working, then he came with his Isabella. So sad." Antonio shook his head.

Kyra looked up. *Isabel? My mother?*

"He always made a point to see us when he was in Boston. The last few years, he'd stop in on his way to or from the Cape. Before he died, he was stopping in regularly, often with a young man." Donna patted her husband's hand.

"This man?" Tarek pulled up a picture of Brendan Delaney.

"Yes. That's him. Nervous fellow." Antonio pursed his lips.

"You knew my parents?"

The older couple swiveled their heads to look at her.

"Ed and Isabel Gibson? You knew them? Both?"

"You're Edward's little girl?" Donna squinted at her, studying Kyra's features.

"Yes. I didn't know they lived in Boston."

"Oh, yes. It must have been over thirty years ago, now." Donna nodded. "They lived just up that way." She waved to the city beyond the diner walls.

"They moved to New York City," Antonio chimed in, eyeing Kyra with a sympathetic smile. "But Edoardo never forgot his friends here."

That sounded like her dad, cultivating relationships all over the world.

Something inside of her cracked.

He had the time to see a couple that ran a diner but not his own kid.

She steeled herself, and plastered on a pleasant smile, determined not to let these people know that their words affected her. She caught Tarek watching her, his head tilted, and she looked down at her hands clasped under the table.

"Do you know why he and Mr. Delaney were coming in so often?" Tarek asked.

"Edward was writing a story. Do you know what he was writing about, Antonio?"

"Wind, I think?" Antonio said, rubbing his chin.

"Wind?" Tarek repeated.

"The young man carried a backpack. It had a picture of a windmill and a bird." Donna talked with her hands. Her rings flashed under the fluorescent lights.

Tarek pulled up the homepage of Wetun Energy. Its logo was a silhouette of a seagull flying in front of a wind turbine. Antonio pulled his glasses back out of his pocket and peered through the lenses. The corners of his mouth drew down.

"Yes, that's it," Antonio said, jabbing a thick finger at the phone screen.

"Did they tell you what they were discussing? Did you overhear them?" Tarek pushed.

"The young man was always whispering. Could never

hear what he ordered." Antonio heaved a heavy sigh.

Tarek's phone rang. He glanced at the screen and excused himself, pressing the phone to his ear. Antonio pointed him toward the back of the restaurant, but he didn't get more than ten feet when he turned around, catching Kyra's eye.

"Donna, Antonio, we need to get back to the island. This information has been very helpful. Thank you."

"Detective Tarek, always busy solving crimes." Antonio chuckled and waved to someone behind the counter. An employee brought over a paper bag and a coffee tray. "Take! Take."

Kyra eyed the table, dismayed at all the virtually untouched food.

Donna stood and embraced Tarek. She put her hand to his cheek. "Come back soon." She turned to Kyra, giving her a hug. "You, too."

Kyra went rigid in Donna's embrace and awkwardly patted her on the back.

Antonio and Donna followed them to the door and waved them out.

"What I don't understand," Kyra mumbled, "is why my dad was talking to Brendan at all. What information could he have had? Was it about Wetun? He was an old ex-employee. That doesn't mean he'd have access to proprietary information. Or was it about Senator Hawthorn? It doesn't sound like they interacted with each other." She glanced up at the detective, wondering what he thought, but Tarek wasn't listening.

He was already back on the phone. From the one-sided

conversation, it sounded like he was talking to someone at the station. Kyra half listened, wondering if he was going to share what he learned.

"There's been suspicious activity on Brendan's bank accounts with large deposits from an anonymous offshore account."

Kyra chanced a peek at his face. Was he actually sharing information? Trusting her? Was she a colleague? A partner? She smiled to herself at the idea of being a partner like in a buddy-cop show.

"I'm driving back to the island now. Are you flying, or do you want a ride?"

"You don't mind?" Kyra asked, relief pooling in her stomach. She'd been dreading the flight and Joel's history lessons.

"No." He shook his head. "It's self-serving. I really need to see your dad's notes."

It was like being doused with a bucket of icy water.

Oh.

Chapter Seventeen

K YRA OPENED THE front door to her father's house. The three-hour trip from Boston had been exhausting. She'd been unable to sit still, squirming in her seat, attempting awkward, one-sided small talk. Tarek, too, was frustrated. He'd mostly ignored her. He made calls to the office, barking questions at his colleagues, then cutting them off or hanging up, when he didn't like their answers, all the while mumbling under his breath. When they'd finally boarded the ferry at Woods Hole, Kyra left him alone with his computer and the spotty Wi-Fi. She'd bought a coffee in the café and sat outside as they sailed back to the island. Tarek set her bag down on the inside of the door.

BANG! A white cannonball landed on the console table.

"*Arrrghhh!*" Kyra's heart stopped. Her hand flew to her chest, and she stumbled back. "Mother shit!"

Cronkite gave her a withering stare and jumped to the floor, landing without a sound. He tossed his tail and sauntered out of the foyer.

"I think you may be a dog person," Tarek deadpanned, and Kyra whirled around. The corners of his mouth twitched. His green eyes sparkled. She tried to glare at him, but her breaths were coming out in pants.

"I think you may be right," she conceded when her breathing slowed enough to talk. Her heart still banged against her ribs.

Tarek's phone buzzed. He read the incoming message, his expression darkening. "I'm being summoned to the station to brief my captain. It shouldn't take more than a few hours. I'll call you later to follow up on Ed's notes?"

"Okay. Later is fine. Thank you." He gave her a quizzical look. "For the ride." Tarek tipped his chin and backed out of the foyer.

Right, just here for the notes.

She shut the door with more force than necessary and flipped the deadbolt.

Kyra wandered through the house, turning on the lights, checking all the locks. She found herself in her guestroom, her bag half unpacked. She sat on the edge of her bed. Her skin felt too tight, her chest too full. She needed to think.

When she was stressed or stuck at work, she'd go to the gym or run along the Thames. Something about the measured breathing, the intentional steps quieted her mind, and helped her organize her thoughts. She picked up her running shoes.

I haven't seen South Beach yet.

Kyra walked down to the cove and found the sandy path that ran along the water. She could imagine her father taking the same route to the beach, lugging his beach chair and laptop, probably an umbrella or a book. Bushes with large berries ranging in color from soft peach to a bright terracotta created a barrier between her and the water.

She heard the waves crashing against the sand before she

could see the beach. The pounding got louder on the other side of the dunes. She stopped to catch her breath and take in the coastline. The crests were white, and the wind tossed sea foam into the air. The sea had a turbulence, a violence unique to the Atlantic Ocean. She walked down to the darkened sand, packed hard by the waves.

Kyra turned east, her back to the house, and began to run. She became accustomed to the sand, first firm, then squishy, falling away as she pushed off with each step. She altered her stride and increased speed as her confidence in her footing grew. Her mind settled. She focused on her breathing. As she ran, she worked through what she knew.

Ed was investigating Wetun Energy and Senator Hawthorn. The senator and his family have financial and political ties to Wetun. Did Ed know about Dr. Brian's investments? When Ed died, the police looked into the senator's son. Then Chase's friend was murdered. Does Chase know something? Is that why the family is protecting him?

Kyra's step faltered and she slowed her pace. She wanted to know what Tarek thought about all of it. Her father. Brendan. Chase. Her.

Ali had been wrong when she'd brought up her fling in Majorca. Kyra had let herself get swept away not just because she was on holiday, but because she wasn't tied to that place, to those people. She'd never see that man again. They didn't even exchange numbers. This island was different. It didn't feel temporary. Her parents had roots here, and she could, too, if she wanted them.

Do I? Want them?

The beach ended and Kyra slowed to a stop. The sea had

broken through, creating a swirling connection between the Atlantic and the Edgartown harbor, severing Chappaquid-dick from the rest of the island. She stooped down, her hands on her knees, and sucked air into her raw lungs.

She didn't know what wanted in the coming weeks or months. Her future, always a clear path in front of her, was suddenly murky and unfocused. But she did see her next step clearly. She would do everything she could to find out what happened to her father. She owed him that much.

I need to see Ed's notes.

Kyra turned back.

And I can't do it alone.

Kyra jogged up to the house and climbed the stairs to her front door. She paused on the step, letting her heels dangle off the edge, stretching her calves. She reached for her toes and froze. There, lying just to the side of the door, next to the mat, was a flathead screwdriver.

She reached for it. She turned it in her hands. It was large, bigger than something you'd find in a home toolbox, and old. The green paint on the wooden handle had worn away in spots. She looked at the door. Marks marred the white paint next to the new keypad. She ran her fingers along the barely there scratches. *Was this from the locksmith?* She swallowed back a trickle of apprehension.

Did someone try to break in?

"Hi, dear," a voice sang, and Kyra jumped and swung around.

Grace and Charlie were walking across the lawn, hand in hand.

Grace's eyes went wide. "Oh my, I didn't mean to startle

you." Her eyes fell to the tool in Kyra's hand.

"Oh no, sorry. I'm fine." Kyra dropped her hand to her side.

"Look, Char, she runs. She's healthy."

Charlie rolled her eyes in what Kyra now recognized as her characteristic response to nearly everything Grace said.

"How was Boston? Did you find out what Ed was doing in the city?"

"Boston was good. We found a few spots where he was meeting with his source. But now I have even more questions." Kyra made a face and turned back to the door to punch in the code. "Thank you again for helping me and for checking in on Cronkite."

"Of course, dear," Grace said. "No problem at all. We didn't realize you were back. We were coming over to check on him just now."

"Oh, come inside." Kyra paused, glancing back over her shoulder. She didn't want to impose if they had something better to do. "Do you have time?"

"Nothing but." Charlie gave her wife a squeeze.

Kyra pushed open the door and stepped inside. She toed off her sneakers and placed the screwdriver on the console table.

Charlie's brow creased with an unasked question.

"I found it on the porch. The locksmith must have left it when he installed the new keycode system. I'll call him tomorrow."

"Contractors." Charlie took Kyra's arm. "They're always losing things. You have no idea what I've found at some of my properties."

Kyra flicked on the fire in the living room.

"I'm going to get cleaned up." She gestured to her sweaty running clothes. "Please, help yourself. There's wine and snacks in the fridge."

Grace was already heading toward the kitchen, waving Kyra away.

"Go. We've got it handled," she said.

When Kyra came back downstairs carrying her father and Brendan's folders and her laptop, Grace and Charlie were snacking on an artfully arranged cheeseboard.

Kyra stared at the spread. "This was all in the fridge?"

"Grace called Julia. She's at the house." Charlie grinned.

"She's just so wonderful, and it took less time than going to the store." Grace shrugged.

"I guess I need to go shopping. Did she make bread?" She pointed to the fresh loaves wrapped in linen.

"Yes, this afternoon. She's been there for a catering job all day and baked some extra for us." Grace poured Kyra a glass of wine. "Julia tries to keep Char on her diet. We tried low carb for about three hours a few years ago, and Charlie became homicidal."

"Don't come between me and bread." Charlie grinned and took a savage bite out of a baguette.

"It was a dark day," Grace said, nodding with faux solemnity, earning a playful swipe from her wife.

"Does Julia always use your kitchen?" Kyra asked, breaking off a piece of the still-warm bread and popping it in her mouth. *Ohmagod. It's amazing.* She almost moaned.

"For bigger jobs. But she's been taking on more clients than usual." Charlie frowned.

"Yes. I asked her about it. I was worried that maybe she needed money, but she said she was getting offers she couldn't refuse." Grace shrugged. "She's such a superb cook. Everyone wants her. So, tell us about Boston." Grace clasped her hands and leaned forward.

Kyra gave them a summary of what she'd learned about Wetun Energy's wind farm.

"Yes, it's very controversial." Grace nodded. "Even Wes is opposed. He's concerned that with low-cost electricity available, new builders won't be interested in green construction, and he'd lose business." Kyra sat back.

Dr. Alonda had said something like that.

"Of course, there's no evidence anywhere to suggest that," Charlie said. "People still want efficient homes. Personally, I think it has more to do with the new housing development he invested in."

"What do you mean?" Kyra asked.

"Wes invested in a development that will be built along the northern shoreline, and the ocean views marred by unsightly wind turbines may reduce the prices of the new buildings. He also holds the contract for much of the construction. If the wind farm goes through, the project scope may change to reduce construction costs." Charlie's expression softened, and she rubbed Grace's shoulder. "Grace and I were also approached about the opportunity, but after reviewing the proposals, we weren't as optimistic as the developer. I tried to talk Wes out of it. He borrowed from Julia to buy in."

"And your father? Were you able to learn more about what he was doing?" Grace asked.

"Yes, we confirmed that Brendan Delaney, the man who was murdered at Mander Lane, was meeting with Ed regularly. He was the senator's aide, but before that, he worked at Wetun Energy. I think my father was writing some sort of story about the wind farm. I also met a couple who knew my parents." Was she mistaken, or did they share another look? "The owners of the Theatre Café in Beacon Hill?"

"Oh, yes. I've heard of it. It's an institution, but I've never been," Charlie said.

"Ed mentioned he and Isabel lived in Boston for a few years while he finished grad school," Grace added. "And I believe his first job was at a paper in Boston before they moved to New York."

"I didn't realize they'd lived in Boston." Kyra stared into her wineglass.

"Well, Boston isn't as glamorous as London, France, Chile, Marrakech, Hong Kong ... where else have you lived?" Grace asked.

"It was Peru." Kyra choked on a mirthless laugh. "I guess you're right. You know, I've never been to Florida."

"Honestly, you're not missing much, dear." Grace made a playful grimace and mimed a shudder of disgust. "Char has been trying to talk me into buying a place in Florida for the winter months. I keep telling her I'll die first."

"It gets so desolate here in the winter, especially between January and March. It's freezing cold, and everything's closed," Charlie complained. She turned to Grace. "Wouldn't it be nice to have the option of taking a walk outside?"

"Walk? In Florida? So you can be eaten by an alligator or

assaulted by an escaped python? No. I'll take the cold, thank you very much. It kills off all the nasty creatures." Grace crossed her arms over her chest. Charlie rolled her eyes.

Kyra's phone pinged. Detective Collins.

"Were you able to access Ed's files?"

"I haven't tried yet but will soon."

"Nearly done here. I can come by if you wanted help going through them."

Kyra worried her lip.

"Dear?"

"It's the detective. He's offered to help me go through my dad's notes." Kyra frowned.

"Hmm." Grace shared a look with Charlie. "If anyone can help you make sense of Ed's notes, it would be the detective." Grace stood up. She offered a hand to Charlie. "Char and I will get out of your hair, but we want to hear about everything tomorrow. If there's anything we can do to help, we're just next door." Grace turned to Charlie and whispered, "And he *is* handsome, don't you think?"

"Grace. No." Kyra felt the back of her neck warm. *Objectively speaking, yes. Very. But it's not like that.*

Despite her protests, Grace gave Kyra a smile that bordered on villainous.

"Oh, the handsomest," Charlie teased. "A total dreamboat." Charlie threw back her head and fanned herself with her hand.

Kyra let loose a long sigh. Objecting only made it worse.

"I left you more snacks in the fridge, dear."

"You know, in case you get hungry from all the *investigating*." Charlie waggled her eyebrows and her mouth stretched in a Cheshire-cat grin. Grace burst out laughing.

Their peals of laughter could be heard as they walked the path home. Kyra shook her head, smiling. She'd grown rather fond of her neighbors these past few days. She hadn't made many close friends in London. Mostly colleagues and old schoolmates. Grace and Charlie made it too easy to like them. Kyra's smile faded away and she finished her wine. They made it too easy to become attached. Kyra placed her glass in the dishwasher, then sent a text to Detective Collins, accepting his help.

Kyra flipped through the papers from Grace's folder. She found the handwritten note with the list of phone numbers and the partial—what she'd thought was an extension. She pulled out the similar page from Brendan's files. The numbers were different.

Tarek said people write down their passwords.

Cronkite jumped up onto the coffee table and blinked at her.

"Do you think this is it?" she asked the cat, tapping her finger on the page. *Could it really have been here the whole time?* "Here goes nothing." She pulled up the website for SkyCloud and entered the account number from the envelope she'd found in her father's desk, and when prompted for a password or a pin number, she entered his six-digit code and clicked on the log-in prompt. The computer spun as it connected with the servers and reloaded to a new page. "Yes!" she whooped.

"Find something?"

Kyra screamed and flung back in her seat. Cronkite screeched, and bolted off the table, his legs hitting the computer. She caught it right before it crashed to the ground. She turned toward the front door.

Tarek was standing in her foyer, hands up in surrender. "Whoa. It's just me." He closed the distance between them and reached for her but stopped just shy of touching her. His arms fell to his sides.

Kyra pressed her free hand to hear heart, willing it to slow. *Fuck me. I've taken years off my life today.* She dropped into her seat, sucked in a breath.

Tarek stooped down and peered into her face. "Hey, you okay?" The corners of his eyes crinkled.

"You scared the shit out of me."

"I knocked and called out, but you didn't answer. I'm sorry." His tone was sincere, but the corners of his mouth twitched. He was trying not to laugh. And doing a terrible job.

She pressed her lips together and glared.

"I brought dinner?" He pointed toward the front door. Two paper bags sat on the floor where he'd dropped them. His eyebrows slanted in a conciliatory smile.

"Fine," she mumbled, suddenly aware of how close he was to her. She shifted away. "What did you bring?"

"Thai." He stood up to retrieve the bags.

"Thai? You have Thai food here?"

"It's an island, not the moon. Of course, we have Thai food … well, Pan Asian, I guess." He stooped to pick up the bags. He paused in front of the console table. "What's this?" he asked, holding up the screwdriver.

"Oh, yeah. It was on my front porch. I think the locksmith must have left it."

Tarek's expression changed. He examined the tool, turning it in his hands.

"What?"

"Nothing." He placed it back on the table and returned to the living room. He pulled out the cartons and arranged them on the coffee table. "This place is called the Friendly Wok. It's not terrible, and it travels well."

"High praise." Kyra got plates, silverware, and a few beers from the kitchen.

She watched as Tarek made up their plates, overloading each with too much food. He handed her one and sat beside her. Cronk slunk back into the room and curled up in front of the fire.

"Tell me. What'd you find?"

"How do you know I found anything?"

"You were so focused. You didn't hear me knock or call your name. Twice. So, either you found something or you're deaf."

"I got in." Kyra set down her plate and pulled the computer closer. "You were right. He'd written down the pin code. I had it the whole time. Brendan probably has an account number somewhere, too."

A private dashboard loaded featuring a few menu tabs, including ones for SETTINGS, MY ACCOUNT, and MY FILES. Tarek scooted closer to see the screen.

She clicked on the MY FILES tab, and another screen loaded with at least a dozen different folders, each labeled and dated. Most were related to old projects and contained working documents, like outlines, drafts, research, and original source data and photographs. One contained what appeared to be notes and outlines related to the beginning of a novel, and another was labeled ESTATE PLANNING. She ignored that one entirely. At the end of the alphabetical list was a folder labeled WIND.

She clicked on it. The folder had at least a dozen subfolders. She opened the first one. It contained transcripts and recordings of interviews and phone conversations, as well as her father's own dictated notes. Another subfolder contained maps plotted with cell phone pings, not unlike the one Tarek had shared with her. He had also saved copies of financial records from Wetun Energy and its competitors.

"Look. He has audio files." She clicked on one of the phone recordings labeled VOICEMAIL 05AUG.

"The final deposit has been made," a woman's voice said, and the call ended.

Kyra thought the voice sounded familiar, even through the tinniness of a cell phone recording. She replayed the recording three more times, turning her ear toward the laptop.

"Is that Bea? Dr. Alonda's assistant?" Kyra asked.

"Play it again." Tarek leaned closer to the computer, turning his ear toward the speaker. He shook his head. "I can't tell. Does he have anything that says who the caller is or who they called?"

"Not that I can see, but there's a note that the phone numbers are burner phones." She began clicking open the files and scanning the contents, trying to piece together whatever her father had uncovered. She pointed to a document containing his notes from October. "He's arranging a meeting with a new anonymous source. That must be

Brendan." She opened the next document, this one from early November. "It says that the source admitted to arranging a meeting in May between Wetun and the senator before Wetun's presentation of the offshore wind farm proposal to the Energy and Natural Resources Committee." She kept reading and thought of something. "Didn't you say there was strange activity on Brendan's bank account?" She met Tarek's eyes, her brow furrowed.

"Mmmhmm," Tarek mumbled around a spring roll.

He studied the screen over her shoulder, and Kyra held her breath. *Will he tell me?* She steeled herself for what he'd say next, telling herself not to take it personally. *Although he could just subpoena Ed's files from me.* That thought chilled her. She'd be entirely shut out.

Tarek swallowed. "Yes, there were twelve or thirteen suspicious deposits over four months of varying amounts. All came from his brokerage firm but from different accounts. The money was always withdrawn before the next deposit was made. The total was just over seven million."

Kyra blinked in surprise. "Do you know where the money went?" she whispered, afraid if she pushed him too far, he'd clam up again.

"Yeah." He took a swig of beer. "Well, no, not really. The last withdrawal was to his personal checking account. He bought a car the next day. That was in October. Every other withdrawal was a transfer to an offshore account, two in the Cayman Islands and one in Malta. Those all occurred between May and the end of July."

"Do you know why the brokerage firm made the deposits? Who owns those accounts?"

"No." Tarek shook his head. "They've declined to provide any information without a warrant. We should have one soon."

Kyra frowned, disappointed.

"But the brokerage firm is part of the financial-services company used by Wetun Energy for its employee retirement and benefits packages." He shrugged and reached for a carton of dumplings. "That could just be a coincidence."

Kyra sat back and chewed on her lip.

Tarek eyed her over his half-eaten food. "What are you thinking?"

"I don't want to say." She glanced at him. "You'll make fun of me."

"Probably but say it anyway." Tarek grinned.

"Does it sound like a buy off? Like a bribe?" When Tarek didn't respond right away, she pointed to the screen. "Look at this. According to his notes, the senator's office presented the Wetun project as the best option for the contract on the eighth of August." Kyra sat back. "Is it odd that Senator Hawthorn made the recommendation just three days after the last deposit was made?"

"May I?" Tarek wiped his hands and reached for the laptop.

He studied the transcripts of the audio files and clicked open documents and spreadsheets, absorbing the information. "Yes. At minimum, it's damning." He pressed his lips together. "Remember Alonda said that the senator has been distancing himself from Wetun?"

"Yes, he was being investigated. I read the DOJ report, what wasn't redacted, anyway." She pulled the copies from her father's folder and scanned them. "It was dated September fifteenth. They found insufficient evidence to support a claim of misconduct," she said, using air quotes. "But there are no details on what the alleged misconduct was."

"And since the investigation, the senator has not renewed his support for the Cape's offshore wind project, right?" Tarek asked.

"I think that's what Alonda said." Kyra thought for a moment. "What were the dates of the deposits?"

Tarek pulled out his phone and showed her. *Four in June, Seven in July.*

"The last one was a withdrawal in October. Brendan bought his car the next day. A Prius. He financed it," Tarek said.

"When I was researching Wetun, I learned it isn't doing well. It's on the verge of collapse. The offshore wind farm contract would save the company. What if Alonda bribed the senator using Brendan as the go-between, but when the DOJ started their investigation, the senator pulled back?"

"And Brendan contacted your dad to expose the conspiracy *after* he'd bribed the senator and the senator successfully survived an investigation by the DOJ?" Tarek pursed his lips. "He'd be legally culpable. Even if your dad didn't reveal his source, the senator wouldn't protect Brendan and Alonda."

Kyra sighed out her frustration. "No, you're right. That doesn't make sense." She grabbed her bottle and sat back.

"We're missing something." Tarek popped the cap on another beer.

"Maybe we come at it from the other side?" Kyra said, standing up.

"What do you mean?"

"Who stands to gain from my father and Brendan's deaths?"

"*Assuming* that the two deaths are connected, and Wetun was bribing the senator, then Hawthorn, and probably Alonda." He spun his beer bottle on the table. "If the deaths aren't connected, and your dad died from a terrible accident, then Brendan's death could be unrelated to Wetun."

Kyra stopped pacing.

"The senator only has motive to kill Brendan and your dad if there was a bribe, he was taking it, and he thought there was danger of exposure. We don't actually know if Phil Hawthorn accepted funds from Brendan. And he was investigated, and that turned up nothing."

"You don't think this is about the wind farm?"

"Look at what we know. We know Brendan visited Chase. Chase's family didn't approve of their relationship. Perhaps they argued and it got out of hand. That would explain Brendan's death, explain why he was on the island, and why the family is protecting Chase. Ockham's razor. Sometimes the simplest answer is the right one." He shrugged.

Kyra frowned, unconvinced.

"A crime of passion is more likely than a premeditated conspiracy." He leaned forward, studying the computer screen.

Kyra sat back down and crossed her arms over her chest. She didn't think it was the simple answer this time. That simple answer didn't account for her father. She tapped her nails against her bottle. It just seemed too convenient that these two deaths connected to the Hawthorn family were unrelated.

Chase seemed genuinely distraught when he heard about Brendan. Could he have been acting? Maybe I am seeing a conspiracy where there isn't one.

Tarek looked at his watch. "I've got to check in at the inn, or I'll be sleeping in my car."

"Oh, okay." Kyra nodded. "What do we do next?"

"I'll submit Ed's notes into evidence and have forensics go through it." He pulled a USB drive from his pocket, and when Kyra nodded, he began copying over the files. "And then if we have a better understanding of the narrative from his perspective, I'll re-question the Hawthorns. I'll also send someone to re-question Alonda."

"I'll go through the documents again too. See if I find anything," she said, at the door.

Tarek's eyes fell on the screwdriver, and a muscle in his cheek twitched.

"Okay. Bolt the door behind me. Call if you learn anything."

She nodded.

"G'night, Kyra."

Chapter Eighteen

Sunday

KYRA RUBBED HER eyes and slipped a pod into the coffee machine. A headache throbbed at her temples. She'd stayed up late, reading through her dad's case notes, then rereading them. She *might* have finished a bottle of one of the nicer French reds she'd found in the wine cellar, and she felt stiff from dehydration and the death-like sleep brought on by too much alcohol.

Kyra pushed up the sleeves of the oversized Columbia Law sweatshirt she'd found in the dresser in her room. She added almond milk to her coffee and took her mug into Ed's office. She stood in front of the French doors and looked out onto the cove. Sunlight refracted off the water like dancing white stars.

She flipped the lock and stepped out onto the back patio. The stone was cold under her feet. She sipped her coffee, letting the sun warm the backs of her bare legs.

I'm certain Ed was assembling a story exposing the senator and Wetun. That must have been why he was on that boat. But what did he hope to learn? If it was murder, did someone lure him there? No matter what way she looked at it, she couldn't sort out how Brendan fit in. *There is one person who might know.*

Kyra took a sip of her now tepid coffee and hugged her arms to her body for warmth. Despite the chill, she liked it out here. The soft ocean sound, the salty tinge to the air, it was peaceful. *I'll miss this.*

She turned back toward the house. "I need to speak to Chase Hawthorn," she mumbled and slipped inside.

A fluffy white menace was waiting for her in the office, by the door. She stooped down to scratch his ears.

"Time for a different tactic, right, Cronkers?"

He followed her into the kitchen, chirped his agreement, then cast a longing look at his empty food bowl. "No, you had breakfast." She made herself another cup of coffee. "Come on," she called to him, walking back to the living room. "Do you know how I can speak to Chase Hawthorn?" The cat jumped onto the couch and blinked. "Me neither," she said, taking a seat next to him. He turned a circle before plopping down in a tightly coiled ball. "Let's check Hawthorn's campaign finances." *What could be more exciting?*

Sure enough, Hawthorn's reelection campaign had received donations from Dr. Maria Alonda and Bea Watson, but neither donation seemed outrageous, and both appeared consistent with other personal donations from corporate executives.

Next, she pulled up the finances for the Energy and Natural Resources Committee and, except for small deposits and debits credited to a lobbyist organization, there wasn't anything strange about the committee's finances.

She looked through the deposit and withdrawal history of Brendan's brokerage account that Tarek had forwarded.

She frowned. *He had almost nothing in there last spring, then all this activity, and then again nearly nothing. It doesn't add up. Where did all that money go? Seven million dollars doesn't just disappear. And if he moved it, why call my dad?*

If he moved it.

She texted Tarek.

"Can you ask Brendan's brokerage firm to provide log-in data? Days, times, and from what IP addresses last summer?"

"Our warrant was served this morning. We should have that data by the end of the day. What are you thinking?"

"It's probably nothing. I'll let you know."

Kyra turned back to her laptop. She was still on the home page for the Energy and National Resources Committee when she noticed the Featured Committee Updates section. She clicked it. As of March, the committee had heard proposals from all the energy contractors and were considering eight different proposals. Wetun Energy and BoSOil Petroleum were the only applicants from the Northeast, and Wetun was the only offshore wind farm proposal. Kyra pressed her lips together, thinking.

There was a noise at the front door and Kyra started. Irritated at the disruption, she walked to the foyer to see Wes Silva trying to open the door.

She yanked it open. "What are you doing here?"

Wes glowered at her. "I told you. I need to check the heating system." He held up his keys.

"I've had the locks changed," Kyra snapped, pointing to the new keypad. "Your services are no longer needed. Now, kindly get off my property." She tried to push the door closed, but Wes stopped it with his boot.

"And what are you going to do about it?" He shifted his body, towering over her.

"I'll call the police." She stood straighter, challenging him. She didn't glance behind her, where her phone sat on the coffee table.

"What, you mean the one you're fucking isn't enough for you?" Wes sneered.

Kyra reared back like she'd been slapped. She stared him down. "Get. Off. My. Property." She spoke through gritted teeth, her words slow and measured. "Now."

Kyra stepped back to close the door. She leaned into it, using her body weight.

Wes grunted and moved his boot.

The door slammed shut. Kyra stumbled against it. She turned the deadbolt. Wes Silva stood on the other side, glaring at her through the glass. With all the self-control she could muster, she turned her back on him and walked to the living room.

Furious, she grabbed her phone and called Detective Collins. Before he could say anything, she hissed at him. "What the fuck have you been telling people?"

"What?"

She could hear the confusion in his voice, but she ignored it, scanning her yard. She couldn't see Wes. Moving quickly, her phone still tucked against her ear, she double-checked the locks on the glass doors.

"Wes Silva tried to get in the house again. What have you been telling people?"

"What? Are you okay? Is he there now?" Kyra froze. *The study.*

She ran for the office. Her hand struck the doorframe, just as Wes Silva pushed the door open and stepped inside the house.

Kyra heard a whooshing in her ears. Forcing herself to at least sound calm, she enunciated each word, "I have called the police, Mr. Silva. I won't tell you again. Leave."

Wes shrugged, a sneer plastered across his mouth. He slung an empty backpack over his shoulder and stepped toward her, his boots thudding on the floorboards, slow, deliberate.   .

"Kyra!" Tarek's voice was loud, commanding through the phone she still held to her ear. "Get out of the house. Go to Grace and Charlie's. I'm coming."

Kyra backed out of the office, keeping her eyes on Silva. Once her toes touched the living room rug, she turned and bolted for the front door. She had to stop to turn the lock; her hands shook. She threw a glance behind her shoulder. She didn't see him. *Where is he?*

Kyra yanked the door open and ran across the front yard toward the path connecting her property with the Chamberses'. She ran down the path and across their lawn, hardly feeling the rough ground against the soles of her feet. She bound up the stairs onto their porch and banged on their door. Nothing. She pressed the doorbell. It rang through the house. Kyra scanned the drive. Their car was missing. She craned her neck for a view of the path, but the house was in the way. *Is the following me?* Her breathing came fast. *Where do I go?*

"Kyra." Tarek's steady voice came over the phone. He had stayed on the line.

"I'm here," she whispered, gripping the phone. "Charlie and Grace aren't home."

"It's okay. The Edgartown police are on their way. They'll be there soon." She concentrated on his voice. "Kyra, I want you to take their driveway and get to the main road. Go."

Kyra held in a sob and turned toward the driveway.

"I'll stay on the line."

Kyra ran down the gravel driveway and turned onto the street. She followed it around the bend, hoping she was running toward the main road. Her lungs burned. After what felt like miles, she found Herring Creek Road, wide and sandy.

"I'm here. On the road," she told Tarek, her breathing raspy.

"I'm almost there. Just stay where you are."

"I don't think he followed me."

Kyra looked down the road. She stood on the bike path and willed the police cruisers or Tarek's Ford Explorer to appear. Kyra heard the low whine of the truck before she saw it. The engine revved. The grill glinted in the sun as it barreled toward her. She dove off the bike path, into the brush, just as Wes Silva sped by. She landed on her shoulder with a yelp at the impact.

Kyra lay on the ground, stunned. She wasn't sure if Wes had seen her and tried to hit her, or if her brain in survival mode had overreacted. She shifted her arms and legs. Nothing was broken, and she slowly got to her feet. Her shoulder throbbed. Her hands and knees were bleeding. She hobbled back to the street, just as Tarek drove up. The SUV screeched to a stop, sliding on the sandy road.

He jumped out and ran to her. "Kyra!" His arms went around her.

She slumped against him, letting him support her weight.

He pushed her hair away from her face, scanned her body, searching for injuries. "Are you okay?"

"Yes." She nodded. "I'm not hurt." She gave him a weak smile, trying to reassure him.

His hands ran down her arms and wrapped around her waist. "I got you."

He helped her into his car and called the station. Where were the dispatched officers? What about Silva?

He glanced over at Kyra, scanning her face. A muscle in his jaw moved. He put the car into drive and gripped the steering wheel, his knuckles white. Kyra closed her eyes and rested her forehead against the cool window.

When they arrived at the house, two police cruisers were already in the drive. Three men in uniform were standing outside the open front door, talking. At the sound of Tarek's car, they turned, and one with a shiny bald head strode toward them, hand raised. Tarek stopped and got out of the SUV.

"Detective," the first officer greeted him. "The situation seems to have rectified itself." He waved toward the house. "No one's home."

"No shit." Tarek walked around to the passenger side. He opened Kyra's door. "Come on, lean on me." He turned to the officer. "Does she look like she's fucking home?" Tarek reached for Kyra and, supporting her, led her to the front door. He set her down on the step and motioned for her to stay put. She leaned against the railing. "Where's Silva?"

"He's not here. I did a walkthrough of the house. It doesn't look like anything's been disturbed," a younger officer said. "Wes is a good guy, ma'am. I'm sure this was all a misunderstanding."

"He broke into my house. He threatened me," she said, unable to keep her voice from shaking. "He's been trying to get inside since I've arrived."

The three officers exchanged a look.

"There's no evidence of a break-in," the third officer said and shrugged.

"The way we've heard it is you've been real nasty. Won't let Wes do his job," the bald one said. "He's got his tools and gear here, and you won't let him have his property back. From where I stand, that's theft." He hooked his thumbs in his belt.

"I beg your pardon?" Kyra gaped at them.

"We're just telling you what we've heard," the third officer piped in. "Wes don't want no trouble. He's just an honest guy trying to get by."

"You summer people." The bald officer clenched his hands into fists.

"What on earth are you talking about?" Kyra pulled herself up using the railing.

Tarek stepped in front of her. "That's enough." He nodded toward the cruisers. "You can leave. I'll take care of her."

"I'm sure you will." He sneered and spun on his heel.

Kyra's cheeks heated with shame. She shook her head

unable to understand what was going on, what these men were implying, or why.

The third officer snickered as he strode to his cruiser and got in. The second officer, the young one, followed the first, avoiding eye contact with either Tarek or Kyra.

Once the cars left her driveway, she snapped at Tarek, "What the fuck was that?"

"*That*," Tarek said, turning around, "was a giant asshole." He ran his hands through his hair and reached for her, helping her into the house. "They're all friends with Silva. I knew they wouldn't arrest him, but I didn't think they'd be so hostile. I'm sorry."

He guided her to one of the kitchen stools.

"What's going on, Tarek?"

He moved to the sink and dampened a paper towel. With a sigh, Tarek kneeled down and cleaned the scrapes on her knees and feet. Despite his gentle touch, she still flinched. "Sorry," he mumbled, and reached for her hand. He picked away the gravel imbedded in her palm. "There's a strange social balance between the summer crowd and the islanders. The island relies on the money brought in by the tourists, but it's hard to depend on people who don't see you. It fosters a lot of resentment."

"But I'm not a summer person. I've never been here in the summer. And even if I was, that doesn't give anyone the right to break into my house."

"I'm not sure he was talking about you. But you're right." He started on her other hand. "You're lucky. You could have been hurt."

Summer people. Off islanders. Mainlanders. If their intent was to make her feel unwelcome, alone, and vulnerable, they'd succeeded.

"It's fine," she lied, pulling her hand back. "It doesn't hurt. Thank you."

"Don't mention it," Tarek muttered, standing up, but his brow was still furrowed, his jaw set.

His phone rang. He glanced at it and frowned. "I've got to take this."

"Go ahead. I'm fine. I'm going to take a shower." She pushed herself off the stool and headed toward the stairs, trying to hide the stinging in her feet.

The hot water bit at her scrapes, and the river-stone flooring irritated her raw feet, but Kyra found some small comfort in the mild pain and more in the hot water sloughing off the trauma of the morning. She was thankful Tarek had stayed. He was getting in touch with a security company now. She'd heard him calling as she'd changed out of her clothes. Clearly, he was more concerned than he'd let on. She didn't believe Silva was trying to collect tools he'd stored at the house. A normal person would have said that days ago. *What's here that he wants so badly?* Her mind went to the screwdriver she'd found yesterday, and a shiver ran down her spine despite the hot water. *Silva's?* Had he tried to break in while she was in Boston?

Kyra rinsed the suds from her body and turned off the water. She dressed in comfortable slacks and a soft sweater— clothes that didn't catch on her torn skin.

Tarek was sitting at the island on his phone when she entered the kitchen. He looked up and ran his eyes over her, his gaze assessing. He looked like he was going to ask how she felt, but instead he glanced at the basement door. "I want to check the house, see if Silva really did leave his things here or if he took anything. You should call your lawyer and insurance provider, let them know what happened. And you're getting a security system. I mean it," he said, his voice stern.

She nodded. *Yeah, I know.* Kyra sighed at having more things added to her never-ending to-do list.

They went downstairs, Tarek's hand on her elbow offering support if she needed it. Other than the wine cellar, Kyra hadn't really come down here. Not since Grace had given her the tour. The basement was broken up into three rooms: the wine cellar, a storage room, and the utility room containing the HVAC, water heaters, and electrical panel. The storage room contained cleaning supplies, beach stuff, various boxes with labels of things typically stored in basements, like CHRISTMAS and CABLES. Tarek gave the room a cursory once over, while Kyra stood in the doorway.

"Doesn't look like anything's been disturbed. I doubt there's anything valuable down here. Nothing worth assaulting someone over." Her voice sounded forced and strained. She pointed. "The HVAC is in there." Kyra tried the knob, and the door swung opened. *It* was *locked.* Kyra wrapped her arms around herself. How many times had Wes Silva been in the house and she hadn't known about it? When she'd been sleeping? The thought made her sick.

Tarek stepped in first and turned on the light.

The HVAC system consisted of two large units from which duct work spidered out in all directions. Behind the units was a large wall panel full of dozens of valves, switches, and pipes.

"Does this mean anything to you?" she asked, taking in the organized chaos.

"Nothing at all." Tarek snapped photos of the system with his phone. "I'll send this to the office. See if someone can find an expert."

"There isn't anything here he could have left, right?" she asked, looking about the room. "I don't see any tools or…" She didn't know what she was looking for. "Should we check the wine cellar?"

Tarek ran a hand through his hair. "Yeah."

They retraced their steps to the temperature- and moisture-controlled room.

"I can't tell if he's taken anything," she said, surveying the racks of wine and stacks of cases pushed to the side. "There's enough here to get the island pissed a hundred times over."

"I almost hope he was sneaking in to steal bottles of rosé." Tarek mocked, and Kyra let out a weak laugh. He grinned at her, but it didn't reach his eyes, still full of concern. "We should check the rest of the house."

They inspected the first floor, leaving the office for last. Kyra walked around the room, eyeing the piles and clutter.

"It was a mess before," she said, shrugging. "It's still a mess. Wait, my laptop."

She returned to the living room and found her computer where she'd left it on the couch, partially covered by the throw blanket. "Nope, he didn't take it." She made sure it turned on. "I've no idea what he was looking for."

Her eyes went wide. Her heart jumped into her throat.

"Where's the cat?"

"You think he stole the cat?"

"No, but what if he got out?" she asked, her voice shrill, as she succumbed to panic. But she didn't care how she sounded. Images of Cronk being hit by a car, his broken body flashed before her eyes. "Cronk!"

"I'm sure he's here." Tarek's long fingers wrapped around her wrists. "Calm down. We'll find him."

Kyra, caught in his dark-green eyes, nodded even as she swallowed back tears.

He let her go and called for Cronkite. "Where's his food?"

Kyra showed him. Sure enough, once a few kibbles hit the bowl, they heard a *thump* from above. Kyra let out a breath, relieved, embarrassed. *How can I be so attached to a cat I've had for less than a week? I don't even want him.*

She blamed it on the surge of adrenaline that had left her jittery, but when Cronk finally ambled in, she scooped him up, hugging the wriggling demon to her chest. She cradled him as she sat on the couch, crooning softly, promising she'd always keep him safe.

Tarek's phone rang. He pulled it from his pocket. "Collins. Yes. Really?" He sat next to Kyra on the couch. "You're sending that over? For how long? Yeah, and it was widely communicated? No … yes … yes." Kyra listened to the one-sided conversation with increasing impatience. "Thank you. Evans? Good work." Tarek hung up and turned around.

"Well?"

"Well, what?" he asked. The side of his mouth twitched.

Kyra pouted, annoyed.

"Fine." He grinned as if pleased to have coaxed her out of her meltdown. "It turns out that the phone your father was calling was, in fact, Brendan's, which we knew, but now it's officially confirmed. It was paid for by the senator's office, and it had been since the number was issued about eighteen months ago and assigned to congressional aide, Brendan Delaney when he started on the senator's staff. They pulled the call logs. There are four calls in October to his brokerage account, right after he bought the car. He'd never called them before, at least not from his cell phone. About a week after he bought the car, he made his first call to Ed Gibson but to his regular phone, the one that's missing. After that, he made dozens of calls to your dad's burner phone."

Kyra pressed her lips together.

"Another thing. We got some more information about the storm. The one that would have allegedly caused your dad to seek refuge on *The Island Pearl*. It wasn't sudden, but slow-moving. It would have worsened over the course of the night. There was a weather warning, and many of the businesses on the island closed early. The storm hit around midnight."

"What does that mean?"

"I'm not sure yet." Tarek frowned. "But it sure as shit means your dad wasn't on that boat because of any storm."

Chapter Nineteen

"I'M EXPECTED AT Mander Lane," Tarek said when he came back to the living room.

He'd taken another call in the office. He'd been on and off the phone in there all morning.

Kyra stopped pacing. She'd been unable to relax since this incident with Silva and the police. Anxious and unsettled, she kept double-checking the locks on the doors and peering out the windows. She'd felt Tarek watching her, either concerned or annoyed. She couldn't tell. He'd made her breakfast, but she couldn't eat. He'd told her to lie down, but she couldn't sleep.

"Now?" she asked.

"Mmmhmm," he hummed, his lips pressed in a line. "Are Grace and Charlie back? Can you go there?"

Kyra shook her head. She'd called them. They were on the mainland for the day, seeing a specialist for Charlie's diabetes.

"They'll be back this afternoon."

"I can drop you off somewhere. Or have an officer stationed here."

"The local police don't give me much sense of safety." Kyra swallowed. "Maybe I can come with you?"

I could speak with Chase Hawthorn. The thought popped into her head. *Tarek hasn't been shy about seizing an opportunity when he sees one.* But she still felt a tiny bit guilty for using him. Tarek narrowed his eyes at her.

"I can see the animals? Pick up some things at the farmer's market." She raised her shoulders helplessly, playing on his sympathies. Kyra was sure he was going to say no.

Tarek let out a long breath and nodded. "Yeah. Let me call ahead. Get your things."

THEY DROVE PAST the turnoff for the airport. Kyra smiled to herself. She was learning her way around the island.

Tarek cleared his throat. "The call I took in your office?" he said, glancing at her. She nodded for him to continue. "We've confirmed via his credit card statements that Brendan bought ferry tickets at Woods Hole on Sunday morning, right before the nine thirty ferry departed. It's likely he took that boat. We're questioning the crew. They also found his rental car parked at the Palmer lot. It was due to be returned on Tuesday."

Kyra nodded. *This isn't news. Obviously, Brendan was on the island. He died here, and presumably he had intended on returning home at some point.*

"The team also checked the Hawthorn family. Chase took one of the Cape Air flights to Logan on Sunday at two p.m. So, it is possible they missed each other, but there was also a window where they overlapped and were both on the island. Margot Hawthorn has been on the island since early

April. She's come and gone a few times, but mostly she's been here. The senator arrived by private plane on Saturday morning from DC."

"So, they were all here when Brendan died, except Chase. But we knew that already."

"No, we don't know exactly when Brendan died, just when the fire was set."

Kyra pressed her lips together. "You think he and Brendan fought, Chase shot him, and then left the island?"

"Not necessarily. But Chase's alibi isn't as airtight as we thought. He could have intentionally caused a scene in Boston to have his photo taken, creating an alibi."

Kyra contemplated Tarek's theory. "And the fire?"

"Someone else could have set it."

"But why?"

Tarek shrugged. "To protect him? Destroy evidence?"

Kyra mulled on that. *It is possible.* "What about Adele and Dr. Brian? When did they arrive?"

"The team is looking into that now. In the meantime, knowing what we do about Wetun, Brendan's general involvement with every aspect of this case, the wind farm, and now the trajectory of the storm in January, I want to get more specific information about the family's activities last Sunday and on January third. I'm speaking to the senator, his wife, Chase, and some of the staff."

"But not Adele and Brian?"

"The team hasn't been able to get in touch with them yet."

"And Brody?"

Tarek cocked his head. "I've asked for his travel records,

but that may be more difficult to get. The military protects its own." He grimaced. "With any luck, the Lees flew into the private airfield, but we'll also check the commercial flights and ferry manifests. If they walked onto a ferry, though, it'll be difficult to confirm without a warrant to pull financial records. I'm betting that Brian Lee wouldn't stoop so low as to walk onto a ferry with the commoners."

Based on her experiences with the Lees, Kyra agreed.

"But even if they were on the island, other than the husband's tenuous connection for buying stock, I don't see how they could be connected."

"If Dr. Brian learned about my father's story and that Brendan was a source, that information getting out could cause the stock to tank, and he'd lose a lot of money, right?" Kyra shook her head. "No, that's shit. He could just sell the stock."

"I'll learn a lot from what the Hawthorns don't say over the next few hours."

"You think they'll talk to you?"

"This is just an informal meeting, information gathering. They can decline to speak to me if they want, but if the Hawthorns aren't forthcoming, I've enough to make a formal inquiry. And if it gets to that, those interviews won't be in the comfort of their living room." Tarek turned onto the long gravel drive and drove up to the house.

The Porsche was still in the driveway. A blanket of yellow pollen dulled the red paint to a burnt orange.

"I'll go down to the market," Kyra said, unbuckling her seatbelt.

"Are you sure?" He ran his eyes over her face. "Grover

knows you're with me. I'm sure…" His voice trailed off.

"I'll be fine."

"Okay. If you need anything, call me. Immediately."

Kyra nodded and walked down the drive.

There were a few cars in the parking lot. Kyra peeked inside the farm stand, cramped with shoppers, and decided to wait at the restaurant.

It wasn't busy, just a few tables were occupied. Kyra was waiting for the hostess when she spotted Sara sitting at a table in the corner, surrounded by papers and her laptop, her forehead scrunched in concentration. When she looked up, Kyra raised her hand in a wave. Sara's eyes widened with recognition, and she waved back. Sara slid aside a stack of papers and offered Kyra the empty seat.

"Hi," Kyra said, sitting down.

"Hi. Are you the chauffeur again?"

"No, more like a babysitting charge." Kyra shrugged. "I'm just waiting for the detective. He's interviewing the family. Do you have to speak with him?"

"Yes, I think they have me as one of the first ones." Sara checked her watch. "I hope it's quick. My mare is about ready to drop her foal, and I'd rather be with her."

"Will she be okay?"

"Oh, yes." Sara nodded, her excitement palpable. "She's healthy, and the vet and Chase are with her now."

Kyra wondered why the senator's playboy son would help deliver a baby horse, or why Sara seemed pleased that he was there. *Maybe I can sneak down and talk to him.*

"Would you like something else, Sara?" a waitress asked and picked up a plate containing the remnants of Sara's lunch.

"Can I have some tea? Would you like some?" she asked Kyra.

"Yes, please. Thank you."

"Two teas, Jill." The waitress nodded and disappeared.

"What are you working on?" Kyra asked, glancing at the pile of papers Sara had moved aside.

"Scheduling." Sara took the pages, fanning them out and frowned. "I'm already short-staffed this summer, and Margot wants to host events. You know, like weddings." Sara closed her eyes, her expression pained. "She wants to demo the old barn and set up a pergola or tents. Thank goodness we have to wait until the police are done with their investigation. I hope it takes months." Sara went quiet, and her cheeks flushed. "I'm sorry. I didn't mean it like that. Of course, I want them to find out what happened to Brendan as soon as possible." She bit at her fingernail and glanced up at Kyra a frown tugging at her mouth.

Kyra remembered the tasks board in Sara's living room. She didn't begrudge her for not wanting to take on more work.

"Did you know him? Brendan?" Kyra asked.

"No, not really. I met him a few times last fall when he came to the island with Chase. He was very clean."

Clean?

Jill returned with their tea. She set it down along with a plate of French Macarons.

Sara's whole face transformed with a wide grin. "Thank you."

Jill gave them an indulgent nod.

"They're my favorite," Sarah said to Kyra. "Especially the pistachio." She popped the green cookie in her mouth. "I really don't know why Brendan would have been at the old barn."

"What do you mean?"

"When he's here, Chase splits his time between working here on the farm and at the marina. Brendan didn't seem interested in Mander Lane. The guys from DC rarely are. He preferred to stay at the house or go into town." Sara huffed. "The few times Chase convinced him to come to the fields, he'd complained." She grabbed another cookie.

Ah, clean. Sara's two-way radio handset bleeped.

"Sara," she said, pressing the button on the side.

"It's Beth. They're ready for you in the senator's office."

"I'll be right there." Sara closed her computer and collected her things. "What will you do?"

"Might I go see the animals?"

"Oh, sure. Just say you spoke with me, and no one will trouble you. I'll see you later."

After paying for her tea, Kyra followed the path she and Tarek had taken a few days earlier. Kyra was watching the antics of two tiny lambs playing along the fence when she ran smack into a broad chest. She stumbled back. Hands reached out, grasping her shoulders, steadying her.

"Oh shit. I'm so sorry," she stammered and looked up. And up.

Chase Hawthorn was very tall.

His hands fell to his sides. "Are you okay?" he asked, squinting at her.

"Oh, yes. Sorry. I wasn't paying attention." Kyra waved

to the lambs.

He rubbed his forehead and stared at her, like he was trying to place her. She watched as recognition seeped into his handsome features, smoothing them out.

"You're Grover's friend. The one with the police." He stepped back, increasing the distance between them, and wiped his hands on a dirty rag he'd pulled from somewhere. "What are you doing here?" he asked, his eyes wide with curiosity.

Now that she could see them properly, she noticed they were a startling blue-green, the color of an alpine lake.

"Sort of. Mr. Grover was a friend of my father. I'm not really with the police. I'm just hanging out while the detective speaks with your family. I thought I'd visit the animals while I wait. Sara said one of the horses was in labor?"

A muscle in Chase's cheek twitched. He pulled his baseball cap off and dragged his dirty hands through his shaggy blond hair. Chase's eyes were red rimmed and bloodshot, his features gaunt and hollowed out. He looked like a man who was barely holding on.

He slapped the hat back on, brim forward, and walked over to the fence. Propping one leg up on the lower rail, he rested his elbows on the top one and leaned against it. She came up beside him, mirroring his stance, and looked out at the pasture.

Chase waved toward the corrugated metal and plastic barn. "She was. Marigold had her baby about twenty minutes ago. A boy."

"Really?" She smiled. "Are they okay?"

"The vet said they're both perfect." Kyra noted the hint

of pride in his voice. "Sara will be sad she missed it."

"What will you do with the foal?" she asked.

"He'll live on the farm. We'll train him up as a pleasure horse, I think."

"For you?" she asked.

With his stylishly unruly hair and movie-star good looks, Kyra had a hard time seeing him as a farmhand.

"I'm not much of a rider, but maybe." Chase shrugged. "It's Sara's call, but she might let me help."

"I didn't know you worked here. On the farm, I mean."

"I don't officially, but I try to help out when I can. My dad doesn't think it's a bad idea, but my mom…" He broke off like he'd said too much. He shook his head, then looked in the direction of the charred skeletal remains of the old barn.

Kyra followed his gaze. "You know, I really am sorry about Brendan."

He stiffened and turned to face her, suspicion darkening his eyes. "You knew him?"

"No, but my dad did. I think they were friends, or at least colleagues."

"What do you mean?" There was a new hardness to his voice. "Who's your dad?"

"Edward Gibson. He was working with Brendan, but he died last January." She chose her next words carefully. "Last January, he fell off your family's boat and drowned." She kept her voice neutral, trying not to be unnecessarily cruel, but observed his reaction as he absorbed her words.

Chase went rigid. With something that sounded like a hiccup or a sob, he dropped his head, his chin almost to his chest. "Oh … I didn't know," he said, his voice low, strained, and raspy. He took a few deep breaths, then he straightened to his full height. He repeated his words louder, his tone laced with anguish. "I didn't know Ed was your dad." The way he said her father's name, Kyra realized Chase had known him. He looked at her. His eyes darted back and forth between hers, like he was trying to read her or make her understand.

"I don't remember being on *The Pearl* that night." Chase shifted his weight and looked away. He coughed.

Kyra shifted again, dropping her foot to the ground.

Does he think he could have had something to do with Ed's death?

"How did Ed know Brendan?"

"They were working on a story together. I'm pretty sure it had something to do with the Cape Cod wind farm." Kyra frowned.

She probably shouldn't be sharing this with him. He was one of the detective's most likely suspects for both murders. She glanced toward the barn. They were alone. She was suddenly aware of how close she was to Chase. *If he had killed Ed and Brendan, he'd kill me too.* She stepped away, just out of reach of his long arms. He didn't seem to notice.

"The detective and I found my father's case notes." She watched him closely, but he didn't react. "Do you know anything about it? The offshore wind farm?"

"Brendan." He swallowed, then tried again. "Brendan used to work for a wind company. He was big into clean energy. He mentioned the Cape program a few times, but something changed last fall."

"What changed?"

"I'm not sure. He just didn't support the offshore wind project anymore." Chase shrugged. "And he didn't want to talk about it."

"You and Brendan were close, then?"

Chase stilled, and a muscle in his cheek ticked. Kyra got the impression he was deciding whether he could trust her.

"He worked for my dad." Chase kept his eyes glued to something in the distance. "All I remember about that night, the night Ed died, is drinking at the Nest. Margot had been on my case for days. I don't even remember about what. I took a cab into Edgartown just to get away from the house. I do that often. I drank there and woke up at home the next day. And Brendan," he continued, his voice scratchy and raw, "I didn't know he was coming to the island. I'd spoken to him the night before, told him Margot was giving me shit about the campaign and some fundraiser. He never mentioned he was coming. I went to the city to get away." He shook his head. "We had plans to meet in a few weeks. If I'd known he was here..." He sucked in a ragged breath.

Chase's phone rang, and he pulled it from his back pocket. "Yeah?" He listened and hung up. "I'm being summoned by your boss." He looked at her, his eyes wary. "Are you coming?"

Kyra thought of saying no, but she heard the soft plea in his voice like he was asking for anyone to have his back. *He's so broken.*

She nodded before she fully thought it through. "I can walk with you."

Gratitude shone in his eyes.

Kyra walked beside him, taking care to stay in the center of the path. Chase stuffed his hands in his pockets and rounded his shoulders, becoming smaller, like he was collapsing in on himself. If he noticed Kyra kept a wide distance between them, he didn't say anything.

"Chase, did Brendan ever mention my dad?"

"No, I don't think so."

"What about a woman named Dr. Alonda?" Chase stopped walking. He pulled his hands from his pockets and adjusted his hat.

"Maria Alonda?"

"You know her?"

"No, but Brendan mentioned her once or twice. I think she was an old boss, or mentor. They had a falling out last fall. I'm not sure about what." Chase pressed his lips together. "It happened just before we came here for the weekend actually," he mumbled, almost to himself. "I only remember because he was in a terrible mood the whole weekend. He spent most of the weekend working. He took my car one day."

"Do you know what he was doing?"

"He said sightseeing." Chase shrugged, his expression pained. "He ended up flying home early."

They arrived at the back door. Chase stared at the doorknob as if mentally preparing for whatever came next.

Kyra placed her hand on his arm. "I promise I'll do everything I can to find out what happened to Brendan. And my dad."

Chase lowered his gaze to hers, his expression wary, but something flickered behind his eyes. Kyra thought it might be hope.

Beth pulled the door open and ushered him in. "Chase, they've been asking for you." Kyra stood frozen on the threshold. "Please come in. It's freezing out there." Beth shut the door behind them. "Margot wants you cleaned up before you speak with the authorities. She's already upstairs." Beth wrung her hands together.

"Bye, Ms. Gibson," Chase said, and disappeared down the hall.

"Hi," Beth said with a shaky smile. "How's Marigold? Sara said you were looking in on her?"

"Chase said she and the foal are doing well. She had a little colt. I didn't see them, though. How are the interviews going?"

"Well enough, I suppose. Mr. Grover was taking questions while they waited for Chase. Mrs. Hawthorn is last."

What I wouldn't give to see Margot put in her place.

"They've asked for coffee while they wait." Beth pulled two trays from a cabinet.

"I can help," Kyra offered, thinking she might be able to sneak in, hear what Chase and Margot had to say.

"Oh, thank you." Beth gave her a grateful smile. Kyra imagined Beth didn't get offers for help often. "The cups and saucers are in there." She pointed to a cabinet. "I hope the detective is easy on Chase," Beth said as she added coffee grounds to a pour over coffeemaker. "It hasn't been easy for him, you know."

"It hasn't?"

"Not just with Brendan or even the rumors around Mr. Gibson's death earlier this year." Beth cast a sympathetic

251

look at Kyra. "He's trusted the wrong people in the past. It's gotten him into trouble. Drinking and drugs, the media. He's constantly being watched, judged." Beth set down the carafe and looked at her hands. "I've known him his whole life. He's not the person the media makes him out to be. He wouldn't hurt a fly, much less a person. Not on purpose."

Kyra stopped pouring milk into the porcelain creamer and set the carton down. "Not on purpose? What do you mean?"

"I didn't mean that." Beth's words came out in a rush. "I'm just. He..." Beth looked at Kyra. "Chase wouldn't hurt anyone."

"I'd better get this to them." Beth lifted her heavily laden tray.

"I can take this one."

Beth led Kyra down the hallway to a room with a closed door. She called out to Grover, and a moment later, he opened it, ushering them in.

The room was large, with mahogany wainscotting and hunter-green wallpaper. Oil paintings depicting hunting scenes in ornate frames hung on the walls. A large desk stained to match the wainscotting was set to the back of the room, and a tufted leather couch was pushed up against a wall. She felt like she'd left the real world and wandered into the Monopoly man's office, a parody of elegance and power.

On the far side of the room was a conference table where Detective Collins and Grover were conducting the interviews. Beth beelined for a credenza sitting against the wall behind them. Tarek raised an eyebrow at Kyra and his lip quirked like he was trying not to smile. She inclined her head to the tray. *I'm helping. And eavesdropping.* Kyra followed Beth to the back of the room to set up the coffee service.

The door banged open, slamming against the wall. Kyra jumped, nearly overturning the carafe, but righted it just in time. Beth froze. Margot Hawthorn strode into the room.

Society pages described the senator's wife as "stunning," but today, her angular features were pinched and severe. She swept into the room on a cloud of Chanel No. 5 and stalked to the table where Tarek was reading over some documents. Margot smoothed her designer skirt and took a seat.

"Your son was next," Tarek said, turning his attention back to his notebook.

"Our attorney." She leveled a glare at Mr. Grover. "Excuse me, our personal attorney, has advised my son to decline to speak with you until he is present. As he is in Washington, you won't be speaking with my son today."

Margot's gaze fell on Kyra and her nose wrinkled in distaste. She glanced away, dismissing her. "Beth, coffee."

"Of course, Margot." Beth poured two cups of coffee and glanced at the detective.

"Black, one sugar," Kyra whispered, and Beth nodded her thanks.

"Proceed, Detective," Margot said, the words dripping from her lips like acid.

Kyra pressed back against the wainscotting, surprised she hadn't been asked to leave. Beth placed Margot's coffee in front of her and took a position next to Kyra against the wall.

"Thank you for your time today, Mrs. Hawthorn."

"I didn't have much choice, Detective."

"What was your relationship with Brendan Delaney?" He pushed a photo of Brendan across the table.

"I had no relationship with Mr. Delaney." Margot didn't even glance at the photograph.

"Have you ever met him?"

"I couldn't say. My husband has many associates, and we often entertain, but I don't recall this particular man."

"Then you didn't know he was coming to Mander Lane Farm last Sunday?"

"Certainly not."

"Where was your son the night Brendan died?"

Margot clenched her teeth. "In Boston. You know that. There are photographs in the newspapers."

"But your son seems to think Brendan came to the island to see him. Did Brendan come to the house to see if Chase was home?"

"I don't know why you would think that. I do not know what business my son would have had with my husband's employee. As I've already told you, I have no recollection of seeing that man at this house or anywhere else, on any occasion."

Tarek nodded. "How about January third?"

"What about it?"

"Where were you on January third?"

"Where was I?" she repeated and frowned. "Grover, where was I?" Grover consulted a diary in front of him.

"You were here, ma'am. You had tea with your winter book club and afternoon meetings with Beth and Sara regarding the spring scheduling for Mander Lane."

"Well, there you go." Margot waved her hand at the

book.

"What about your son? On January third?" Tarek asked.

"Chase was in town."

"Where?" Tarek prompted.

"My son was in Edgartown, at a restaurant. I'm afraid I don't know the name," Margot said with a sigh. "It's not an establishment I would frequent."

Kyra wondered what kind of establishments this witch would deign to frequent. *Executions? Human sacrifices? Fur farms?*

"You can't remember where *you* were on January third, but you remember where your son was?" Tarek countered.

"Yes. He's my son. He's more important to me than a book club. I do remember we read and discussed a biography of Eleanor Roosevelt."

"Do you know what time he returned home that night?"

"I believe it was nine or ten. Why? What does this have to do with my husband's employee?"

"You saw him come home then?"

"No."

"Then how do you know what time he came home?"

"Detective, there was a storm." Margot pressed her fingers to her forehead, between her eyes, and breathed out a heavy sigh. "Everything was closed, and residents were instructed to stay indoors. My son is a responsible young man. He would not have been out if the authorities had ordered us home."

Her story sounded rehearsed. *They've probably been telling the same one for months.*

"So, you really cannot confirm his whereabouts that

evening."

"I told you, Detective, my son was home by ten. Are you calling me a liar?"

"Were you acquainted with Edward Gibson?"

"The reporter? Barely."

"Care to elaborate, Mrs. Hawthorn?"

"I believe he played golf with my husband and Grover. He's been a guest at our house here and in DC, but I've never had more than a brief conversation with him. He has a house somewhere in Edgartown, I think."

Kyra bit back a retort. *What a bag o' shite. Margot knows exactly where my house is.* She'd made that clear at the fundraiser.

"He was writing a story about Wetun Energy. Do you know the company?" Tarek asked.

"I cannot say that I do."

"What about Maria Alonda?"

Margot's cheek twitched at the executive's name. "No. Does she work for the company?" *Did she pause?*

"She's the CEO."

"Perhaps." Margot raised a shoulder in an elegant shrug. "My husband is on the energy committee. It's possible we've crossed paths. Did this woman kill Mr. Gideon or Mr. Delaney?"

Kyra's body went rigid.

"Gibson," Tarek corrected. "She attended your husband's campaign party."

"There were many attendees that I'm not personally acquainted with. Case in point, *you* were there."

Touché, you icy harpy. Kyra begrudgingly gave the woman

credit.

"Brendan Delaney was an ex-employee of Wetun Energy Industries." Tarek pushed a paper across the table. "Senator Hawthorn was investigated by the Department of Justice for inappropriate conduct. Was your husband taking bribes from Wetun Energy in exchange for supporting their bid for a wind-farm contract?"

Margot ignored the paper. "My husband was cleared of those ridiculous rumors." Margot's voice rose. Her hand came down on the table with enough force to rattle the cups on their saucers. "Philip has the utmost integrity. He cannot be bought." He'd rattled her.

"What about the other committee members?" Tarek prodded.

"I can assure you, I do not know," she said through clenched teeth.

"Are you happy with the work being done for you by Wes Silva's company?"

Silva? Where's Tarek going with this? Even Grover sat straighter in his chair.

"Of course," Margot responded, surprised. "He's an excellent contractor. This house is entirely carbon neutral, and the new barn will also meet our strict sustainability requirements."

"What do you mean by *sustainability?*"

"Mander Lane is entirely organic and renewable. We only employ growing and husbandry practices that balance the current use of the land against the future need. Sara can explain it in greater detail, but we're very proud of our accomplishments here." Margot recited the words like she had said them a thousand times—without emotion or entirely understanding what they meant.

Kyra remembered the bottles and vials of chemicals and antibiotics in Sara's apartment.

"That's very conscientious of you."

Kyra suppressed a smile. No one else would have known Tarek was being sarcastic.

"Yes, it is," Margot said. "Is that all? I've an engagement."

"Yes, thank you, Mrs. Hawthorn. You're free to go. We'd like to speak with your daughter and her husband next."

Margot didn't respond. She pushed her chair back with a screech that had the hairs on the back of Kyra's neck standing on end. The senator's wife left the room, her heels *clicking* on the floor. Her coffee remained untouched.

"Well, that went better than I expected." Grover gave Tarek a grim smile once Margot was out of earshot. He stretched, and his eyes found Kyra. "I apologize. Ed was a welcome guest. Margot was out of line."

"Why pretend that she wasn't acquainted with him, then?" Tarek asked.

Grover sat back in his seat. "Margot being Margot, I suppose." Kyra got the sense that Grover often apologized for Margot.

"It's fine." Kyra turned to Beth, but Margot's assistant had slipped out unnoticed. Tarek was gathering up his papers and Kyra approached the table. "Mr. Grover, is the house really carbon neutral?"

"What do you mean?"

"I'm just wondering how environmentally compliant Silva's construction work really is." She shrugged. "My dad had a system put in at the house, but I'm not sure it works properly." She explained about the locked utility room and Wes had been dropping by unannounced to check the system.

Tarek stiffened when she glossed over this morning's events. Grover glanced at Tarek, then the door.

Grover shifted uncomfortably. "Entirely off record?"

Tarek nodded and snapped shut his notebook. He leaned back in his chair, crossing his arms over his chest.

"I told Ed not to use Silva. He's a con man. The systems all have traditional power access to supplement the geothermal and solar energy, but the reality is we power and heat this house on standard electricity and propane. The bills actually increased."

"Seriously?"

"Yeah. His father ran the company and secured the contract with Mander Lane, but he retired before starting the job. Wes took over and leveraged the contract with the Hawthorns to secure new contracts for geothermal systems all over the island. He made promises that were too big to keep. Phil and Margot are working with off-island experts to fix the issues with the HVAC system, but they want to keep their dispute with Silva quiet. The optics would be terrible for the senator if it got out that he was duped on the energy contract for his own house. Doesn't instill a ton of confidence in his judgment."

"But you hired him to do the new barn?" Tarek asked.

"It's a confidential settlement agreement. The family

isn't suing him, and in exchange for a release, he's *assisting* in the build. We have an off-island expert in green agricultural construction overseeing the work. To his credit, Silva has cooperated with us."

Kyra could see the practical benefit of the arrangement, even if it sounded insane.

As if reading her thoughts, Mr. Grover raised his palms to the ceiling. "It sounds complicated, but politics is ninety-nine percent public perception." Grover's phone buzzed and he checked the screen. "Hmm, Adele and Brian are at the yacht club. I can have a car bring them here if you like?"

"No, thank you. I can follow up with them there." Tarek slid his notebook into his pocket.

"I'll let them know to expect you."

"Are you ready?" Tarek asked Kyra.

She nodded, relieved to leave Mander Lane.

Kyra followed Tarek to the door when, impulsively, she turned around. "Thank you, Mr. Grover." She extended her hand to him. "I'm not heading back to London for a few more days. It'd be nice if you came by the house sometime, just to chat about my dad. I'd like to hear some of your stories."

"I'd like that, very much." Grover gave her a sad smile and her hand a gentle squeeze.

Chapter Twenty

TAREK DROVE THEM back to Edgartown. Kyra went over the conversations she'd had with Chase, Sara, Beth, and Grover.

"So how did you do it?" Tarek asked, interrupting her thoughts.

"Excuse me? Do what?" she asked, turning to look at the detective. He glanced at her, his expression amused.

"Get invited into the senator's office."

"I carried the coffee. It worked in *Dirty Dancing*." Kyra shrugged.

"Operation Watermelon?" He huffed a laugh.

"I'm surprised you didn't kick me out."

"It wasn't an official interrogation. I didn't Miranda them, and I wanted your opinion." She blinked back her surprise. "What do you think of Margot Hawthorn?"

"Other than being a right bitch?" Kyra pressed her lips together in distaste.

Tarek grinned.

"I think she's lying for Chase, but I don't understand why. I don't think Chase knows either." *Is Margot that fiercely protective of her son? Or the senator's reputation?* "But I don't think he could have hurt Brendan."

"You talked to him?"

Kyra couldn't read Tarek's expression, but he didn't look angry. *Actually, he looks … pleased.*

"I ran into him down by the fields. He helped deliver a foal."

"What did he say?"

"Nothing really." Kyra pressed her lips together.

She didn't feel entirely comfortable sharing Chase's story. He hadn't confided in her, not really, but sharing his grief still felt a bit like a betrayal.

"He told me he was drinking at a bar in Edgartown on January third. He has no memory of what happened after the bar. He said Brendan and Dr. Alonda had a falling out last fall, but he didn't know what they were arguing about." Kyra tapped her fingers on the armrest. "I knew Alonda was lying when she pretended she'd never heard of Brendan." Kyra chanced a glance at Tarek, but his eyes were on the road. "I just can't think of a reason Chase would kill my dad. Even if it was an accident, and Chase was involved somehow, I still don't understand why Ed was on that boat."

Maybe Chase was in trouble and Ed tried to help him? No, Ed never did anything that didn't benefit him.

"The motive I've come up with is that Chase knew about your dad's article and wanted to protect his family."

"I'm pretty sure Chase knew my dad, but I doubt Ed would have confided in him. If Chase found out about the article, I bet the rest of the family knew about it, too. And if Chase did know, if he wanted to protect his family or Brendan, wouldn't he just tell his father? The senator would have resources to bury it. You said people don't quickly resort to murder."

No, we're missing something. Ed was on that boat for a reason.

Tarek parked the car at the bottom of Main Street and turned to her. "Are you sure you don't want me to drop you off at the house?"

"No, I'll wander around, maybe go shopping." She gave him a timid smile.

Actually, there's something I want to see.

"Okay." Tarek gave her a long look. "I doubt this will take long. If you need anything, call me."

Kyra grabbed her bag and walked down to the marina. She pretended to window-shop while watching Tarek continue up the street and enter the yacht club. As soon as he was out of sight, she turned her back on the town and scanned the boats. There, she spotted what she was looking for. It was still tied up in the third slip where it'd been the other night when they'd talked with Brody. The yacht was even more luxurious in the daylight. She glanced around. The few nearby people were busy, and no one noticed when she hopped off the pier and onto the stern of *The Island Pearl.*

From the back of the boat, Kyra climbed up to an open-air deck, which contained a lux seating area. There was another set of stairs leading to an upper deck and a glass doorway into the interior cabins. She ascended the stairs and popped her head above the floor of the upper deck. Empty. *Ed wouldn't have come up here during a storm.* She returned to the main deck and tried the glass door to the cabins. It slid open.

She slipped through, careful to shut the door quietly behind her, and crept down a short hallway to a gourmet kitchen. There were empty glasses and bottles of champagne discarded in the sink. Kyra's heartbeat ticked up. *Adele should be at the yacht club with Tarek. There shouldn't be anyone here.*

Even still, Kyra strained her ears, but the only sound was the creaks of the spring lines. She moved beyond the kitchen, nay *the galley*, into a formal dining and living space complete with an electric fireplace and a television above the mantle.

Kyra wasn't sure what she was looking for, but this was where Ed had died. She owed it to him. She slunk through the communal space, hugging the walls. The back of her neck was slick with sweat.

Toward the front of the cabin, she came upon a spiral staircase.

She descended to the lower level, nested in the hull. At the base of the staircase, she faced a hall with three doorways leading in different directions. She peeked through the open one to her left. The room was a multilevel sleeping area. It was tidy and undisturbed. Kyra caught the faint musty smell of disuse from the linens. She opened a closet door. Empty. The Hawthorns didn't keep many personal items on their yacht.

She retraced her steps back toward the spiral staircase and tested the closed door. It opened to reveal a luxurious suite. This room was not tidy. It had been inhabited. Recently. The bed was unmade, the coverlet and sheets askew. Discarded clothes and more empty champagne bottles lay on the plush carpeted floor, moving slightly with the rocking of the waves. A built-in desk was littered with glasses and the remnants of a meal. *Someone's living here? Adele? Brody?* Kyra crossed the floor to another doorway, careful not to disturb the clutter on the floor. It was another room—an en suite bathroom and a generous walk-in closet.

Kyra stepped into the bathroom. She absorbed the decadence of the space, her eyes resting on the soaking tub nestled under an oval window. *Is that necessary?* The door to the walk-in closet was slightly ajar. She pushed it open and stepped inside. It was full of clothes; however, despite the glossy wooden shelving and hanging racks, the clothes were scattered around the room on the floor, mostly in piles, and one of those large, waterproof duffle bags lay in a corner. Kyra noticed the coastguard emblem on the side. *Definitely Brody.* Shoes—men's—were strewn about as well, resting where they'd fallen from being kicked off. A strange, earthy moldy scent lingered in the closet reminding her of stale, unwashed towels and she pressed a hand to her nose. She turned to leave. She stepped over a pile of laundry, and her foot hit something hard. Kyra paused and toed the dirty clothes. Her eye caught something, a matte, gray metal casing. With a grimace and a snort of disgust, she pushed aside the laundry to uncover a laptop.

She yanked it out from under the clothes and opened it. The screen was cracked, but there it was. Taped down next to the touchpad was a Post-It. "USERNAME: E.K.GIBSON / PASSWORD: KUDDLEBUG."

"Holy shit!"

Chapter Twenty-One

KYRA STOOD IN the closet, the laptop open in her hands. Her breathing came fast. *Ohmygod.* A loud noise sounded from above. Kyra stifled a scream, nearly dropping Ed's computer. She looked around for a place to hide. With the laptop clasped to her chest, she hid behind the open closet door, her back pressed against the wall. She strained her ears. Heavy footsteps clunked on the hardwood floor above. Someone was in the kitchen. She heard them opening cabinets, moving about. She fished her phone out of her bag to text Tarek. No service. *Fuck!*

"What?"

She heard a muffled voice. Kyra inched as close to the doorway as she dared and tipped her head to hear better.

"I'm here … What do you mean you're not coming?!" the voice demanded, volume increasing.

It sounded like a man. *Brody.*

"What do I do, then?"

Kyra closed her eyes and concentrated on his voice. He was walking, his footsteps getting softer, then louder. *Pacing?*

"Fine. Call me when you're ready."

A cabinet door slammed. His footsteps faded away. Kyra crept forward, forcing her shoulders to relax, her breathing to slow down. She waited a minute more, straining her ears for any sign he was coming back. Hearing nothing, she stepped forward.

Light flooded the bedroom. Kyra slammed back against the wall. She clamped her free hand over her mouth.

"Are you fucking kidding me?" he snarled. "You want me to leave?" He shuffled around the bedroom.

Through the closet door's slats, she glimpsed his shadow as he moved about, but he didn't step into view.

"That cop and his girlfriend are where? Fine. I'm leaving. I'll be in O.B."

Kyra heard a jangle of keys, and the lights went off. She heard him on the deck above.

Kyra remained frozen against the wall for what felt like an eternity. The pounding in her chest eventually subsided, and her breathing returned to semi normal. With a relieved sob, her knees gave out, and she slunk to the floor, shaking. She pushed her hair out of her face and sucked in a deep breath. She slipped the laptop into her bag. Gathering what remnants of courage she had left, she snuck out of the closet, up the stairs, and outside.

Kyra climbed up onto the pier and hurried to a bench across the parking lot and out of sight of *The Island Pearl*. Her body vibrated, and she felt light-headed from the adrenaline. She stared out at Chappaquiddick without seeing it. Her internal voice berated her for being so reckless, so stupid. Her phone pinged. She pulled it from her pocket. Tarek.

"I'm just about done."

She had to concentrate to text him back, steadying her

shaking hands on the touchscreen. *"Heading your way now."*
She took another steadying breath and walked up Main
Street and to the yacht club.

She hadn't noticed it when she'd been here last, but
across the street from the yacht club was a pub, the Crow's
Nest. *Chase said he had been at the Nest the night Ed drowned.
That must be it.*

Kyra entered the club. The same hostess from the other
night greeted her. After explaining why she was there, the
hostess directed her to a table at the front of the deserted
dining room. Tarek was already sitting there with Adele. In
front of the senator's stepdaughter was a lowball glass full of
amber liquid. Tarek had a coffee mug.

Kyra slipped by their table, ignoring Tarek's questioning
look. She nodded to the bar, conveying she'd wait for him
there. She sat at the far end, out of the way but still close
enough to hear, and placed her bag on the chair next to her.
Brian Lee was camped out on the other end. He gave her a
sly smile she bet he thought suave. She couldn't stomach
talking to him right now, her nerves still too raw. She pulled
out her phone, pretending to be busy. The bartender
brought her a water, and she gulped it down. She was
tempted to break out the laptop. *Would Adele recognize it?
Dr. Brian?*

"Michelle, get me another," Adele called and clinked her
rings against the glass.

Tarek cleared his throat and shuffled some papers. "Just a
few more questions, Mrs. Lee. Can you tell me when you
arrived on the island for Christmas?"

"Christmas Eve. Why?"

"According to your mother and stepfather, your visit was unexpected."

"Mother can be flaky, especially with her many social events." Adele's tone was dismissive. "She miscounted her guests. We were expected. I'm *always* expected."

Kyra stole a glance at Brian, but he was leaned in, speaking to the bartender.

"And how long did you stay?"

"I left after the New Year, maybe the second or third."

"Which was it?"

"I don't recall. My husband was needed back at work. He's a doctor."

Michelle placed a fresh glass on the table.

"Do you remember a severe storm?"

"No."

"What about this past week? When did you arrive?"

"Wednesday for my mother's event." Adele gave a loud sigh.

Kyra remembered that Beth said Adele came in earlier in the week, but she'd stayed elsewhere. That Dr. Brian arrived Wednesday morning.

I bet she was with Brody on The Island Pearl.

"Did she remember to include you on the guest list this time?" Tarek asked, and Kyra could picture him raising his eyebrow in feigned innocence. *Asshole.* She grinned into her glass.

"Of course," Adele snapped. "What are you suggesting?"

"Did you know the victim, Brendan Delaney, Mrs. Lee?"

"No."

"Did you know your brother was seeing one of your

stepfather's employees?"

"It wouldn't surprise me. Chase is not discreet. I'm sure he's screwing half the island."

"Do you know Officer Brody McAllister?"

Adele didn't respond right away, and Kyra resisted the urge to turn around.

"Officer McAllister is in the Coast Guard, and he often looks after your family's boats, does he not?"

Kyra wondered why he didn't just come out and ask her about the affair. She slid another glance at Dr. Brian, still flirting with the mildly annoyed-looking bartender. She remembered how he'd behaved the day of the party in the alcove, and again at the photoshoot. How Tarek had stood up, prepared to intervene.

Tarek won't ask anything that might endanger her safety.

Kyra's chest felt full. She snuck a glance at the detective. She wondered if perhaps she may have misjudged him. Maybe he wasn't so singularly focused on solving his case.

"Oh yes, of course. I knew that my mother had arranged for a caretaker for the family's vessels." Adele's voice was muddled, like she was talking into her glass.

"What about the night of the senator's fundraiser? Where were you?"

"At the party, obviously."

For part of it, anyway.

"Mrs. Lee, what is your relationship with the senator?"

"My relationship?" Kyra could hear the confusion in her voice.

"Yes, are you close?"

"No. I barely know the man. I was already a teenager

when my mother married him."

That's the first truthful thing that woman has said. Despite herself, Kyra felt a pang of pity for Adele. Her father hadn't publicly disowned Kyra like Margot had done to Adele, but they shared the pain of being an unwanted daughter.

"What about your mother?"

"Am I close with my mother? Hardly. There isn't much room for the illegitimate daughter when you're a senator's wife."

Kyra winced at the familiar sound of bitter resentment.

"Your parents favor your brother?"

"Half-brother. He fits the narrative better, even if he's a blithering idiot."

"You aren't close with Chase either?"

"No." A glass slammed down on the table. Hard. Kyra jumped.

"I don't see how my relationship with my family has anything to do with Chase murdering his boyfriend, or that reporter."

"You believe Mr. Gibson was murdered?"

"I think you do, Detective Collins, or you wouldn't be asking questions about it."

"Why do you think Chase murdered those men?"

Kyra turned around.

"He's unstable." She shrugged. "Always has been. I'm done." She pushed her chair away from the table.

"I've no further questions right now, Mrs. Lee, but please don't leave the island yet. And if you think of anything..." Tarek handed her a business card.

Adele took it between her fingers and dropped it into her

empty glass. She turned around and glared at Kyra before stomping away.

Mrs. Lee disappeared upstairs, leaving her husband at the bar. Kyra tossed a few dollars down for the bartender and grabbed her things. Tarek was already at her side when she slid off the barstool.

He looked down at her, a smile playing at the corners of his mouth. "Pleasant woman. Takes after her mother."

Kyra stifled a laugh. "She's lying." She followed Tarek toward the door.

"Yes, she is."

"Did you already speak with Brian?"

"I did."

Kyra wanted to know what else the Lees told Tarek. She also wanted to tell him what she'd found on the Hawthorns' boat even if she was apprehensive about how he'd react.

"Did he say anything helpful? Brian Lee?" she asked once they were outside. The sun had come back out, and she turned her face into it, savoring the warmth.

"Oh, he confirmed they arrived on the island on Christmas Eve, but he said they flew out early on January fourth, after the storm. He also said he arrived on the island on Wednesday, the morning of the party. He flew Cape Air both times. I'll confirm that. Other than that, he was chatty about the stock purchase. I didn't get the impression he was hiding anything. He said he bought the stock after Adele got a tip from one of the caddies at the golf course. He thought it was a good idea to invest in green energy. It never occurred to him that there could be a conflict of interest. He said he offered to give it back, but the DOJ said that wasn't necessary." Tarek shrugged and stepped off the curb. "I'll have the team follow up to confirm, but I'm not sure there's anything there."

Kyra put a hand on Tarek's arm. "Can we pop in there?" She pointed to the Crow's Nest.

"Um, sure … In the mood for a warm beer?"

"No." She made a face at him. "We don't drink it *warm*. It's just not ice cold like it is here. I want to see if anyone in there remembers Chase on the night of the storm."

Tarek raised a hand, motioning to her that he'd follow, and they crossed the street to the pub.

The bar was dark, but that's where its resemblance to Gully's place ended. Gully's was warm and cozy, inviting. The Crow's Nest was dingy. What little lighting there was came from dirty windows and an old television hanging from the ceiling. A long bar took up the left side of the room, and about a dozen mismatched barstools were scattered about. A drink rail ran the length of the opposite wall. There were a few patrons hunched over their drinks. They sat mostly silent, their attention divided between a KENO monitor and a grainy, muted broadcast of a Red Sox game.

The bartender shuffled toward them. "What can I get you?" he asked, and Kyra pulled up a picture of Chase on her phone.

"Do you know this man?" She held her phone up to the bartender. He adjusted his baseball hat, leveled her with a stare, then glanced at Tarek. Tarek pulled out his badge.

The bartender sighed and nodded. "Yeah, Chase Hawthorn."

"Were you working the night of January third?" Kyra

asked. The bartender appraised her and again glanced at Tarek.

"Please, answer the question," he said.

The bartender made a resigned noise then scrunched his face in thought. "I don't remember." He shook his head.

"It was the night of that big storm?" Kyra pressed.

"Oh." He stood up straighter. "No, I wasn't working that night."

"Do you know who was?" Tarek asked.

"Yeah, Daphne. She does some night shifts."

"Can you provide us with Daphne's contact information?" Tarek pulled out his notebook.

"I can, but she's in the back. I can get her." At Tarek's nod, the man motioned for them to stay and disappeared through a door.

A few minutes later, a woman came in. Kyra guessed she was about forty but could have been much older. Her dark-blond hair was pulled away from her face and tied in a messy bun. She was dressed in leggings and a crop top that showed off her trim, toned figure. She pulled on a hoodie, leaving it unzipped.

"Can I help you?" she asked.

"Daphne?" Tarek said as he pulled out his badge.

"Mmmhmm."

"I'm Detective Tarek Collins, and this is my associate, Kyra Gibson. We have a few questions for you."

"What's this about?" Her eyes narrowed and she pulled the sweatshirt tighter around her.

"Were you bartending here the night of January third, the night of the storm?"

She looked up past them, thinking, then nodded.

"Do you remember seeing this man?" Tarek held up his phone with the photo of Chase.

"Oh, sure." She blinked. "Chase is a regular."

"You remember him being here that night? Do you recall when he left?" Tarek asked.

Daphne gave him an odd look. "Yeah. I remember. I drove him home. Why?"

"You drove him home?"

"Yes, the storm was coming in, and the bar was closing early. He was in no shape to drive, and it's not so easy to find a cab in the off-season, especially when the weather's bad." Daphne explained it like Tarek was slow.

"He drank at the bar while I closed up, then I drove him home." She frowned, the lines around her eyes deepened with concern. "Did something happen to him?"

"No, nothing like that. He doesn't remember how he got home, so this is helpful. Do you know when you left the bar?" *At least someone takes care of that poor kid.*

"Probably around eleven-ish, maybe a little earlier. It was a slow night, even before the whistles to shut down blew, so it didn't take long to close up."

"You have a good memory," Tarek said.

Kyra's eyes snapped to him.

"Nah." Daphne shook her head. "I remember because I don't often drive patrons home, and the storm was getting bad. Chase may be a pain in the ass, but I wasn't going to leave him."

"Did you or Chase go on the Hawthorns' yacht that night?"

"No. Well, I don't know what Chase did before he came in. But he was there, in that seat"—she pointed to one near the register—"when I started my shift and didn't leave until we left."

"About what time did you start your shift?"

"I start about five."

"Thank you, Daphne." Tarek handed her a card and invited her to call if she thought of anything else.

Daphne turned to leave, but Kyra stopped her.

"Thank you for making sure he got home safe."

Tarek raised an eyebrow at her and frowned. Daphne just nodded.

"The Hawthorns will be glad Chase has an alibi," Tarek said when they stepped back outside.

Kyra followed Tarek to his car. "It's almost like someone wants us to think he did it, but they're doing a terrible job at it."

"You think he's being framed … badly?" Tarek asked as he navigated the car back toward Kyra's house.

"It sounds insane, I know. But it makes sense. He had access to both the yacht and the barn. He knew both victims. He has a motive, no matter how farfetched. I just don't know why. Why go to all that trouble?"

"Or who."

"Obviously. Do you think Adele really thinks he did it? Or does she just hate him that much?"

"I don't know. She seems to believe he's capable of it."

"And do you?"

Tarek clenched his jaw. "I learned a long time ago, everyone is."

Chapter Twenty-Two

THEY PULLED INTO Kyra's driveway and parked in front of the garage. She stared at the house. Images of Silva breaking in and the confrontation with the bald officer flashed before her eyes.

Tarek grasped her hand. "Hey, it's okay. I'll go in with you."

She'd gone still. She nodded, both grateful and completely embarrassed. Her chest constricted. She knew she was overreacting. *This is so stupid. Nothing even happened. I'm fine.*

He gave her hand another squeeze. "It'll be okay, promise."

They entered the house. Tarek led her through the rooms, turning on lights as they went, chasing out the few shadows that lingered untouched by the afternoon sun. Only after they'd walked through every room, and he'd checked every closet, nook, and cranny, did they return to the kitchen. Kyra prepared Cronk's dinner and placed it on his mat just as he trotted in. He gave her a cheerful meow and turned to his bowl. Kyra smiled at the big fluff ball. She pulled down a few wineglasses and opened a bottle, while Tarek slipped off his tie and put his bag on a chair. She handed him a glass as he settled into a seat at the island.

"Thank you." Kyra gestured to the house, then sat and sipped her wine. "I know I'm being ridiculous."

"You're not, and don't mention it. The security company will be able to do the install late next week. You'll already be back home by then, but I think you should have it done. You'll feel safer when you're here."

Kyra nodded. An emptiness loomed in her chest when she thought about going back to London, to her empty flat, her old life.

"Until then, do you want to stay in a hotel?"

"No. If the doors are locked, no one can get in. I'm safe."

Tarek nodded and spun his wineglass. He looked like he was going to say more, maybe convince her to leave.

"I want to show you something," she said, cautiously approaching the topic.

"What?" He gave her a curious smile.

She retrieved the battered laptop from her bag, placed it in front of him, and opened it.

He stared at it, then looked up at her, his brow furrowed.

She tapped the Post-It note. "It's my dad's."

"Where did you get it?" he asked, his words slow and measured.

Kyra told him about sneaking onto *The Island Pearl*. Detective Collins remained quiet. He listened while she talked, but a muscle in his jaw twitched, and he pressed his lips together when she got to the part where Brody almost found her. She took in his stony face.

"You're mad?" she asked, disappointed.

"You're damn right I'm mad. You could have been hurt,

or worse. What the fuck were you thinking?" he asked in a quiet voice.

"I know. I shouldn't have done it." She pushed the laptop toward him. "But it proves my dad was on the boat."

"We knew he was on the boat." He paused. "Or at least we suspected it, since they found his jacket on board. This was a stupid, unnecessary risk."

"But the police didn't find his laptop when they searched it, right?"

"No." Tarek sighed and ran his hands through his hair.

"Brody is living there."

"So what?"

She got up and walked back and forth. "Do you think he was living on the boat when my dad died?"

"To our knowledge, no one was living on the boat." Tarek pushed the laptop toward her, as if its proximity to him was offensive. "I can't use it." His voice was strained, and he avoided meeting her eyes, staring down at the counter instead.

"What do you mean?"

"You acquired it illegally. We didn't have a warrant. Anything on there is inadmissible. You know that." Tarek glared at her, his cheeks flushed. His voice was hard. "You can't just go off and do whatever you want. It's not just dangerous, but it affects my investigation. You know better."

Kyra flinched. "Fine," she hissed through her teeth. She grabbed the laptop and stormed to the office. She dropped into Ed's enormous desk chair and sucked in a breath.

Everything he said was right. *I do know better.* She was angry with herself for her impetuousness, her temper and she felt guilty for snapping at him. *He's sitting in my kitchen trying to keep me safe.*

With a frustrated growl, Kyra yanked open the desk drawer, searching for a power cord. She found one and plugged in the computer. The battery light came on. She waited, drumming her fingers on the metal casing, until the computer charged enough to turn on. Kyra pressed the power button. Although the screen was cracked, it booted up right away. Kyra entered the password: Kuddlebug.

She ran a finger along the Post-It note. When she was a little girl, her father would tuck her into bed at night. He'd wrap the covers around her and give her a rib-crushing hug, repeating in a singsong voice *snug as a kuddlebug.* She wondered if he knew that wasn't how the rhyme went.

She logged into the computer, and the home screen came into view. His background was a photo from years ago. It had been taken when she graduated from law school. He had flown in from who knew where for the occasion, and Ali had insisted they take a picture together. He had his arm around her shoulders and grinned like a proud dad. She was scowling. Kyra remembered she and Ali had argued that morning because she had wanted to skip the ceremony and go to brunch without her father. Kyra swiped at the stinging in her eyes.

She searched the files on the computer. She scrolled through the date stamps. Nothing had been updated since his last upload to his cloud storage a few hours before he died. "Ugh." She snorted, frustrated with herself. Tarek was right. The laptop wasn't going to be of any help.

On a whim, she opened his email client. There were

hundreds of unread emails, mostly ads, newsletters, and other junk that bogged down an inbox. He had a saved draft, though, and it was from January second. She opened it. *Probably an email to Brendan.* Her mouth fell open. It was addressed to her.

Kay,

I hope you had a nice Christmas. I'm sorry we weren't able to see each other. I tried calling, but it went straight to voicemail. By now you know that I've been speaking with Alicia. I invited her and Cam to visit me on Martha's Vineyard this summer, and I'd like to invite you to come with them. I'd love to show you where your mother spent her summers as a girl, show you the place she called home.

I wanted to tell you in person or at least over the phone, but you're very good at avoiding me. Alicia seemed to think you may consider reading an email at least, so here goes:

I know I was a terrible father after your mother died. I didn't know how to raise a little girl, and I was heartbroken after her death. I told myself that the best life for you was a stable one with your aunt. But if I'm honest, I left you there because I was afraid. I'm so sorry. I only hope it's not too late and you can forgive me.

Please consider coming to Martha's Vineyard this summer or anytime. I love you.

Love,
Dad

Kyra sat back, stunned. She wrapped her arms around

her body like she was holding herself together. She knew Ali had been talking to her father, that he had been trying to contact Kyra for months. But Kyra had never suspected this was why he'd wanted to talk to her. To apologize. To acknowledge what he'd done. She remembered avoiding his calls at Christmas. She'd spent a few days with Ali and Cam, then flown to Taghazout with some friends for a beach vacation. When he was pulled from the harbor, she'd been sunbathing in Morocco. Kyra wiped away the tears streaming down her cheeks.

Without warning, the lights went out, pitching the room into shadow. The laptop screen blacked out before coming back on, relying on its battery.

"Kyra!" Tarek shouted.

She jumped, startled, then felt relief. He hadn't left.

"I'm okay," she called. "I'm in the office."

Tarek appeared in the doorway.

"I'm fine, really."

He narrowed his eyes, taking in her tear-stained cheeks.

"Grace said the power goes out."

"What did you do?" he asked, giving her a soft smile that didn't reach his eyes.

"I don't think it was me. I only plugged in the computer." She frowned and fussed with the laptop cord.

Tarek walked to the window and peered outside.

"It might just be the wind or a brownout. There doesn't seem to be a storm."

"There's a generator. I can get that started." *Maybe.*

"I doubt it'll be out for long. If it doesn't come back on soon, we can start it."

We? He's going to stay? Kyra paused, but the thought didn't bother her. Actually, she felt safer with him here.

"Was there anything on it?" Tarek walked toward her and motioned to the laptop.

Kyra considered the question. There was nothing that would help with the case. But that email? The one that Ed had never sent. Maybe it had been worth the risk.

"No, not really. Mostly … personal things."

"Kyra." Tarek stepped toward her, but she brushed past him and rushed upstairs.

KYRA STEPPED OUT of the shower and wrapped the plush towel around her body. She used her hand to clear the steam from the mirror and looked at her reflection. Her eyes were red and puffy. She splashed cold water on her face and, using the pads of her fingers, tried to pat out under her eyes. With a sigh, she gave up. If Tarek hadn't guessed she'd runaway to bawl her eyes out, he'd know now.

She stepped into her bedroom. The ceiling fan spun in lazy circles. *Power's back.* She heard Tarek's voice from the living room, talking to someone, and closed the bedroom door to get dressed.

Kyra descended the stairs to find the detective camped out on the couch, Cronk snoozing next to him. He idly pulled on the cat's ears while reading a book. His head came up, and he gave her a smile. "Hope you don't mind? I pulled it from one of your dad's shelves." He held it up. *Treasure Island.*

"No, help yourself. Stevenson?"

"It's actually pretty good."

I know. That was my copy.

Kyra's phone pinged, and she fished it out of her pocket. "It's Grace." She skimmed the text. "Their club is hosting a beach party on State Beach tonight. She's inviting us."

"Us?"

"Yeah, it says 'you and the handsome detective should come.'" She turned the phone to him, feeling heat spread across her cheeks.

"Oh, my car outside." He chuckled. "That woman should do my job. She'd be excellent at it."

Kyra huffed a laugh and sat on the couch, sandwiching the cat between them. Cronk gave a big stretch and started purring. She scratched his chin.

"We should go." Tarek marked his space in the book and set it aside. "It'll be a nice distraction from," he paused and studied her face, then gestured around the house, *"everything."* From the way he was looking at her, he definitely knew she'd been crying. "And we couldn't possibly deny them my handsome face."

"No, of course not." She smiled despite herself.

"In the off-season, they can set a fire on the beach. It's fun."

Kyra nodded not really convinced, but giving in. "I'll let her know."

"I NEED TO make a quick stop at my hotel." Tarek glanced at

Kyra from the driver's seat of the Range Rover. "Grab warmer clothes." He gestured to her thick sweater and jeans.

Kyra nodded and stared out the window. She was jittery and exhausted. The long, confusing day was taking a toll.

Tarek pulled into the driveway of a small inn and left her in the car. Without thinking about the late hour, she pulled out her phone and called Ali.

"Kay?" she answered on the third ring, her voice groggy.

It was well past midnight in London. That Ali refused to set her phone to silent had irritated Kyra to no end when she was younger, and she felt her lips stretch into a weary smile.

"Is everything okay?" Ali whispered.

Kyra heard her aunt's muffled voice whisper to Cam and the soft click of a door closing.

"It's fine." But Kyra's voice hitched. *Not fine.*

"Kay," Ali said in the stern voice she only reserved for the rare serious conversation.

Under command of the Ali-voice, Kyra crumbled. She told her aunt everything, the attack with Wes, the Hawthorns, the boat, the laptop, the email, Tarek. Ali didn't say a word until Kyra stopped talking and drew in a ragged breath.

"That fucking bastard," Ali hissed, and Kyra hiccupped a laugh, realizing she didn't know which of the people she'd talked about had elicited Ali's fury.

"Who?"

"All of them, obviously. Which one are we most pissed at? I'll start there."

"Where are you?" Kyra pictured her aunt's open-concept townhouse.

"The first-floor loo, actually. Don't judge me. Ignatius is

part bat."

Kyra sobbed and laughed at the same time. The combination made a strange choking sound.

"You know, because of the hearing? Bats have excellent hearing."

Kyra laughed, bending over her knees. Fresh tears stung her already sensitive eyes.

I'm half delirious. Bat biology is hardly this hilarious.

"How do you know that?"

"One of the books I've read nineteen gajillion times to the little shit. Did you know there's a lizard that can shoot blood from its eyes?! Its fucking eyes! This is in a fucking children's book! I swear I'm not cut out for modern parenting." Kyra could hear the pride in Ali's voice.

"You're a fabulous modern parent."

"Yeah, well. I'm glad you found the note from your dad," Ali said, picking the person who troubled Kyra the most. "He'd have grown the balls to send it eventually, you know."

"Do I?" Kyra wasn't so sure.

"Ed was a workaholic, a coward, and a rank cockwit, but I never doubted how much he loved you and my sister." The Ali-voice was back.

Kyra blinked, and a tear slid down her cheek.

"Where are you now, babes?"

"In a carpark waiting for Tarek."

"Oh? Waiting for him? Why?" Kyra grimaced at her aunt's smug tone.

"He's getting some things from his hotel room. We're going to a beach party."

"Good. He'll take you to a hotel tonight then, right?"

Kyra didn't like lying to her. "Yes, he's got me sorted. I'll be safe. Don't worry." She saw Tarek walking toward the car carrying a bag. "He's back. I'll call you in the morning."

"First thing?"

"Promise. Love you." Kyra hung up just as Tarek opened the door.

He took a long look at her, the phone clutched in her hands, and frowned. "Is everything okay?" he asked, sliding into his seat.

"Just telling Ali about the day. A lot happened." She offered him a thin smile.

"Hmmm, I'd say. Ready?"

Kyra nodded.

UNLIKE SOUTH BEACH near her house, State Beach was flatter, calmer. They parked and walked up the path, over a small dune, to the beach below. It stretched out toward Nantucket Sound, where the two merged.

"Heyoo!" a cheerful voice called from a group of people a few yards down. Grace waved, her entire body shaking.

Tarek laughed and raised his hand in acknowledgment.

"Grace." Kyra embraced her friend. She couldn't help grinning. Grace's enthusiasm was infectious.

"How are you? Where's Charlie?"

"Char's over there." Grace gave Tarek an enthusiastic hug, then pointed behind them.

Kyra recognized Charlie's wild curls dancing in the

breeze; she was squatting on the ground, her back to them.

"She's fussing with the fire." Grace dispensed with introductions, listing off at least two dozen names while pointing to the people milling about, setting up tables, chairs, and a tent, before excusing herself to supervise.

The other revelers were a mixture of neighbors, beach friends, and Charlie's colleagues, all members of an unofficial beach club. Even Mr. Entwistle was in attendance, looking strangely comfortable in seersucker shorts, a dress shirt, and a V-neck sweater. Kyra didn't know how she felt about his very visible, very pale knees.

A cheer erupted from the crowd. Charlie had gotten the bonfire lit.

Kyra found a seat by the fire on a driftwood log. She'd lost Tarek, having excused herself when a conversation with a man in a Celtics sweatshirt delved into a deep analysis of the New England Patriots' draft prospects. She stretched her toes toward the flames, relishing the heat.

"There you are." Tarek sat down beside her and offered her some food from his plate.

She shook her head, still full from her own sampling of the clambake's vast selection.

"Not a Patriots fan?" he asked her, picking up and eyeing a barbequed chicken leg.

"I'm not sure I've ever seen an American football game. I've been to a few Chelsea matches, though."

"Soccer?"

"Football." She made a face at him making him laugh.

"It feels like we haven't seen you in forever." Grace's voice interrupted them. She was pulling two beach chairs over. "Tell me…" Grace stopped midsentence. Her smile wilted off her face as she narrowed her eyes, taking in the scratches on Kyra's hands, visible in the firelight. "Oh, my. Kyra. What happened?" Grace dropped into her chair and leaned forward, scanning Kyra's face.

Tarek explained what had happened with Wes Silva.

"I can't believe it." Grace pressed her hands together, massaging her knuckles. "I've known Wes since he was a teenager. He's always been polite. He was a foreperson on the renovation of our house."

"Believe what?" Charlie appeared. Her gaze bounced between Grace and Kyra. After Grace repeated the story, Charlie wrapped her arms around Kyra, hugging her close. "Are you alright?"

"Just a few scrapes and bruises. I'm fine, really." Kyra attempted a smile. *I must look terrible.* Tarek rubbed her shoulder, and she resisted the urge to lean into him.

"I thought he might be struggling," Charlie murmured and plopped into her chair. Something that resembled guilt pinched the corners of her eyes. "I never thought he'd break into your house or attack you." Charlie's expression was apologetic. "I'd heard rumors that there are issues with his geothermal installations. They aren't working correctly. One of my clients even accused him of stealing materials from their site for new builds. He visited his house over the winter, and the system wasn't working. A pipe burst. There was a lot of damage. Honestly, though, I didn't pay attention. It could have been anything. A malfunction. The homeowners setting the temperature too low. There are so many construction disputes on the island. Everyone blaming everyone else. But recently, the claims against Wes have been more consistent from homeowner to homeowner. I should have paid more attention."

"But why?" Kyra asked, confused. "Does he not know what he's doing?"

"It's a common contracting problem. Use the money designated for a current job to pay for the materials for another or move materials from an unsupervised site to a supervised one. Rob Peter to pay Paul. He must have real money problems." Charlie shook her head.

"Oh, my." Grace put her hands to her mouth. "That's why Julia's taking so many catering jobs."

"But my dad still used him?" Kyra asked.

"Yes, Wes's company, Forrest & Co., renovated your house. Ours, too. He started on your property just as he was ending his contract with the Hawthorns. That was about five years ago."

"Ed never complained to me that the system didn't work, or his bills were higher than expected, so I never suspected there was a problem with the build." Grace twisted her hands together, her rings glinting in the firelight.

"Kyra's house has been sitting empty these past few months. The bills went to the lawyer, right?" Tarek asked. "It's possible Silva's been stealing parts while the house has been empty, to use in other projects. He's told her he has a key and seems to be used to coming and going as he pleases." Tarek rubbed his forehead, thinking something through. "Or is it possible he's not trying to take things but put them back? Have you turned on the HVAC system?"

"No, I've been using the fireplace for heat. But he asked

me that, too. Maybe it doesn't work? If the house was going to sell, it'd be inspected. If it failed because the system was missing parts, Wes's scam would be exposed."

"Before we knew you were coming, we'd expected to have everything wrapped up before the season starts in May." Charlie avoided Kyra's eyes. "He would have had plenty of time to put things back."

Kyra flushed with guilt at the memory of her first conversations with Mr. Entwistle, asking him to take care of it because she was too busy to deal with it.

"This is my fault. I engaged Wes's company for maintenance. I do on all the geothermal houses. I asked him to make sure everything was in working order once I knew you were coming." Charlie reached out for Kyra's hand. "I'm so, so sorry."

Kyra shook her head. "You couldn't have known."

Kyra let out a ragged sigh and rubbed her arms against a chill that had nothing to do with the cool weather. *Maybe I should stay in a hotel tonight.*

"I've talked to a security-system installer," Tarek told Grace and Charlie. "Unfortunately, they can't get here until after Kyra's headed home."

"That's a good idea. What do you think, Char?" The firelight cast shadows, enhancing the worried creases around Grace's eyes.

"You think?" Charlie asked. "We rarely even lock our doors." She picked at the arm of her beach chair.

"Murder, theft, vandalism. These aren't things we're supposed to worry about here." Grace's voice pitched up.

"I'll take care of it, Grace." Charlie reached out and

grasped her hand. "Don't worry."

AS THE SUN fully set, the fireside became more popular with the partygoers, and Kyra wandered down to the shoreline. The full moon glowed, basting the beach in diffused light.

"Hey, how are you feeling?" Tarek asked, walking up.

"I'm fine." She pushed her hair out of her face. "I'm just thinking."

Tarek fell into step beside her, and they wandered down the beach, away from the party.

"I spoke to my team. The Hawthorns confirmed no one's been using or staying on *The Island Pearl*, then or now. No laptop was seen onboard in January, either."

"Really? Did you tell them we know Brody's living there?"

"No. Then I'd have to explain why I suspect that."

There was no condemnation in his tone, but Kyra still cringed. "So, what does that mean?"

"Other than someone, maybe Brody, brought the laptop onto the boat after the accident? Nothing. We don't know how Brody got it. He could say he found it on the sidewalk or bought it at a secondhand store."

What Tarek didn't say was that because of her, they wouldn't be able to ask him about it.

"Another thing." He stopped walking and pulled out his phone. "I asked about the IP addresses logging into Brendan Delaney's brokerage account. Most were different and probably using a VPN since we geolocated them to various foreign countries. Only two are the same. Both geolocated to DC, one in early April when a modest deposit was made, and the other in October when he withdrew the funds he used for the down payment on his car."

Kyra started walking, her bare toes sinking in the sand. He fell into step beside her.

"What do you make of that?" he asked.

"I'm not sure."

"That's the problem with this case. It could be connected, but I feel like I'm missing something. I can't put my finger on it." Tarek slid his hands in his pockets. After a few beats, he said, "Our motive theory is that this is all related to your dad's story about Wetun Energy, but we've confirmed it, and Maria Alonda has pretty airtight alibis for each murder. She was skiing with her family in Vermont in January, and all the board members confirmed she was on the video conference call from her home office last Sunday. She wasn't on the island." He looked out to sea. "She doesn't strike me as the type of person who'd take out a contract. I don't have enough to subpoena her financials either."

"But that doesn't mean she wasn't bribing the senator. Didn't you say Brendan's brokerage firm also manages retirement benefits for Wetun employees? So, Wetun could have access to those accounts?"

"Yes, potentially."

Kyra stopped walking. "What if Brendan didn't know?" Her words spilled out before her mind had fully caught up. "What if Brendan wasn't aware of the funds being transferred using his accounts? He logs in to buy a car and sees all this money moving. Chase said that Brendan had a falling out with Alonda and withdrew his support for the offshore wind farm, for Wetun Energy, around that time. What if he figured it out? Then he called my dad?"

"Figured it out? What's *it*?" Tarek asked. He used his toe to dig up a shell buried in the sand.

Kyra chewed her bottom lip. *What* is *it*? She felt it. The answers were there, just out of reach.

"Hear me out. Why would they use Brendan's accounts?"

Tarek cocked his head to the side. "He had access to both Wetun and the senator. If the DOJ had looked, they would have found the deposits and the withdrawals. The optics are bad for Brendan." Tarek shrugged. "But in a vacuum, he's not doing anything wrong. It just looks strange. But no one's watching a low-level congressional aide." Tarek paused. "No one's watching a low-level congressional aide," he repeated, his eyes glittered in the moonlight. "He was their cover." Tarek started walking again, faster this time, and Kyra struggled to keep up with his long strides in the sand.

"Tarek," she huffed.

"Sorry." He slowed down and gave her that crooked smile that made her insides warm. "Thinking." He spun his hand around his head, wheels turning. Then he frowned. "That doesn't explain the murders, though."

"But doesn't it? Someone must have figured out what Brendan knew. And we know it's not Alonda. Who else would have motive to kill my dad and Brendan?"

"The Hawthorns?"

Kyra knew he was thinking about Chase. "What about

Margot Hawthorn? She was on the island when both murders happened, and she had motive. Stopping the release of my dad's story and getting rid of Brendan."

"You think she's strong enough to overpower your dad and throw him overboard?" Tarek asked, confirming Kyra's doubts. "I don't think it's possible." He shook his head. "She also has alibis. Beth and the senator claimed she was home on the night of Ed's death, and she was in the house with her husband when the fire started."

"Realistically, how strong are those alibis?"

"Not very. Both Beth and the senator are unreliable because of their close relationships with Margot. But that doesn't mean either of them is lying."

"Do you think they are?"

"I don't think so. Beth doesn't strike me as a deceptive person. I've no doubt the senator would lie if he thought it necessary." Tarek stopped walking. He looked out onto the Nantucket Sound. "He'd do anything for his wife, but I found his story credible. I'm not as sure he'd do the same for his son, though." He looked down at her and his eyes narrowed. "You're cold."

"A bit." She hadn't even noticed she was shivering.

"Come on. I'll take you home."

TAREK PULLED INTO her driveway and walked with her to her front door. Kyra figured he'd leave, but he followed her inside and did another sweep of the house, checking each room. Kyra waited nervously in the kitchen. She didn't want to be left alone in the house, and it was probably too late to find a hotel. She debated asking him to stay but was embarrassed by her neediness. *For fuck's sake, I live alone in a city of over nine million people, and I'm not frightened.* She was still chastising herself when she heard the television go on. Kyra followed the sound into the living room to find Tarek lounging on the couch. He'd taken off his shoes and propped his feet on the coffee table. He was flicking through the channels.

"What are you doing?"

"I don't have cable at the inn, and there's a new episode of..." He looked at the screen. "The local news."

"I'll be right here. If you need anything, give a shout."

He was staying.

"Thank you." She said, her voice breathy with relief. Tears welled in her eyes, and she turned away. "Can I get you anything?"

"I'll be fine. Goodnight."

"Goodnight, Tarek."

She walked upstairs. She let herself relax as she slid under the comforter feeling safe, knowing he was just downstairs.

Chapter Twenty-Three

Monday

K YRA'S EYES FLUTTERED open. Cronk was stretched out alongside her. The room seemed to hum with the contented rumble of his purr. She stretched and sat up, trying not to disturb him. The room was bathed in a pink light, harsher than a sunrise. She checked her phone. It was well past eight. The sun had been up for hours.

She pushed back the covers and padded to the window. Outside, everything was awash in a rosy, golden haze. The cove, only just visible, twinkled amethyst. Despite the warmth in the room, the hair on the back of Kyra's neck stood on end, and she rubbed away a chill. Something unsettling tugged at a memory. Shaking it off, she dressed and made her way downstairs. She checked the living room, but Tarek was already gone, the blanket neatly folded over the couch. Her heart sank a bit.

Cronk beat her to the kitchen and yowled for his breakfast. While her coffee brewed, she fed her mini-yeti and shot off a text to Charlie and Grace, thanking them for the previous evening.

She pulled her mug from under the machine and stared out at the cove. She texted Ali, updating her about the beach party and thanking her for the midnight support, leaving out not staying in a hotel and Tarek sleeping on her couch. Just the thought of that conversation made her head hurt.

"Would you and Cam want to come visit the island later this summer?"

"Is that an official invitation?"

Kyra chewed her lip. *Is it an invitation?* Did she want to come back? For Ali to show her the island? To play with Iggy on the beach?

"Yes. Official. This summer."

"YES!!!" Ali texted back, followed by a bunch of balloon emojis and a calculator.

She must mean calendar. Kyra grinned. While not at all definite, she had the glimmer of a plan to return. And soon. In only a few months. The discomfort of discontent that had been building over the course of the last week eased like she'd been stooped over, climbing a steep hill, and she could finally stand up straight.

Cronk jumped onto the kitchen island and bumped his head against her hand. "You like that idea, don't you? Coming back?" She scratched his chin, and he flopped over on his side, his floofy tail twitching. Kyra noticed the notepad. Tarek's. *He must have left it.* She slid it out from underneath the cat and flipped it open.

Tarek's notes were a jumble of his thoughts and idle doodles. She thumbed through the pages until she found his most recent entry. He was building a case against Chase for Brendan's death. He suspects that someone in the family, maybe Phil or Margot, set the fire to protect him.

Kyra snapped it shut. She tapped her nail on the cover.

"I just don't believe it, Cronk. I want to talk to him again."

The cat blinked his big green eyes at her.

Kyra picked up her phone just as it rang. Assaf. *Shit.* She ignored the call and texted Beth asking for Chase's number. Within seconds, her phone pinged with Chase's contact information.

"Hi Chase, this is Kyra Gibson. We've met a few times at your family's farm. I have some information about the night Ed Gibson died that you may want to hear, and I was hoping to ask you a few more questions. Can you meet me at Café Joy in Edgartown? Thanks."

To her surprise, she received a response almost immediately. He'd be there in thirty minutes. She debated texting Tarek, but he'd insist on coming with her. *I think I can get more out of him alone.* Kyra pulled on a windbreaker and grabbed her purse.

She stepped off the porch and froze. A police cruiser sat in her driveway, the engine idling. The driver's-side door popped open, and a man in a police uniform stepped out. "Miss Gibson?" The man took off his hat and held it in front of him. "I'm Officer Mark Evans with the Massachusetts State Police." He pointed to his badge on his chest. "Detective Collins requested a security detail for the house. For you."

"I … uh, I'm sorry?" She glanced at the officer's car. It was the same color as Tarek's. Officer Evans wasn't with the Edgartown police.

"Yes, ma'am, oh sorry, *miss*." He gave her a bashful smile and took a cautious step toward her, like he was approaching a frightened animal. "I'm assigned to stay here and make sure no one enters the residence unless you or Detective Collins allow it." Kyra just stared at him. That she didn't run away seemed to make him more confident, and his features stretched into a goofy grin. "I'll just be in my vehicle, ma'am, ugh, *miss*." He pushed his shaggy reddish hair out of his face and shrugged. "If you need anything, just give me a yell." He slapped his hat back on his head.

"Please, call me Kyra." The man gave her the impression of an overgrown golden retriever. "I was just going to go out for coffee."

"Okay, *Kyra*." He bobbed his head. "I'll be here if you need me."

She gave him a weak wave and climbed into her SUV.

KYRA PUSHED OPEN the door to Café Joy, and a bell jingled. The brightly decorated coffee shop was busier than the last time she'd been there. *Was that really only a week ago?* So much had happened in a few short days. She'd tentatively made a go at keeping her father's house, stumbled onto a mystery, made new friends in Grace and Charlie … and Tarek. Last Saturday, packing her bags in her London flat seemed like another lifetime.

Nina was behind the counter again. She gave Kyra a wave and gestured for her to sit anywhere. Kyra settled at a table a little out of the way by a window and set up her laptop.

"Coffee?" Nina asked, holding up a carafe.

"Yes, please. Thank you," Kyra said, wrapping her hand around the warm mug. "I'm also meeting someone."

"We officially opened for the season yesterday." Nina handed her two menus. "We have a lot more options now. I'll come back to check on you and your friend."

"Ms. Gibson?" a soft voice said, and Kyra looked up from her laptop. Chase stood a few feet away from the table, hands stuffed in his jeans' pockets and his golden hair flopping down over his forehead.

"Kyra." She gestured to the chair across from her. "Please, sit."

Chase pulled the chair out and sat down. He pushed his body close to the wall, his shoulder wedging up against the window like he was trying to melt into the building.

"Thank you for coming."

"What did you want?" His blue-green eyes were dull and bloodshot, but he held her gaze.

She had expected to see suspicion, maybe fear, but she could read nothing on his slack, sallow features. *He's given up*, she realized, and her heart lurched.

"I wanted to ask you a few questions about Brendan. Would you mind?"

Chase shook his head, but his expression was pained.

"Did he have money problems?"

Chase frowned. He rolled his lips like he was carefully choosing his words. "He wasn't wealthy, if that's what you're asking. I don't know how much he made working for my dad, but he seemed okay. He insisted we split expenses, like meals. He never mentioned having money trouble."

"Do you think he could be bought? Would he take money to use his influence to persuade your dad to vote a certain way?"

Chase's eyes narrowed. "Are you asking me if Brendan was bribing my father?"

Kyra swallowed. Perhaps she'd pushed too far. She gave a nod. Her hands tightened on her coffee cup.

"No. Brendan wasn't that kind of person. He actually believed in politics." Kyra heard the scorn in Chase's voice. "But even if he wasn't an idealist, Brendan didn't have any influence with Phil. Phil probably didn't know he existed before he died. Senator Hawthorn is much too important to trouble himself with such trivial affairs as what aides work in his office. He leaves that to Grover." Chase cleared his throat and looked down at the table. He sat up and his eyes locked on hers. "Brendan knew something, didn't he?" He leaned forward, his voice a hoarse whisper, "What did he find out?" Chase Hawthorn was no fool. He just played one.

"I'm trying to piece it together."

Nina came by to refresh Kyra's coffee and pour one for Chase. He added cream and stirred.

"I know you didn't kill my dad," Kyra whispered once Nina was out of earshot.

The spoon stopped moving.

"You didn't have anything to do with his death."

Chase sat frozen for a beat. Two. Then he deflated. His face went slack. His shoulders rounded in, making him small. He sucked in a ragged breath.

"You were given a ride home by the bartender from the Crow's Nest the night my dad died. Do you know Daphne?"

"The bartender at the Nest?" He blinked. "Yes, I know

her."

"I spoke to her. The night of the storm, January third, you were at the Crow's Nest. The bar closed early because of the storm. It was raining pretty hard. Daphne said you sat with her while she cleaned up, and she took you home. You never went to *The Island Pearl* that night, or at least not after the bar. My dad died sometime after seven p.m. You couldn't have killed him."

"I wasn't there?"

"No. But why do you think you were?"

He closed his eyes, and his head fell forward.

"I didn't … don't remember, and my mother…" Chase looked up. His eyes flicked back and forth between hers, like he was searching for something. He glanced away. "My mother thinks I did it." Chase shuddered. "She convinced my dad. They've been trying to protect the campaign. Keep it out of the media. Keep me out of the public eye." His voice was flat.

Kyra realized he wasn't angry. He expected nothing less from his family. The campaign came first.

"But why?" she asked. "Why would they think that?"

He shrugged. "I'm not sure the reason matters to them. I was in Edgartown. I blacked out. I'm a disappointment. That's enough for them. Mother thinks Ed was using me to get dirt on the family. She's always been suspicious of him, of the media in general." Chase stared out the window. "That isn't true, though. Ed was always nice to me. He never asked about Dad or politics. He'd ask me about sailing or the farm. Sometimes he'd talk about you, his daughter, a big-time lawyer in England." Chase's mouth twitched.

Kyra started. *What? Me?*

Chase turned to face her, then dropped his eyes to his coffee. "Last year, I got into trouble. With another boat. I guess it's what I do." He shrugged. "Get wasted, do something destructive. Stupid." His voice cracked. "There's more." He gave her a helpless look.

"What do you mean, *more?*" She shifted in her seat, nervous.

"They're convinced I killed Brendan, too. Or that I'll be arrested for it. The truth doesn't matter, just what the people believe." He said it like he'd been fed that line his whole life.

"What do you mean?" Kyra asked. "You were in Boston when he died."

"I was in Boston when the fire started. The lawyers say the police will argue that I killed him and left. Someone else started the fire. I probably paid that person off."

That is what they're saying…

"Did you?"

"No!" His face blanched, but he held her gaze. "I'd never have hurt him. I didn't even know he was coming to see me … or *if* he was coming to see me. I didn't know he was on the island. If I'd known, I'd have told him not to come, to meet me in Boston or somewhere else."

"But why would they think that?" Kyra asked.

Chase finally broke eye contact and stared at the table. His hands clenched into fists and his shoulders raised and lowered. He was quiet for a long time.

Finally, in barely a whisper, he said, "Because I have the gun."

She leaned forward and grasped the table.

"What?" Her brain was spinning.

"A few days after Brendan died, I found a gun in my room. It was hidden between my bed and the wall. There's a crawl space back there. I'd hide weed there when I was a kid."

"Is the gun yours?"

"No. Before this week, I'd never touched one. I don't know how it got there."

"Who else knows about the crawl space?"

"I'm not sure. Mom might know. Beth and the staff, probably. My sister. It connects our rooms. I'd crawl through to see her when I was little. She hated that." The ghost of a wry smile fluttered across his lips before he cleared his throat. "After I found it, I told Mom, thinking we'd go to the police. Maybe the gun could be tested or … or something. But she flipped out. Accused me of sabotaging Phil's career. Destroying her life. She made me promise to get rid of it and never talk about it again. I don't think my dad even knows."

"Why are you telling me this?" she asked, her voice a hoarse whisper.

Chase looked at her. Under the gaze of his piercing eyes, she felt exposed.

He shrugged, but it was a halfhearted motion. "You seem to want to help. To find the truth about what happened to Brendan and Ed. Even if they accuse me, I want that, too. For them."

Kyra searched his face for any sign of dishonesty. She let out a breath.

"Did you get rid of it?" She almost hoped he had, for his sake.

She couldn't keep this from Tarek, and once he had the murder weapon, the detective would arrest Chase. But maybe if they brought him the weapon together, they could persuade him that Chase was innocent?

"No, not yet. I hid it until I could take the *Neamhnaid* out. Throw it in the ocean."

"The *Neamhnaid*?"

"Margot's sailboat."

Kyra thought for a moment, chewing her bottom lip, thinking through their next step.

"Chase?" She'd made her decision.

"Hmm?"

"Where did you hide it?"

Chapter Twenty-Four

KYRA DROVE UP island, following the barks of her GPS to Menemsha. She remembered Tarek pointing it out to her on one of their drives. She turned off the main road, and the little fishing village came into view. Cottages and outbuildings were sprinkled along the harbor. Commercial fishing vessels were docked and tied along the decks. Further out, moored in the deeper waters, were only a few pleasure boats, including a large ketch with *Neamhnaid* painted on its navy-blue hull in a bright, almost iridescent, pearl-white paint.

Kyra parked and made her way to the marina. Her hair whipped around her face. The village was deserted. The only activity came from the cormorants as they pierced the water's surface in search of fish. The buildings along the water's edge that supported Menemsha's fishing industry—boat repair, fish packaging, fishmongers, a filling station. All were shut up. A carved wooden sign hung above a takeaway clam shack's order window. CLOSED. It banged against the shingles in the wind. The increasing cloud cover cast the little village in shadow, giving it the air of abandonment. Kyra rubbed away the goosebumps on her arms.

Chase said he'd hidden the gun in the family's boathouse. She stood at the edge of the marina. There, at the far end of the dock, beyond the fishing boats, were a few small, gray cedar-shingled buildings. One was decorated with old nets and once-colorful buoys, now faded from the salt and sun. A ragged American flag flapped from a pole on the roof. Kyra walked over to the cluster of boathouses. Little more than sheds, really. A plaque was nailed to the door of the third one. HAWTHORN. *This is it.*

A padlock hung from the door. Kyra cast furtive glances up and down, checking she wasn't seen. She used the combination Chase had given her. The lock sprang open. She unlatched it, pulled the door open, and stepped inside.

The interior was small and, to maximize space, the Hawthorns had erected free-standing shelving units. *He said he hid it in the shelves in the back.* Because of the shelves full of equipment, she couldn't see the back of the room. Careful not to disturb the items on the floor, she walked around the shelves to the back of the shed.

The back was just as crammed with gear. Extra sails were tied and stowed. Ropes were coiled in piles on the floor. Fishing rods stood propped against a wall. Kyra searched the shelves for the gun. She pushed aside buckets of netting, gas canisters, deflated beach balls, and moldy towels. *Where is it?* She rolled her shoulders against her growing apprehension. *I should have called Tarek.* She closed her eyes, anticipating what he'd say to her when he found out what she'd done. Like *The Island Pearl* but so much worse.

She bent down to search beneath a stack of grimy life jackets. Her foot connected with the side of a metal pail, and it scooted along the floor, hitting the fishing rods. They crashed to the ground.

"Fucking hell." She squatted down to pick up the mess.

She stretched for a rod.

Something hard and cold pressed against the base of her skull. Kyra froze.

"Get. Up." a voice growled.

Kyra inched to a standing position instinctively holding her hands up at shoulder height. She hadn't heard the door open. Hadn't heard anyone enter.

"I'm sorry. I was just borrowing some fishing things." Kyra shifted to turn around.

Her assailant rammed her shoulder with the butt of the gun, and she slammed into the wall.

"Don't fucking move," a man snarled.

Kyra tried to keep her voice calm. "I won't. I'm sorry."

"You nosy bitch." He sneered and pushed her against the wall.

She felt his hot breath on her ear.

"You couldn't just stay out of our fucking business, could you?"

Kyra swallowed. She recognized the man's voice.

"Brody, please," she pleaded, her voice shaking. "Please, put the gun down."

He pushed her again. Hard. Kyra's cheek struck rough wood, and she cried out. Brody pressed his body against her, pushing her into the wall. She went rigid.

"Keep your fucking mouth shut."

He yanked her arms behind her, and she let out a yelp. *He's going to kill me.* Her mind went blank with terror. She barely registered her hands being bound behind her. He pulled the restraints tight, yanking on her shoulder. The sharp pain pierced through her panic, brought her back.

Come on, think! Think! Her law firm's women's safety presentation came back to her. *Make your assailant acknowledge you're a person. Use his name.*

"Brody, please," she whispered. "Brody, please let me go."

He didn't respond.

She let out a cry when he wrenched her against him. He half carried, half dragged her out of the boathouse and down the dock. He tossed her onto the floor of a small, dirty rowboat. She flopped on the metal hull and gasped, the wind knocked out of her. Brody jumped into the dinghy, tossing the wet spring lines on her. She tried to pull her legs under her to sit up, but he shoved her back down with his boot. The back of her skull struck the hull. Kyra saw stars.

"Move and I'll put a bullet in your brain." Brody turned and yanked on the outboard motor. Once. Twice. It growled to life.

Kyra felt the boat propel forward. *Where are we going? Where's he taking me?*

"Brody, please. Please let me go." She couldn't see where they were going from the floor of the boat. "Brody, where are we going?"

He didn't so much as glance at her.

She changed tactics. She made her voice commanding. "Brody, take me back right now. Detective Collins and Chase Hawthorn are expecting me. They will come looking for me," she lied.

Brody scoffed, his eyes flicking from her to something

beyond the boat. He guided the dinghy through the rocky surf. Frigid water splashed over the sides, soaking her clothes. Kyra clenched her teeth to keep them from chattering.

He cut the engine, and the boat slowed. Kyra tried to sit up but was knocked back by a wave. Brody reached for the line and tied down the boat.

"Get up," he growled and hoisted her to her feet. He heaved her over the side, and she collapsed against the transom of the *Neamhnaid.*

Brody yanked Kyra to her feet and pushed her toward the interior of the sailboat.

She twisted and kicked out at him. "Let me go," she screamed.

He slapped her. Her head snapped back. She tasted blood on her lip.

"Shut the fuck up," he howled, his face inches from hers.

He opened the door and shoved her through. Kyra tumbled down a flight of stairs and slammed to the floor.

She lay there, stunned, her heart and head pounding. The door clicked shut. Kyra rolled to her side. She tested her arms and legs, making sure nothing was broken. She tugged at the binds on her wrists, choking on her rising hysteria.

Calm down. I need to calm down.

She took a few deep breaths, trying to center herself. She bit into her cut lip, focusing on the sting.

I need to get my hands free.

She tested the binds. Gritting her teeth against the pain in her shoulder, she pulled her bound hands around her butt and under her legs, one at a time. With a little maneuvering, she was able to get her hands in front and pushed herself into a sitting position.

She reached into her jacket pocket and pulled out her phone. She stared at it, blinking. No service.

"Fuck, fuck, fuck!" She bit back a sob.

The sailboat rocked, throwing her off-balance. Righting herself, she looked around the dark cabin. She got unsteadily to her feet, and the boat lurched, throwing her against the wall. Leaning into it for stability and using the flashlight on her phone, she found the light switch. She flipped it, and the room flooded with a warm light.

Kyra was in a sort of vestibule surrounded by darkened doorways. *Sleeping quarters? A kitchen?* She crept to the closest one and peered inside. A bedroom. *Where's the galley?* She needed a knife, scissors, anything she could use to free her hands or as a weapon. She tried the room directly across. It was pitch black inside. She felt along the wall for the light switch and flipped it. She saw the body crumpled on the floor at the foot of the bed, dark curls splayed out on the carpet.

"Charlie!"

She sucked in a breath and scrambled to her injured friend. Charlie was unconscious, bleeding from a nasty cut on her forehead.

"Charlie? Charlie, are you okay?" Kyra fell to her knees and pressed her hands to Charlie's face. She shook her shoulders. "Charlie? Charlie, wake up."

The other woman stirred. She moaned softly, and her eyelids fluttered.

"Charlie. Oh my god. Wake up. *Wake up!*" She shook her again.

"Grace?" Charlie muttered, her voice thick.

"No, it's Kyra."

"Kyra?" Charlie's eyes slowly focused on Kyra's face, then widened with recognition. "Kyra." She grabbed for Kyra's hands and swiveled her head around. "Where are we?" She tried to sit up.

"Wait, don't move. Let me help you. Are you hurt?" Kyra helped Charlie into a sitting position, leaning her against the footboard. Charlie put her hand to her head and flinched.

"A man hit me," she said. "I was supposed to meet Grace at L'Huître. I was early and wandering around." Charlie shook her head like she was trying to clear it. "I went to see the horses. Adele and a man were there. I surprised them, and then... The man hit me." Confusion and pain clouded her eyes. "Where are we?"

"We're on the Hawthorns' sailboat."

"The sailboat? Why?"

"Listen to me." Kyra grasped her hands. "Adele is having an affair with a Coast Guard officer named Brody McAllister. Brody brought me here, too."

"But why? What's going on?"

"I think they killed Brendan. And my dad." Kyra's voice was barely a whisper.

Charlie's brow furrowed. "What? Why?" Her eyes went wide. She shook her head, as if trying to clear it. "What are you talking about?"

"Brendan and my father were investigating a bribery conspiracy. Wetun Energy is trying to buy the senator's support for their offshore wind farm and using Brendan as a cover.

After he and Ed died, someone close to the family has been trying to throw suspicion on Chase."

Charlie didn't look convinced. "That doesn't make any sense." Her voice cracked. "Is he going to kill us?"

"We're going to get out of here." Kyra didn't answer her question. She was terrified she knew the answer. "Can you stand?"

Charlie nodded and got to her feet, clutching the side of the bed.

Kyra's vision swam, either from the wild rocking of the boat, a concussion, or both. She pressed her bound hands to her eyes. Suddenly, there was a loud noise from above. Kyra yanked Charlie back against the wall.

"What the hell, Brody?" a woman's voice shrieked from above. *Adele.* "What the fuck were you thinking?"

"She was in the boathouse. She knows," Brody yelled back. "I had to do something."

"Knows what?" Adele's voice came out like a snarl. "What could she possibly know?" Adele let out a string of curses. "Now what? What are we going to do with them?"

"We stick to the plan. We just leave earlier. Tonight. We have the money. We have the boat. We pack. We go. We'll be in Cuba in a week. We go from there."

"Jesus fucking christ, Brody," Adele screeched.

Then there was silence.

"We need to get help. Do you have your phone?" Kyra whispered.

Charlie patted her jacket pockets. "It was in my purse. You?"

"No service." She held up her hands. "I need to get free.

Stay here?"

Charlie nodded, wrapped her arms around herself, and sank to the floor.

The galley was sparse but tidy. She checked the drawers and cabinets, searching for anything that might be useful. It wasn't well stocked. There was almost no food and only a few bottles of water. Finally, in a drawer, she found a paring knife.

Kyra rushed back to Charlie and handed her the knife. "Can you cut the ropes?" She held out her hands. Charlie tried to saw through the binds.

"Hold still," Charlie commanded, but her hands were shaking. The knife slipped.

"Ow," Kyra hissed through her teeth and jerked back.

"Oh my god," Charlie sobbed and dropped the knife.

"Try again. Please."

Charlie picked up the knife. She took a steadying breath. After a few more swipes, the ropes fell away. Kyra pressed on her wrist to slow the bleeding.

"I'm sorry," Charlie whispered.

"It's not deep. I'll be fine."

Kyra led Charlie into the kitchen, where she found a towel. Charlie helped her tie it around her wrist. Kyra pointed to the bare cupboards. "They have no food. No water. They can't leave without supplying the boat."

Charlie followed her back to the bedroom.

"They were able to sneak us on the boat, but they can't risk anyone seeing us while we're in the harbor. There's no way they can get rid of us without going out to sea, and they don't have supplies. They can't leave yet. We just need to bide our time until one or both of them leave. Then we escape."

Charlie nodded and rested her head against Kyra's shoulder. She shivered, and a few tears slid down her cheeks. Kyra stilled under the other woman's weight and wrapped her arm around her. Charlie's skin felt hot. Her face was pale, and her cheeks were flushed.

"Charlie," Kyra whispered. "Do you feel okay?"

"I'll be fine," Charlie said, raising her chin. "Just tell me what we need to do."

"Is there another way out?" Kyra asked.

Maybe we can make a swim for it? She wasn't confident Charlie was strong enough, and by the way the boat was rocking, she could tell the waves were getting bigger. She clung to the bolted-down furniture to keep from being tossed around the cabin.

Kyra remembered something and her stomach sank. "Charlie, do you have your insulin?"

Charlie shook her head.

Fuck. Kyra kicked the bedpost. She needed to get help. "Stay here."

Kyra searched the interior of the sailboat, checking the other cabin doors and compartments, looking for a radio, phone, something to communicate. She found the engine room behind the stairs, the bathroom, a locked door to a closet near the bow, but no exit or comms system.

She backtracked through the cabins to the stairs. She crept up to the door to the back deck and tested the handle. Locked. Kyra pressed her weight against it. It was made of a lightweight composite, intended to protect the inhabitants from the weather. She was sure she could break it down if she needed to, but she couldn't overtake Brody and Adele. She pressed an ear to the door.

"We have to wait until they leave," Kyra said and slid to the floor next to Charlie. She pulled the comforter from the bed and flung it over them.

The minutes passed slowly, and the rocking got wilder. She had to brace herself against the bed to keep from falling over. Kyra swallowed back nausea and closed her eyes. Something rumbled outside. Charlie grabbed her hand.

"Is that a motor?" Charlie whispered.

Kyra strained her ears. *Could it be the dinghy's outboard motor?* She wasn't sure. Kyra motioned for Charlie to stay and crept back up the stairs. She pressed her ear to the door. She didn't hear voices, couldn't make out any specific sound.

"Kyra?" Charlie called from the bottom of the stairs. In the dancing dim light, the sheen on Charlie's cheeks, the greenish pallor of her face, was more prominent.

Charlie held on to either side of the stairwell. "Are they still on the boat?"

"I don't know. I can't hear them. How long have we been here?"

"I don't know. It's dark out. But it could just be the storm."

Kyra swallowed. *Storm?* "There's a storm?" Kyra's eyes met Charlie's.

Thunder erupted. The boat quaked.

Charlie gasped. Her fist flew to her mouth.

Kyra stifled a scream and grabbed the wall. "It's okay. You hear me?" She was reassuring Charlie as much as herself.

"We need to get off this boat. Now." Kyra pushed her bodyweight against the door. It bowed. "I'm going to break it down."

Charlie nodded, wringing her hands at the bottom of the stairs. Kyra stepped back and slammed her entire body against the door. It bucked but held.

Charlie scrambled up beside her.

"Together." Kyra nodded. "On the count of three. One! Two! Three!" They rammed their bodies into the door. It shuddered but didn't give.

"Again." They threw their bodies against it. With a loud crack, the lock gave way. They tumbled through into the rain and onto the wet deck of the *Neamhnaid*.

Kyra grabbed a bench and pulled herself to a standing position. Charlie tried to stand but fell back.

"Charlie!" Kyra reached out to help her.

The sky splintered with lightning. The boat lurched. They gripped the rail to keep from being thrown.

"Oh. My. God." The wind tore Charlie's words from her lips. "They've cut the mooring!"

Kyra froze, stunned. Her gaze followed Charlie's out-stretched arm, pointing toward the now-distant shoreline. She searched for the little Menemsha harbor. Rain lashed down, blurring her vision.

"Stay there," Kyra ordered and scrambled toward the *Neamhnaid's* helm.

Free of its anchor, the boat rocked and rolled, thrown by the waves crashing into the hull on one side and over the rails on the other. Her soaked sneakers slipped on the teak decking slick with seawater and rain. She pulled herself hand over hand along the rails, gasping for air. *Get to the steering column. Get to the radio.* A loose sail whipped and snapped in the wind, missing Kyra's head by inches. Rain pelted her face with such force it stung. *Please*, she begged. A sob bubbled out.

She pulled herself into the seat in front of the steering wheel. Her fingers ached with cold. *Where's the island?* She swiveled her head around, looking for anything recognizable. But on all sides, all she saw was black, churning water merging with the dark, angry sky. She searched the dashboard. *Radio?! Where's the fucking radio?!*

With a whimper of relief, she grabbed the handset and slammed her hands on the buttons. "Mayday! Mayday!" she screamed, her voice cracking.

Nothing.

Kyra pulled the handset away from her mouth, and gaped. A strangled sound escaped from her throat. The wire swung, unattached to the console. She swallowed back bile. The entire comms system had been ripped out.

She dropped the handset and punched the steering wheel with a horrified scream. She squatted down, cowering under the steering column, out of the onslaught of the rain. Kyra needed a plan. *We have to get off this boat.* She stared at the broken radio. Her heart thumped. *I saw an engine room down there.* If they could start the engine, they could get control of the boat. *Drive it back?* Kyra stood up and ran her hands along the cockpit dashboard, but nothing looked like it controlled the engines. No ignition button, no key. *Where's the engine control?* Her eyes slid to the stern of the boat, to the door down to the hold. *There must be a cockpit down there.*

Kyra scrambled back to Charlie. Lightning lit up the sky for a split second, blinding her, and Kyra lost her footing. She slipped and slid along the deck, hurling toward the hungry sea. She flailed her arms, clawing desperately for anything. Her fingers latched onto a rope. She howled as her arm was wrenched from her shoulder socket, and her slide jerked to a stop. She pulled herself up, hand over hand. The edges of her vision turned black from the pain. She hauled herself back along the deck to the hold. The door flapped back and forth on its hinges, the locking mechanism useless. She yanked it aside with a shout and stumbled inside. Charlie had taken shelter from the rain and was sitting at the bottom of the stairwell, resting her head against the wall.

"Charlie!" Kyra called. She slipped on the rain-soaked stairs and tumbled down.

"Oh god." Charlie rushed to her and grabbed her shoulders. "Did you call for help?"

"They cut the radio." Kyra's voice cracked with despair.

Her breaths came in short pants. *Keep it together. Keep it together.*

"Oh god." Charlie put her fists to her mouth. "Oh god."

"Charlie, we need to start the engine," Kyra said, willing her voice to stay calm. "We need to get control of the boat."

Charlie just shook her head. It dawned on her the same time Charlie's eyes drifted toward the bow. The locked closet door.

"We'll have to break it down," Charlie wheezed, reading Kyra's mind.

Kyra nodded, bolstered by her friend. "Together."

"Together," Charlie agreed with grim determination.

They rammed the door. Kyra's shoulder exploded in pain at the impact, and she bit back a scream. The latching system gave way, and the door popped open. The interior cockpit, just a steering console and a captain's chair, was for navigating the boat through a harbor. From the small window, they could see the bow dipping and rising. Waves crashed over the side, rolling the boat. The port side dipped under the water. Charlie screamed as they were thrown against the control panel from the force of a wave.

"Charlie!"

The boat righted itself with a groan and a sharp snap.

"I'm okay," she said, but her voice cracked. She gripped the steering console, her knuckles white. Charlie pushed the ignition button, but nothing happened. Her eyes went wide. Kyra stared at the control panel, her stomach dropping. *No! No. No. No.*

"They may not be hooked up," Charlie said.

"What?"

"The engines. They disconnect them when the boats are stored for the winter."

"They disconnect the engines?" Kyra repeated the words thick in her mouth. "Like a car battery?" She sucked in a breath. "The engine room. Stay here."

The *Neamhnaid* lurched.

"Go!" Charlie yelled.

Kyra ran back toward the engine room behind the stairs. Water streamed down the stairwell from the broken hold door. She held onto the walls, anything, to keep from slipping in the icy water. Her teeth chattered. She entered the engine room. A wave hit the *Neamhnaid* with a crash, and the boat rolled. Her feet left the floor. Kyra screamed. The boat righted itself again, throwing Kyra to the ground. The lights flickered and went out, pitching the room into darkness. Kyra kneeled on the wet floor in the pitch black, frozen in terror.

Suddenly, red lights glowed as the emergency system engaged. She let out a relieved sigh that stuttered like a sob.

The engine room was a mess. Debris had been flung everywhere since the boat had been set adrift. She stumbled to the panel that controlled the engines. No power. Kyra ran her hands along the wires and followed the connectors with her eyes. Everything looked connected.

A wave hit the boat, and she fell, barely stopping herself before her face slammed into the engine casing. That was when she saw it—a single, unconnected cable dangling underneath.

"Like connecting a battery," she whispered and said a silent prayer to all the gods, her uncle Cam, and his shitty MG.

Lying down on the wet floor, Kyra reached under the engine bay, her fingers splayed, feeling for the cable. It swung just out of reach. Kyra extended her arm, reaching as far as she could, and the tip of her middle finger touched something. She stretched, and with the lurch of the boat, the cable swung into her palm. She grabbed it. With a cry, she pulled the cable up and plugged it into its port on the control panel. The bright red ready-light flicked on.

"Try it now!" she hollered her voice cracking.

There was a loud rumble and a clicking. The starter tried

to turn the engines.

Kyra screamed to try again. "Please, start. Please. Please." Kyra slammed her hand on the panel. "Fucking *start*!"

The starter clicked and clicked, and then, with a guttural roar, the engines caught. Kyra sagged against the console. The boat rocked and spasmed. *Charlie.* She ran, slipping and sliding back to the cockpit.

Charlie was standing in front of the steering column, holding the wheel, struggling against the force of the sea. "Help," she begged through gritted teeth.

Kyra grabbed the wheel, and together, hand over fist, they forced the *Neamhnaid* to change direction. The boat rumbled and seized as it fought the current and the waves tacking port side. Inch by inch, they turned the bow into the waves. With each inch, the rocking subsided.

"We've got to hold it here to keep from capsizing," Charlie said through gasps. Sweat beaded on her brow. "But the boat won't last long. It won't be able to take the pounding." Charlie's voice wavered. Something in her tone alarmed Kyra.

"Charlie? Are you okay?"

Charlie's voice wasn't shaking, her entire body was. Kyra swallowed.

"No. I don't think I am," Charlie said, her voice so soft Kyra could barely make out the words.

"You stay with me, Charlie. Hold the boat." Kyra grabbed Charlie's shoulders, forcing her to look at her. She pushed her down into the chair. "Hold the boat. I need you." She ran to the kitchen and yanked out the drawers. *Sugar.* She found a small box containing coffee supplies and a few packets of sugar. Holding them and a water bottle, praying she didn't drop them in the water, she made her way back to the cockpit. "Here. Eat this." She tore open the sugar packets, handing them to her, then pushed the water bottle into her hands.

Charlie slumped back in the chair. "Thank you," she said, her voice resigned.

Kyra wrapped her hands around the steering wheel and fought the boat, keeping it straight. The engines groaned and stuttered, but the *Neamhnaid* moved forward into the waves. Slowly climbing up, up, then down with a bone-shattering crash, again and again and again.

She didn't know what direction they were traveling in, where they were going, or if anyone would be able to find them, but she'd cross that bridge when she came to it. For now, she just needed to keep the *Neamhnaid* afloat and Charlie alive.

Chapter Twenty-Five

Tuesday

K YRA'S ARMS AND back ached with the exertion of keeping a continuous hold on the steering wheel, fighting the constant shudders and pulls of the boat. The minutes extended into hours, but she kept watch out the window, her eyes glued to the horizon, or where she thought the horizon should be in the churning darkness. *Just keep the boat moving forward.* She had to sail into the waves to keep it from capsizing. That was what Charlie had said. Over and over, the boat slammed back into the water's surface after cresting a wave. She heard crashes, groans, and snaps from above, but the *Neamhnaid* stayed true. She barely noticed when the swells became less violent, the crashes less shocking. The rumble of thunder distant.

"Kyra?" Charlie gripped her shoulder, and she winced. "Kyra, look. The storm. It's over."

Kyra raised her eyes from the swirling gray water. It was still dark, and rain pelted down in sheets. Was it her imagination? *Is it calmer?* She dared to hope.

"It's over?" She slumped into the captain's chair, exhausted.

Charlie wrapped her arms around her, and Kyra sobbed

against her shoulder. Awareness seeped in, and she pulled back. Charlie was so cold.

"You're freezing. Are you okay?"

"I think so." Even in the dim red emergency lighting, Kyra saw that Charlie's face was pale, and her lips blue.

"We need to get you warm."

Kyra scrambled to the bedroom, her sneakers squishing in the soaked-through carpeting. The bedding was soaked too. She searched the closets for towels, clothes, anything. Nothing. She went back to the engine room. Maybe there was a first-aid kit? She found it among the rubble. Inside she found general supplies, a flare gun, and there, at the bottom, a packet for one of those mylar emergency blankets. Kyra returned to Charlie and wrapped the plastic film around her shoulders. "Keep your feet out of the water."

"Thank you." Charlie's voice was soft. "Kyra, we need to turn off the engines."

"What? Why?" Panic lanced through her body.

"We need to conserve gas." Charlie tapped the fuel gauge. They had less than a fifth of a tank. "I don't know how to sail." She raised her eyes to Kyra's, defeated.

"I don't either."

Despite every nerve telling her not to, Kyra turned off the engines. The rumbling stopped, and the *Neamhnaid* descended into silence. Without the forward momentum, the boat slowed to a listing roll, and the incessant rocking started again. She tried the radio handset. It wasn't cut, but Brody had destroyed the console at the helm. It was dead. Kyra checked her jacket pocket for her phone. It was gone. She wasn't surprised. It was probably on the bottom of the ocean. Kyra pushed away her growing despair.

"I could fire a flare?"

"It's better than doing nothing. Try." But there was no hope in Charlie's weak voice.

Kyra went back to the engine room and gathered the flare gun and a few shells. She left the hold and returned topside. Kyra sucked in her breath and swore as the wind hit her, slicing through her wet clothes. It was freezing. She read the instructions, loaded the gun, and aimed it into the sky. Kyra pulled the trigger. She bit back a scream as the recoil twinged her torn shoulder muscles. A bright-white light streaked upward, leaving a trail of red smoke. She switched hands and fired two more rounds. Kyra went back to Charlie and folded herself around her shivering friend under the filmy blanket. *There's no need to conserve flares or gas. If we aren't found soon, we won't make it.*

A HORN BLASTED jarring Kyra awake. Her eyes flew open. She was still squeezed in the captain's chair with Charlie. Light streamed in through the tiny cockpit window. Charlie was still asleep, her breath shallow but consistent. The *Neamhnaid* rocked, a gentle listing back and forth. The horn blasted again, closer this time, and Kyra covered her ears.

"This is the US Coast Guard!" a voice blared over a loudspeaker.

Her heart skipped and banged against her ribs. She broke out in a cold sweat. She didn't know what to do. If it was Brody, they were as good as dead. But if Charlie didn't get medical attention immediately, she was going to die. With a gulp of air, Kyra untangled herself from Charlie and stumbled out of the cockpit and up the stairs.

"Mayday!" she screamed, her voice hoarse and scratchy from salt and dehydration. "Help!" She waved her arms, ignoring the searing pain in her shoulder, and scrambled to the stern.

A blue-and-white Coast Guard vessel drew up alongside the sailboat.

"Help! Please!"

A man came into view, and her heart stuttered. Her knees gave out, and she crumbled to the floor at the sight of Tarek running toward her. Right behind him, she recognized Chase Hawthorn. Chase leaped over the rails and tied off the two boats.

"Kyra!" Tarek ran to her. He shouted something to the crew, and two more men carrying cases and emergency equipment came running.

"No, Charlie. Help her, please. She's diabetic." Kyra waved them away and pointed toward the hold. The medics ran down. Kyra slumped against Tarek. He pushed her hair away from her face and peered into her eyes.

"Are you hurt?"

"No."

Chase squatted down, his blue-green eyes level to hers. "You good?" he asked, his head cocked to the side, appraising her.

She nodded.

"All right, then." Chase turned as the officers emerged from the stairwell carrying Charlie.

They strapped her onto a stretcher and loaded her onto the Coast Guard vessel.

"Let's get them back to the island," Chase said to Tarek.

Tarek gathered Kyra against his chest and carried her to the other boat. He handed her over the rails to Chase. Chase carried her inside and gently deposited her in a chair. Someone wrapped a blanket around her. Chase pushed a hot cup of coffee between her icy fingers. Tarek sat next to her and pulled her against him. She leaned into him, letting him hold her.

"Charlie?" she asked, her voice cracking.

"We have an ambulance waiting for us. Her vitals are stable."

Kyra rested her head against his chest. Tarek's arms tightened around her. She let her eyes close and soaked in his warmth, giving in to the exhaustion. She felt his lips move against her hair. "You're safe. We got you."

Chapter Twenty-Six

Wednesday

T HE AFTERNOON SUN beamed through the wall of windows overlooking Crackatuxet Cove. Kyra blinked, getting her bearings, trying to place where she was. She sighed when she remembered. She'd refused to stay in the hospital, and the doctors only agreed to let her go home because Detective Collins promised to stay with her. Pushed beyond exhaustion and numb from the pain meds, she didn't have the strength to argue when Tarek tucked her into her father's bed. He had seemed reluctant to let her out of his sight.

Kyra sat up. Her muscles objected, and she sucked in a breath, wincing at the sharp pain in her side. She had two cracked ribs. Her left shoulder throbbed, and everything else felt stiff and bruised. Tarek was snoozing on the couch, Cronk stretched out on his chest. Kyra made a soft noise to the cat, jealous they were cozied up together. Cronkite lifted his head and yawned.

Tarek's eyelids fluttered, then popped open. He twisted his head. "You're awake."

He was at her side in an instant. "How do you feel?"

"All right," she rasped.

He disappeared into the bathroom and returned with a glass of water. She gulped it down. "Thank you." Her voice already felt less scratchy. She attempted a smile.

"You've been asleep for most of the day." He checked his watch. "How's your shoulder?"

"It hurts, but not so bad," she lied.

"I bet."

"How did you find us?" Kyra asked, her eyes welling up.

Tarek pulled a chair up to the side of the bed. He stared out at the cove. "After you left the coffee shop, Chase hunted me down. He told me the whole story. Eventually, we figured it out that it must have been Adele. She knew about the crawl space, and she'd lied about when she arrived on the island. She was with Brody, on *The Island Pearl*, before her husband arrived. We followed you to Menemsha, but by the time we got there, the *Neamhnaid* was already gone. At first, we thought Brody and Adele had used it to escape, then we found your car, but we couldn't find you. We notified the Coast Guard, who prepared a search mission.

"They found Adele and Brody late last night refueling *The Island Pearl* in Nantucket. They were taken into custody, and Adele accused Brody of kidnapping her, of murdering Brendan and Ed. Once they told Brody Adele had turned on him, he told us everything, signed a confession, and agreed to testify. Adele intercepted calls between Wetun and the senator and found out about the bribes. She set up the offshore accounts and transferred the funds out of Brendan's account. Wetun probably thought the senator received the money. When Brendan became suspicious, they watched him and learned he'd gone to your dad. She used what she knew to lure Ed to the boat, promising to share evidence she had of Phil accepting the bribes. She or Brody struck him and tossed him overboard.

"When they were unable to find Ed's notes on his computer, she persuaded Brendan to go to the farm. They shot him and set the barn on fire using a fertilizer accelerant from Sara's supply. They hid the gun in Chase's room, hoping it'd be uncovered during a search. They set up Chase to take the blame for both murders." Tarek turned to Kyra.

"But why?" Kyra's voice was a whisper.

But she knew. She knew that Adele, rejected over and over, had finally been pushed past her breaking point. She wanted to be free of the family that didn't want her. Adele saw an opportunity, and she took it.

Kyra swallowed. "Why Charlie?"

"Charlie was just in the wrong place at the wrong time. Adele and Brody were in the middle of planting evidence in Chase's equipment locker. Brody reacted. He hit her and stowed her on the boat. You're lucky." Tarek took her hand, ran his thumb along the bandage at her wrist.

"Chase had installed a GPS system on the *Neamhnaid* to help navigate during races. We located you by tracking the signal, but it shut off when the emergency system engaged." Tarek's face paled. "We couldn't send a rescue party out until the storm subsided." His voice caught. "We had a general idea of where the *Neamhnaid* was, and Chase knows these waters better than anyone. He calculated your drift direction based on the currents and wind speeds. Once the storm calmed, we were able to send out the search crew. Then we saw the flares." Tarek turned back to her. The dark purple circles under his eyes somehow made them appear greener. "He saved your life."

"Remind me to send a gift basket."

Tarek huffed a laugh.

They were quiet for a few minutes.

Tears slid down her cheeks, and Tarek moved onto the bed. He held her while she cried against his chest. Kyra cried because she was safe, because she had survived. She cried for Charlie, for Chase and Brendan, even for Adele. She recognized herself in Adele's anger, what she could have been, and murmured a soft thanks to her aunt, her rock, and her best friend. Tarek ran his fingers through her hair, soothing her.

Finally, when she had no more tears left, she pulled away. "What happens now?" she asked, her voice raw.

He sighed, stroking her back. "We've notified the FBI, who will take over the investigation into Wetun and Alonda. Another investigation will be opened to relook at the senator. Chase has been exonerated of both crimes, and the prosecutor is making a statement. Last I heard, the senator and Margot were going back to Washington."

"What about Dr. Brian?"

"He left for the mainland after we spoke Sunday afternoon. He's been in Washington this whole time."

Tarek's phone rang. He untangled himself and crossed the room back to the couch.

He answered it, talking quietly, then held the phone to his chest. "Are you up for some visitors?"

IT TOOK AN hour. Twenty minutes of struggling on her own, fifteen minutes of arguing with Tarek, and twenty-five minutes of soul-destroying mortification after she accepted his help to get bathed and dressed. Finally, Kyra found herself on the couch in the living room in front of a roaring fire wrapped in blankets. Cronkite was snuggled in her lap, watching everything through one half-open eye.

"Knock, knock," a voice said from the front door as it cracked open. "Can we come in?"

"Come in." Tarek stood.

Grace fluttered into the room. "My dear girl." She ran to Kyra and hugged her too hard. Kyra hissed through her teeth at the sharp pain. "Oh my." Grace jumped back. "I'm so sorry." She grabbed Kyra's hands so tight her rings bit into Kyra's skin. "Thank you. Thank you." Tears welled in Grace's eyes. "You saved my Charlie."

"Oh, leave her alone, Grace." Charlie rolled her eyes. "We had it under control the entire time."

Tarek held her elbow. Bandages covered the cut on her forehead, and there were dark circles under her eyes, but she smiled and embraced Kyra—much gentler than Grace. Tarek helped her take a seat next to Kyra.

"She's right, though, thank you. You saved my life."

"We did it together." Kyra squeezed Charlie's hand.

Tarek told the Chamberses the story he'd shared with Kyra. When he finished, they sat in silence.

"We all owe that Hawthorn boy an apology," Grace said, and kissed the back of Charlie's hand. "He's a hero."

"That's certainly how Margot's spinning it," Tarek said, his tone cynical.

Kyra made a face. Just days ago, Margot had been ready to throw her son to the wolves.

"Already?" Grace tsked and shook her head. She looked between her wife and Kyra. "We don't want to stay too long. You both need your rest. Dear, I'm so glad we got to see you before your flight tomorrow."

"I got your email," Charlie whispered. "I'll make sure the house is ready for you and your aunt's family when you're back in July." Charlie gave Kyra's hand another squeeze.

Grace bent to press her cheek against Kyra's and helped Charlie to her feet.

"Oh, I'm so glad." Grace beamed. "You'll love the island in the summer. Come, my love, you're heading back to bed."

Charlie rolled her eyes and gave Kyra a tired grin.

"July?" Tarek asked, after he'd showed the Chamberses out. He leaned against the chimney his head cocked to the side.

Kyra raised her shoulder and winced. She hadn't had a chance to tell him she was coming back. She hadn't discussed it with anyone, except for the quick email she sent to Charlie Monday morning, letting her know she was postponing the sale. Indefinitely.

She bit into her lip and looked up at him. "I've put off selling the house. I'm planning on coming back this summer. For a holiday with my aunt and her family. Ali wants to show me the island." Would he want to see her if she came back? "What do you think?"

His mouth hitched into that crooked smile, and he moved to sit beside her. Kyra's heart thumped in her chest. Each beat a sharp reminder of her cracked ribs.

Tarek took her hand in his and pressed a soft kiss to the inside of her uninjured wrist. "I think I like that plan."

Fin.

Thank you for reading *A Chain of Pearls*. I hope you enjoyed visiting Martha's Vineyard with Kyra. I'm excited to share what trouble she and Tarek find themselves in next. If you are too, I invite you to check out *Death at Dark* coming August 2024. A Chain of Pearls is my first book and I've much to learn. I thrive on feedback. Please tell me what you liked, loved, or even hated. You can write to me at raemi.ray@gmail.com and find me on my website at www.raemiray.com. Finally, I've small favor to ask. Please consider leaving a review. Reviews positive and negative are how readers find writers. You have my deepest gratitude.

Until the next ferry over ~ Raemi.

Acknowledgments

Writing a book is a surreal experience. One moment your mornings, evenings, and middles of the night are full of coffee and tea, relaxing sunrises and sunsets… sleep, and the next, they're consumed with drafting and redrafting, highs and lows of pride and anxiety, elation and fear, and significantly more coffee. And then, not at all suddenly, you have a stack of paper and ink, and a niggling sense of accomplishment. But like all achievements, a village of encouraging people supported me, and to each of them I owe a humble and heartfelt thanks.

To Mrs. Amanda, Sarah, and Ms. Martha, who never once laughed, who believed in me, and who were my cheerleaders. To Chris, and our extended family, Dole, Buckovich, Lotze, and Koesler, who introduced me to the island I fell in love with. To Sara Quaranta, Jonathan Starke, Alan Pinck, and the folks at Killer Nashville, who saw something in my story and gave me the confidence to persist. And last, but certainly not least, to the wonderful community at Tule Publishing, especially my editor, Sinclair Sawhney who supported me and pushed me to be a better writer, and storyteller, and without whom this book would not be what it is today. Thank you.

If you enjoyed *A Chain of Pearls,*
you'll love the other books in…

Martha's Vineyard Murders series

Book 1: *A Chain of Pearls*

Book 2: *Death at Dark*

Book 3: *Widow's Walk*

Book 4: *Final Exit*

Available now at your favorite online retailer!

About the Author

Photo Credit: L.A. Brown

Raemi A. Ray is the author of the Martha's Vineyard Murders series. Her travels to the island and around the world inspire her stories. She lives with her family in Boston.

Thank you for reading

A Chain of Pearls

If you enjoyed this book, you can find more from all our great authors at TulePublishing.com, or from your favorite online retailer.

TULE

Made in the USA
Las Vegas, NV
23 August 2025

26817524R00204